THE PAST CAPTURES US FOREVER

Copyright © 2024 MARK M. TILLINGER.

THE PAST CAPTURES US FOREVER

Contents

TWENTY BETTY WHITES AND YOU'RE BACK TO JESUS 1
Story # 1 THE ISOLATIONIST 16
Story # 2 A DREAM BUSINESS 34
Story # 3 PRIDE AND PLUTO 58
Story # 4 FORGED AND FRAMED 92
Story # 5 THE MURDERERS' PIT 122
Story # 6 A HEART OF GOLD 154
Story # 7 THE INVASION OF BRAZIL 182
Story # 8 THE WATCHMAKER'S FAMILY 210
Story # 9 LIVING ON MARS 242

Acknowledgement

For their contribution to this project, I would like to thank my wife, Georgina, Elaine Richman, Sheree Richman, Patricia Astor, Jack Wilson, Ben Andrews, Jordan Jones, and Shay Michaels. I would also like to thank a few people who, unbeknownst to them, taught me something valuable about, either myself, or about what it means to be a professional. They are Darlene Love, Steven Tyler, Louis Salemno, and Marvin Segel.

THE PAST CAPTURES US FOREVER

Dedication

For Georgina – Love Forever Captured in Time

THE PAST CAPTURES US FOREVER

A collection of nine stories

selected over time

Copyright by Mark M. Tillinger

THE PAST CAPTURES US FOREVER

TWENTY BETTY WHITES
AND YOU'RE BACK TO JESUS

Introduction

There were five of us from the beginning. Five friends from the same university with different skill sets who, after making some money, decided to create what is known as a think tank. We hated that name, so we called our company, Thinking Outside The Tank, "Tell us what you want, and we'll think about it." Maybe it was a bit flippant, but our off-beat approach caught the eye of our benefactor. And this journey began.

By the time we sat down with the man who would pay the bills, we knew he was someone who had made an enormous amount of money, cashed out and moved on. And this newly acquired freedom allowed him to focus on something less tangible.

"Something whose existence alone," he said, "could be one of humankind's most important discoveries - The SpaceTime Continuum. What is it? Why does it exist? What does it mean for humankind?"

My friends and I were deflated. We were fascinated by SpaceTime and the theory that if you could travel fast enough you would move through time as well as space. Unfortunately, the questions he was asking could not be answered.

His reply was, "I know that."

We added that even if we wanted to move forward, none of us were physicists. When he told us that wouldn't be necessary, my friends and I decided to relax and just listen as he continued:

"When I faced the challenge of what to do next with my time, I thought about whom I admired and what they were doing to see if it might help me find a path of my own. The first thing that came to mind was the scientists working on String Theory. It isn't important to know anything about String Theory, except perhaps that it's one of the avenues of research attempting to theorize a possible leap forward in our understanding of the universe. However, the science behind the theory is not my focus, just as the science of SpaceTime is not my concern. My interest in String Theory lies in the dedication of the String Theorists. They face the possibility of spending their lives in search of something that may not even exist, all in the service of truth. That made an impression on me. Results or proofs are never the primary focus for these explorers. They are part of a grand process that will continue long after they are gone. With that in mind, I allowed myself the freedom to stop thinking about results, as well.

'Next, I considered the money I would spend. Is it frivolous? I don't believe it is. The world doesn't have a money problem. Trying to use that money to solve complex problems across long distances, affecting millions of people, is problematic. Add personal ego and corruption, and the best we can do is buy an endless supply of band aids. Most of these may be necessary, at least for now, but while band aids may stem the tide, they never stop the bleeding. This may be understandable when it comes to world hunger. It is not when it comes to something like equality. Here, there are no alternate interpretations available for exploitation. None. And yet, we find a way. Even though *equality* is a constant. Like the numbers zero or one. One is one, and equal is equal. Of course, all band aids are not equal, which brings us to the band aids in our society made of crepe paper, with no adhesive at all, that may waste billions of dollars every year. As an illustration, I offer the ridiculous episode of the partial acceptance of people who are transgender. To help them feel safe and accepted, it appears the best our society can do is offer them their own bathroom. Now, while I don't want to speak for the transgender community, I don't think their wish list starts with a bathroom. I believe they want what many of us want. Complete equality and acceptance. An understanding that we are different. And thank goodness for our differences. Yet we are still the same. The answer is clear. Everyone should be treated the same - all the time. Unfortunately, since we can't offer what is right, we present a booby prize. The brilliant minds charged with making our decisions for us envision a day when everyone has their own bathroom; Hurrah, Hurray! And no one can find the right door before they pee themselves.

'I decided that if the world can spend trillions of dollars on band aids, I can spend a few dollars on a dream."

Eighteen months after meeting with our benefactor, the six of us are writing this introductory chapter to share our intentions. It begins with this question. If someday we are offered a glimpse into the past through SpaceTime, which stories might reveal what is hidden beneath what we choose to share with others and, maybe more importantly, what we won't admit to ourselves? Because who we are as people at any given time may be a better indicator of why something happens than the event itself. In any case, if we did get the chance to look into the past, no one would need to remind us of the larger stories, such as the life of Jesus or the story of Noah. Or our personal choice, Ancient Greece and Helen of Troy, to see if a face really did launch a thousand ships. If it did, we'd like to see that face.

THE PAST CAPTURES US FOREVER

Of course, these stories are in the past. They already exist on the timeline. So, we set out to collect stories of our own. Stories from different generations and future generations – nine stories in all. With one story to be selected every twenty years. Our team's challenge was to figure out what the story parameters would be and the logistics of a project that extends one hundred and eighty years into the future. This brings us back to the title given to our first chapter, *Twenty Betty Whites and You're Back to Jesus*. If everything goes well, this book will be published in some form almost 200 years from now, so this may need some further explanation.

In January of 2022, the same year we are writing this introduction, the actress Betty White died at the age of 100. The prospective that twenty Betty Whites seems to suggest, we find significant. Two thousand years and the life of Jesus evokes a picture of ancient times. Twenty Betty Whites just doesn't seem that long ago. Time is strange. Ask anyone in their seventies or older, and they will tell you. It feels as if life, our lives individually, goes by in a flash. We have the memories. We know we've lived. It's just that looking back is very different from looking forward when it comes to time. This is somewhat baffling. A minute is a minute, and a decade is a decade, isn't it? It is when you're counting time, not when you're living through it. Additionally, from the standpoint of this endeavor, it is important to remember that once you have lived a year, you move on. But everything that happened in that year still exists on the timeline, somewhere in SpaceTime.

Backtracking a bit, we wanted to explain the use of Betty White as our reference. During a long career almost exclusively in television, Betty White became part of a show about four female senior citizens living together in Miami. Thirty years after its initial seven-year run, this series appears to have reached the status of being beloved. Called *The Golden Girls*, it is broadcast almost continuously all day, every day, on multiple networks, sometimes simultaneously. Our projection is that one hundred years from now, *The Golden Girls* will continue to be broadcast daily, and Betty White will remain a household name. However, even though our choice of Ms. White was unanimous, we would like to acknowledge the runner up in our search, Kirk Douglas.

Kirk Douglas died at the age of 103. He is a giant in the history of film. A bona fide Hollywood legend whose stature will not diminish over time. Film preservation will take care of that. For example, the Charlie Chaplin shorts have been carefully restored, and they are well over one hundred years old. And we expect the beauty of F. W. Murnau's film "Sunrise," made in 1927, to be admired by someone always. However, on average, a person may see a Kirk Douglas movie or maybe just his image a few times a year. You could be hit by ten subliminally effective glances of Betty White a day. It is the saturation of television that guided our decision, not artistry. Also, twenty Kirk Douglases is more of a mouthful. In a project filled with assumptions, the selection of Betty White was the easiest decision we made.

We say this project is filled with assumptions because aside from the science of SpaceTime, virtually everything else is an assumption. Assumptions which do not necessarily lead to answers. However, that doesn't mean that the questions we ask about the existence of the timeline aren't important.

Ordinarily, getting a group of opinionated colleagues, like us, to agree on an assumption can be a difficult task, except when you are able to eliminate the desire for personal gain where people battle just to have their own ideas chosen, it becomes a different process. With this approach, we were surprised by how smoothly the results were achieved. In our case, there is no advantage for any individual. The six of us speak as one. And we remain anonymous. So, as one, this is what our collective imagination will ask our future collaborators to consider when selecting stories moving forward.

Most assumptions in life are derived from existing knowledge. We start with what is known and build on that. In our case, there are very few facts to build on, and we don't expect to prove anything. Our assumptions are based on beliefs. The first of these is that this universe did not just materialize. It was created. And the architect and builder of all we see and all we are is referred to by many as God. This is not a book of religion, however. We are focused on the creation and existence of SpaceTime. And after accepting the premise that God created everything, it's unlikely there were pre-existing limitations on how the universe could be created. The universe could have been created without the timeline. Why not erase time once it becomes the past? The timeline must be there for a reason. It is part of the physical fabric of our world, yes, but keeping the past intact must be essential.

When considering the direct interaction between human beings and the past through SpaceTime, we entertain two possibilities. First, we may someday be able to view the past. Or the second possibility, where we are never able to view our past and the SpaceTime Continuum is there, "For the Eyes of God Only." We do not believe we will ever travel back in time and interact or effect the past in any way. As science fiction fans, we love stories of time travel, but human beings are too busy making billions of mistakes in the present and could never be allowed to alter the universe because someone thinks they can correct other human beings' mistakes in the past. God is too smart to allow that. If we damage the Earth, that's one thing. Do damage in SpaceTime and forget about it.

Our last assumption is a continuation of the idea that many times, the more revealing stories are untold. In many of these, the story being promoted is a distraction while our society does something vintage newspaper reporters would refer to as "burying the lead." It was a lesson that seasoned veterans taught the rookies when their writing placed the headline item of a story in the second or third paragraph. The difference is that when society buries the lead, it buries it six feet under. Telling the stories that would otherwise be buried is one of the main considerations of this project. However, it is not the only type of story that can be chosen.

More of our thoughts on story parameters are included in the legal, financial and logistical documents now housed in a secure storage facility designed to hold our files for the life of this endeavor. These facilities do exist, of course. Governments have documents that they secure far into the future. The military service record of actor Christopher Lee (b.1922- d.2015) is so secret it is being kept in a secure location by Great Britain for the next two hundred and fifty years.

With some of our documents we attempt to anticipate any needs that may arise for our future colleagues. Covering all possibilities is difficult because of the amount of time for which we must account. While working in our favor, at any given time, only a handful of people are required to support this project. Our files introduce the basics. Nine agents will be contracted, one every twenty years, and each agent will be supported by one supervisor and one assistant. That they, like us, will all remain anonymous. Also, although we begin with a scientific concept, this is not a book of science, just as it is not a book of religion, and the agents' assignment will be to sift through everything from internet searches to small town myths to an overheard conversation in a bar, looking for a story. We ask each agent to choose one primary story and one backup, but up to five stories can be saved and stored during any twenty-year period.

In our preparations, we have covered a number of issues that may arise, such as an agent dying in the middle of their tenure. We also stipulate how each agent will be chosen. Stressing how important that choice will be. The stories themselves can be the narrative of one person or that of a family or group. If a story is multi-generational, it must culminate during the period of time in which it is being written. The storyteller is free to use fictitious names or a person's actual name, although because we stay open to the possibility of viewing the timeline someday, we require that each story contains at least one tracking point. A moment, the storyteller can identify precisely where we could find them in time and space. The balance of the documents held in our storage facility are the financial and legal files. The only thing we have to say about these hard copy and digital documents is that out of all the space secured for this entire project, more than seventy percent of that space has been filled with the wonderful language of finance and the law. The specifics of which you will be spared.

There is one last directive given to our agents that we want to mention. After collecting a story, the agent must vet that story factually. And it will be made clear to the storytellers that exaggerations or titillations will not help their story's chance of being chosen, and since they won't know what our choice is based on, the agent will urge them to just tell the truth. The agent may give weight to a personal feeling they may have. A sense that the person they are speaking with is without artifice. Whether it is illusive or not, truth is what we hope to find.

With our preparations complete, the six of us are ready to leave everything for another time. Before we do, we want to include one example of a story in which we believe society "buried the lead."

We considered using a historical reference, but history requires too much background to establish a prospective. We considered politics, but none of us wanted to cope with untangling that web. Needing a scenario that could be understood easily, we returned to popular culture and the story of Tiger Woods and the nine iron.

The flippant, almost snide introduction to this story is intentional. Not as a jab at Tiger Woods. It is a jab at the world's reaction to the story. Where we, the people, direct the media circus to pitch its tent, and we are all distracted by clowns and acrobats. We challenge our future colleagues to do better than we did, to find their way above the high wire and beyond the distraction. To achieve this is actually simple. It involves a reflex that appears to now be hard-wired into the Zeitgeist. Finger pointing - Blame. To find the truth, start by completely removing all the blame. From that point of view, exposing any individual becomes meaningless. What remains is what the event may say about all of us. We believe the essence of this story is an inconsistent thought process that stops when we get to a place where we are entertained. We never consider how we might act under the same conditions that allow us to judge others in any way that pleases us. Until we are the ones being judged.

For the sake of future readers, Tiger Woods is a world-famous professional golfer. The story began with an image in our heads of

Tiger Woods in his vehicle at the end of his driveway with a nine-iron sticking out of the back window of his car that we believe his wife meant for his ear hole. And the world snickered. And the six of us snickered. It was our reaction to this story that was embarrassing. A descent into schadenfreude. The story itself we see as having three parts. First, there was the domestic squabble. Then, the extension into the golfing community. Lastly, there are people whose livelihood or charity work was tied to Tiger Woods and who focused on damage control.

In fairness, people trying to salvage their livelihood or work to keep their charity flourishing is no story at all. We would all do the same thing. As far as the effect on the golfing community as a whole, when the story expanded further into the private lives of the golfers and their families, our need to be entertained must have caused a lot of pain. Is our enjoyment of the disruption of their lives justified because they are rich or even privileged? Most of us usually hate or make fun of those who believe they have a right to judge our morality.

The last element of this tale is the fight between Tiger Woods and his wife. And that is none of our business. Not even if the fight spilled out on the street and could be glimpsed from a neighbor's home. As long as the couple didn't go three rounds in front of the neighbor's children, it's none of our business. Also, we must understand that money means very little in these moments. And the fame makes it worse. Of course, when rich people split up, everyone has a beautiful home, and there are plenty of options, but that doesn't have anything to do with emotions. Also, the standard our expectations pinned on Tiger Woods was absurd. In his thirties at the time of this incident, he was extremely wealthy, and his face was recognized by the entire planet. In our current society, he was offered the life of a Sultan. Not where the power is handed down to him by his father, and the harem is made up of slave girls forced to serve their master. Here, love is offered freely. This type of temptation, we would think, is difficult for most of us to imagine.

None of this is being noted in an attempt to garner sympathy for the individuals involved or that people don't have a responsibility to question their own actions. They should, but again, for us, it isn't about blaming the individual. Now, while we have no desire to create sympathy, we sorely need empathy. It is easy to understand that the rich should empathize with the poor. However, aside from money problems, it is just as important for the poor to be able to empathize with the rich. This may seem counterintuitive, but empathy creates common ground.

To be honest, we frequently say to ourselves, "They have everything, the hell with them." That's the same as the rich saying, "The hell with the poor, let them work harder." Both are ridiculous statements. Why do we let ourselves get away with it? Take our disdain for Tiger Woods's actions at the time. In this country, it is possible that a significant percentage of the population will have extra marital affairs. Even though this is a sore subject, it is important to reference because, in almost every one of these cases, the person having an affair has two choices - Two. The partner they are with and one other person they find who will go to bed with them. If you are a person who has three or four choices, you are either too good looking for your own good, or you're not very picky. Many of us, with only two choices, are powerless to stop ourselves. If Tiger Woods stands in the lobby of a hotel while he is being checked in, he has ten choices in ten minutes. Of course, the attraction of celebrity is nothing new, although it appears to be very different today.

THE PAST CAPTURES US FOREVER

In an interview, the great silent film star Buster Keaton was asked why his marriage ended. Talking about the 1920s, he said that he couldn't blame his wife because he would walk off the set after shooting a scene, go into his dressing room, and find a strange naked girl waiting for him. When asked how often this happened, Buster replied, "all the time." To Buster Keaton, nicknamed Stone Face. He was no Cary Grant. Many of those women may have been trying to break into show business, and there were a few admiring fans, but the numbers were relatively small. And society's view of them, right or wrong, was not one of acceptance.

Years later, Frank Sinatra and the Rat Pack came, but most of their dalliances were with actresses and showgirls. Today, it seems like everyone is in play. Let us put it this way. Brad Pitt walks into a wedding reception. He has not been invited, and he knows no one there. Brad Pitt walks across the dance floor, approaches your Aunt Libby, and says, "Hello dear, what's your name?" Stunned for a moment, she then answers, and Brad Pitt says, "Libby, come with me." In the large majority of cases, Aunt Libby looks at Brad Pitt, then turns to her husband of twenty-five years, and says, "Morty, I have to." In about a third of these cases, the husband understands. And as Aunt Libby and Brad Pitt leave the wedding reception, arm in arm, many of the guests, with jealousy in their hearts, think, "Why did he pick that bitch over me?" This includes Libby's sister. Now, Brad Pitt would never do this, and for the record, Brad Pitt will never, ever sleep with your Aunt Libby. So Libby, stick with Morty. Now, if all these people, male or female, gay or straight, transgender or anyone else, are drawn to Brad Pitt, is that Brad Pitt's fault? It is not. It isn't a matter of fault, and there's no one to blame. It's indicative of who we are in this particular moment in SpaceTime. And for those who think we have entered an age of equality, consider this. If Tiger Woods was having affairs with members of the transgender community, do you think it would have been the same story? Or would the reports have placed transgender as the headline? Transgender, transgender, transgender. And the story would never have gone away, which thankfully it did. So summoning the late great Edward G. Robinson, whose unique voice delivered lines such as, "Where's your messiah now," in the film *The Ten Commandments*, sounding like the pirate Long John Silver, we say, "Where's your equality now, aay?" That may be funnier on the audio book.

Hopefully, this story serves as an example of looking beyond the distraction where society buries the lead. So the next time someone points west and yells they went that-a-way, we stop and ask ourselves what we are actually being sold. Or what we are selling ourselves.

This book is partially inspired by the SpaceTime Continuum. We don't predict what this project may accomplish; however, we believe the journey is worth taking. This may not be a book of science or a book of religion, but it is a book of faith.

We admit that we cannot know why SpaceTime exists. Maybe we are the first experiment, and when our cycle ends, God will start again, reviewing what we did and making adjustments before the second experiment begins. Or maybe we are the second experiment, or maybe we're the sixth. Maybe God just likes to go back and look at dinosaurs once in a while because, in SpaceTime, there are no extinctions. We would find the Woolly Mammoth, the Black Rhino, the first tree. And every cardinal and every camel that's ever lived is still living. We view the past as being behind us. If it's in the past, it's gone. However, that doesn't appear to be the case. The SpaceTime Continuum is not a recording of our lives, and it's not a place where we used to live. We occupy a permanent place where the past is always the present, somewhere. To some people, this may be frightening; to others, it may be comforting. The word that comes to our minds most frequently is mystifying.

If certain scientific predictions are true and a hundred million years from now, the Milky Way collides with the galaxy of Andromeda, precipitating the transformation of our small part of the universe, and the Earth no longer exists, we will always be right here, right now. The future leaves us all behind – the past captures us forever.

THE ISOLATIONIST

Story # 1

THE ISOLATIONIST

Self-confidence may be necessary in order to reach your potential, whereas an excessive self-serving ego is corrosive to the individual who possesses it and harmful to anyone who, for any reason, may be standing in their way.

AGENT NUMBER 1

(2023 - 2042)

The Isolationist

(2023 - 2042)

An ambulance races along Highway 51 in North Carolina. The passenger lying in the back is on his way to the emergency room at Duke Regional Hospital; while following behind, the patient's wife, Emily Kendall, carefully maneuvers through her fears and through traffic to remain close to the vehicle carrying her husband of over thirty years, praying he survives. Feeling weak, Anthony Kendall strains to stay awake and attempts to clear his vision. He glimpses his wife behind the wheel of the car trailing them, and for just a moment, through the rear window of the ambulance, he sees her tears of concern before he loses consciousness.

Anthony Kendall grew up in Philadelphia, Pennsylvania, in the early 1980s. The street on which he lived was lined with townhouses on both sides, and every house was home to a family. Most of the parents were around the same age, which meant that most of their children were of similar ages, at most three or four years apart. When the kids in the neighborhood chose sides for softball, there were always enough friends around to populate two full teams, and there was a large empty dirt lot behind the north side of the street for them to stage their games. At night, everyone would happily congregate at the end of the block. It was a fortunate time and place to raise a family, a wonderful way to grow up, where most of the boys and girls got along quite well, less tethered to the digital world than subsequent generations would become.

All of this camaraderie and closeness changed for Anthony when he entered the 9th grade. His longtime friendships failed to survive the move from middle school to high school, and the loss of those friends appeared to happen abruptly. He had no idea why his life had been altered so radically, but suddenly, he found himself feeling isolated. At the same time, Anthony's connection with his parents also suffered. His relationship with his mother became strained because as he grew, he had less patience for her venomous nature, while his father, unfortunately, appeared to have no interest in him at all. Under the circumstances, Anthony adjusted well to this more solitary type of existence, and it was his ability to adapt that allowed him to remain content despite a lack of understanding of the changes with which he was forced to contend.

Following his graduation from high school, Anthony felt the need to start over, which led to his relocation to New York City. A few friends with whom he had maintained a relationship moved to New York at the same time, but they showed no interest in continuing their association with him, even while they kept in touch with each other. Still, Anthony remained in good spirits despite this obvious snub.

Over the next few years, Anthony would come in contact with different sorts of individuals, some his own age, some older. However, his experiences with each of them would be similar. They would befriend him and then the friendships would become one sided, with Anthony asked to lend them money or do other favors with very little reciprocation. Subsequently, when Anthony stopped doing them favors, the relationship would end. There were other incidents in his life that baffled him, as well. One in particular stood out in his mind. It occurred when he was visiting a neighbor in the building on Jones Street in the West Village where he lived. Using their bathroom, he had removed a ring from his finger. It was his great grandfather's ring, the only family heirloom that had ever been entrusted to him. Anthony walked out of the bathroom without putting the ring back on his finger. Five or ten minutes later, when he realized what he had done, he returned to retrieve the ring, only to find it was gone. Anthony asked his neighbor if he had seen it. His neighbor replied he had not. Entertaining the possibility that he had left the ring at home, Anthony checked without success. He never saw the ring again, and the episode stayed with him as another example, akin to the loss of his friends, that to him seemed inexplicable.

Despite his struggles, Anthony certainly enjoyed living in New York City. He loved the city's energy and worked in different sales jobs to stay afloat. As most young people do when moving to New York, he shared living quarters with roommates to soften the cost of exorbitant rents. He retained only a passing connection with the people he shared his space with, and from time to time, over the next few years, one roommate would move out and be replaced by another, a common occurrence in a city like New York.

In March of 1999, five years after moving away from his hometown, Anthony's father died suddenly of a heart attack at the age of forty-nine. Six months before his passing, his father purchased a fairly large insurance policy in comparison to his means, which some considered fortuitous while others believed it was a prophetic act by his father. In any case, right after receiving his inheritance, one of Anthony's ersatz friends presented him with a business proposal. Still very young, Anthony handed his father's gift over to him as an investment. This friend strung him along until Anthony realized he wasn't going to get the money back. It was a hard lesson to learn, and even though Anthony would still decide to trust people in the future, it would always end in disappointment. These disappointments, together with the loss of his childhood friends, the loss of his great grandfather's ring, and the one-sided relationships he continued to experience, cultivated a feeling in

Anthony that something about his life wasn't equitable, that these episodes were not above board. However, he also knew that it was difficult to differentiate between the instances of disappointment, betrayal, and failure that may be a part of everyone's life from those that felt aberrant and discomforting to him.

Then, around the turn of the century following the fiasco of Y2K, a permeating fear that never materialized when computers were expected to wreak havoc as the digits changed from 1999 to 2000, something wonderful and unexpected occurred in the life of Anthony Kendall. He met Emily Moore. Anthony had been visiting a client downtown in an attempt to make a living and stopped for lunch. At a corner table, working by herself, was, in Anthony's eyes, the most beautiful woman he had ever seen. She reminded him of the actress from the 1950s and 1960s, Audrey Hepburn. Slim and well-dressed, she had an infectious smile illuminating a face that he could only describe as captivating. To his amazement, when she looked up and saw him gazing at her, she didn't look away. Somehow, her smiling back at him ignited his courage, and Anthony walked over and introduced himself. When she invited him to join her, it kindled the possibility of the unthinkable. The notion that after a single glance and one moment of conversation - this was it. She was the one.

Being a Friday, it was no problem for Emily to take the rest of the afternoon off, and Anthony, in sales and an independent contractor, did the same. They spent the day walking the streets of the city in conversation and then had dinner together. Their immediate bonding felt so natural, with a passion almost preordained that it made spending the night together inevitable. And it happened so quickly that Anthony had hope, that the strange forces seemingly affecting everything he tried to accomplish would be left no opportunity for manipulation. By the end of that first night, their love was irreversible, insulated from any attempt of tampering by an outside world previously set on negatively influencing Anthony's life. By the end of the weekend, Anthony and Emily had made plans for him to move into her apartment in the East Village, in lower Manhattan, which he did the following day.

In a relationship that would last a lifetime, there would be only one hiccup between Anthony and Emily. Four years after their kismetic beginning, Anthony was still struggling to make a living. During this same time, Emily found success. She continually advanced in her position at the literary company where she worked and attained a position as vice president, which brought her a lucrative salary and a modicum of prestige. Outside influences began questioning whether Emily had settled too quickly in her commitment to Anthony Kendall. Many around her liked Anthony well enough but thought she could do better for herself. The year that Emily became a senior vice president, the difference in their station in the materialistic world caused a rift. The breakup that ensued was very painful, but fortunately for both of them, it wouldn't last long. Three months after their separation, it became obvious they had made a mistake, so they resumed the kind of love and devotion that transcended social expectations. In fact, their time apart made them even closer. From that moment forward, outside pressures would never again get the chance to penetrate the allegiance between them.

One year later, Anthony and Emily were married. Their happiness would endure as an additional twenty years would pass, but Anthony's experiences with everyone other than Emily would remain cluttered with confusion. One friendship and business association after another continued to provide the same results as they had in the past. Friendships would begin and end, accompanied by extremely limited successes in his work life. Looking back, Anthony noted that each new friendship and job offer was the result of introductions made by a previous encounter as if one person kept passing him off to the next. He wasn't able to shake the feeling that his life, other than his marriage, was a series of failures designed by something outside of his own efforts. When he began a brief affiliation with another connection arranged by a friend, Anthony believed he found his answer. Jeffrey Banks, a man in his mid-thirties, had failed in his latest business venture and was looking to begin again. As always, Anthony approached meeting Mr. Banks with the hope of an opportunity. The two met to discuss the possibility of starting a sales and manufacturing organization together to concentrate on corporate printing, an area where Anthony had worked before and, therefore, had some measure of expertise. It was when the two prospective partners began discussing how to raise money for their startup company that Anthony was finally able to unriddle a life that had been filled with unanswered questions and enigmatic episodes.

While compiling a list of prospective benefactors they might approach for investment capital, Jeffrey asked Anthony about his cousin, Lionel Felder. Anthony was shocked at the mention of this name. Suddenly, he was overcome by a paralyzing sickness that consumed his entire body. He broke out in a cold sweat even though the reason for his reaction was not immediately clear. Questions began swirling in his head. How did this man whom he had just met even know about his cousin? Why would he think that Lionel Felder, a man who had never shown anything but disdain for Anthony, despite the fact that he was indeed the son of his grandfather's brother, be a viable investor for their business? Lionel Felder, whom he hadn't heard from in over 30 years.

Anthony couldn't explain how he knew, but it was as if something divine had planted the answer in his mind, revealing the reason behind the series of questionable events that Anthony believed had surrounded his every move in life. It was Lionel Felder who had corrupted those with whom he came in contact. Isolating him from the rest of society, thereby taking away any viable chance of success and preventing fate from ever stepping in and intervening in a positive way. Even though the idea made no sense, logically, he was certain it was true. Unfortunately, without definitive proof, what could he do?

His thoughts raced through all sorts of retaliatory possibilities. He thought of infiltrating Lionel Felder's residence and killing him or bombing his home. Of course, any plans of this kind were fleeting and ridiculous. He was not a navy seal. He had no expertise in bomb construction. These were reactionary fantasies; even if Anthony had the skills to strike back this way, he would never have felt it justifiable. It was just part of the defensive mental process of a hurt and frustrated soul. Anthony was, therefore, faced with a feeling of helplessness as he realized that he had no recourse. Certainly, he couldn't go to the police or anyone else for help. No one would believe him. The only power he could count on was an inner strength to persevere and appreciate what he did have; his love for Emily and a strong desire to remain happy with their life together.

Lionel Felder did not grow up in a wealthy household. His family had no ties to great institutions of education or the business elite. In spite of his simple origins, Lionel Felder built an empire of riches that would pave the way for him to become a great philanthropist, developing charities that would benefit a substantial number of people in need. On the surface, his charitable foundations, all bearing his name, were impressive. Some might argue that the man's contributions to helping others stood on their own as a testament to good. However, because the true intent of all he accomplished had grown out of a selfish need to promote himself, he corrupted everyone around him in order to advance his agenda, taking advantage of other people's greed to aid in building a stellar reputation for the Lionel Felder name. As a result, he would be afforded far more power than a man like him would be allowed if fairness held any sway in this world.

It is not difficult to comprehend that a person who has accumulated hundreds of millions of dollars, in many cases, would be equipped with an outsized self-serving ego in addition to whatever talents or intellect they may possess. It is more perplexing, perhaps, to understand why such an individual would use their power and influence to negatively impact the life of someone who poses no threat to them–where their overwhelming ego guides them without self-awareness and clouds the decisions they make, generating actions that may appear petty but with results that are not. Concurrently, their material successes often serve as validation, with their public image bolstered by a generous and charitable facade, creating a myth that no one who benefits from serving them will question. Because nothing is as powerful or popular as "me first."

In the aftermath of his meeting with Jeffrey Banks and the belief that Lionel Felder was in control of everyone surrounding Anthony, basically suffocating him, he and his wife had a decision to make. Do they stay in New York, the city they both love or start over and make it more difficult for Anthony's nemesis to affect his destiny? The first decision Anthony made was to sever ties with everyone he knew. As for leaving New York, the couple had one piece of luck on their side. The company Emily had worked for was being sold to a large conglomerate, and she was given the option of staying on with the new firm or accepting a buy out and retiring. Following an assessment of their situation, it was agreed that she would take the buyout and they would move south. It took six months for them to find their new home in the town of Cary, North Carolina, and so, after living in New York for over 30 years, Anthony and Emily moved out of their wonderful apartment on the top floor of the building on Manhattan's Upper Eastside, where they had resided for the last 15 years of their lives. Although they were forced to leave New York by the actions of Lionel Felder, Anthony and Emily Kendall, who were still in love, knew that as long as they had each other, they would be fine. It was true that Emily would now be farther away from her family, but her relatives could visit, and she would continue to stay close to them. Anthony had no family to worry about. Then, one year after their move to North Carolina, on March 8th, 2027, something truly incredible took place.

Anthony and Emily were in the kitchen of their southern-style home. The television, tuned to CNN news, was playing in the background when a live report caught their attention. Aerial video of a building in New York City was being broadcast, where a crane had broken free of its moorings and fallen from the 22nd story of the building on the north side of the street, sending it crashing onto a nineteen-story structure standing on the street's opposite side. The view from above revealed a devastating scene. The report stated that the apartment on the top floor of the building, struck by the 100,000 lb. steel behemoth, had been obliterated. A 75-foot piece of the crane had broken off its boom when striking the backside of the 19th floor apartment and flew a full block away, leveling a five-story apartment house. It took only a matter of seconds for Anthony and Emily to simultaneously recognize the building shown and the apartment that lay in ruins as their home of 15 years, the home they had decided to leave almost exactly one year before.

Initially, they were shocked when they recognized where the catastrophe had taken place; then a feeling of bewilderment overtook them, followed by a sense of relief in having escaped the tragedy. It was a terrible accident that would claim seven lives that day. The couple felt a chill run through their bodies knowing that if they had remained in New York for one more year, their lives would have been forfeited. Beyond the feeling of remorse for the lives that were lost and their understandable gratitude for still being alive, came the astonishing realization of why they had been spared. The couple were saved by vacating New York, the city in which they thought they would live for the rest of their lives, because of the actions of the man who had attempted to sabotage Anthony Kendall's life from the time he was 14 years old.

The series of events was ironic. They truly believed that fate had reached in and pulled them out of harm's way just in time. The episode seemed evidential in one way. No matter how powerful Lionel Felder was, he could not control everything. Anthony even allowed himself to hope that his nemesis might view the incident as a sign, that maybe he would no longer pursue his own egotistical need to satisfy himself through Anthony's grief. That hope was short lived. Anthony understood that someone who serves his own ego without caring about right and wrong would never entertain the possibility that a higher power was telling him to change course. Still, to Anthony and Emily, the entire ordeal fortified their faith. They believed that they had been guided into making the right decision and the universe had spared them to live on.

The following years in their new home in North Carolina were a happy time for the couple, but that didn't mean Anthony let his guard down. Starting over in a new city had wiped the slate clean, however, the hand of Lionel Felder and his determination to control Anthony's journey in life showed itself from time to time. And there were moments when Anthony examined his past attempting to discover a reason for his being targeted by his own relative. He never found an answer. Nothing he could think of was justification for Felder's oppressive actions or offered Anthony any solace when he considered the actions of those who served Felder's malicious intent, those who entered his life under the pretense of being his friend.

Then, five years after the crane incident, Anthony was overcome by a feeling that something untoward was on the horizon. His senses were activated, alerting him to an event from which he would need to protect himself. Anthony felt an opportunity was approaching that would offer Lionel Felder the chance to execute what he perceived to be Felder's end game, and experience had taught him to heed these instinctive warnings. Anthony had made an appointment for an endoscopy, a test performed thousands of times a day without any negative consequences. Nevertheless, feeling certain his nemesis was still out there plotting, Anthony's instinct promoted a forewarning of what was to come. He didn't share his fear with his wife. He didn't tell her he felt his life was in danger. He only reminded Emily that she was the only person in the world he could count on to look out for him, which he hoped would heighten her sense of responsibility during the procedure. Lying on the table waiting for the doctor, Anthony decided, despite the probability he would appear insane, regardless of the disbelief he was bound to encounter, that he had to disclose what he believed was about to transpire.

Anthony's anxiety centered on the anesthesiologist. Somehow, he knew that the person who would sedate him was the one he had to fear. The one he felt was going to murder him in accordance with Lionel Felder's instructions. Even though he couldn't explain his premonition, he was not going to ignore it. The message that had formed in his mind was crystal clear, and the stakes were too high. The bet being placed was his right to survive. Before the doctor entered the room, Anthony's attention was drawn to a woman standing approximately twenty feet away from the examination table where he was seated. She was gripping a clear visor in her hand as she looked his way with a stern gaze and a $1200 haircut. Her demeanor was disturbing. She appeared extremely tense. He had no way of knowing definitively, but Anthony strongly sensed that she was the anesthesiologist. He tried to make eye contact, but she immediately averted his glance. In that moment, he knew that she was a threat, the culprit who was going to overdose him. A moment later, the doctor who would perform the procedure approached. The doctor was about to begin when Anthony asked if he could speak to her. In fact, he insisted. Respectfully, he informed the doctor of his concerns. He did not mix words; he did not hold back. He did apologize for taking an extra few minutes of her time before proceeding to tell his story.

Anthony began by stating that what he was about to say was going to sound insane, but it was a matter of life and death, so he had no choice. Anthony imparted the history of his cousin Lionel Felder's manipulation of his life and told the doctor that even though he knew she wouldn't believe him, he was positive he was going to be murdered on her operating table right then and there. Anthony informed the doctor that he believed the anesthesiologist was going to overdose him and implored the doctor not to allow it to happen. Anthony reiterated the fact that he was not insane. He begged the doctor to take him seriously and not let his cousin's vile wishes be fulfilled. The doctor didn't have much of a reaction, but she agreed to look out for him. Anthony questioned whether she would, even as he allowed her to proceed.

In the reception area, Emily Kendall was reading a health magazine. She looked up from time to time, waiting to be called into the recovery room, anxious to see her husband and take him home. No one came to get her. When she began spotting people that she remembered had been taken through the doors of the clinic after her husband, she became concerned. How she noticed this was perhaps a result of Anthony's remark that she was the only person whom he could trust, creating an acute awareness. Maybe it was just luck. Emily rushed into the back, where the operating rooms were located, frantically searching for Anthony. When she finally found him, he was lying on a table, where he had been left alone, barely conscious, his life slipping away. Her screams for help were heard, and an orderly immediately called for assistance. A few minutes later, Anthony was in the back of an ambulance on his way to the emergency room while Emily, with tears of distress clouding her vision, followed closely behind.

In the emergency room, a doctor would shock Anthony's heart two times in order to revive him as he had indeed been overdosed, with fentanyl. After forty-five minutes of rest, his breathing normalized, and Emily took him home, weak but alive. Within a few days, Anthony would make a full recovery. This was the last time he felt his life threatened by the man who had affected so much of his life. Then, six years later, at the age of 86, Lionel Felder, an admired philanthropist, passed away, as all humans must, rich or poor, vainglorious or humane.

When Anthony saw a notification of Lionel Felder's death, he felt no relief or satisfaction. He still had no idea why he had been victimized by the now deceased philanthropist and knew now he never would. Also, never being able to pin down any actual proof that he was right about his cousin's actions caused him to consider, for a moment, the possibility that he had imagined Lionel Felder's interference in his life. Maybe it was all a rationalization to explain all the episodes that led to a life of missteps, a life without friends, without social success. However, he thought of how fortunate he felt, as well, for the life he had been granted. His relationship with Emily by itself, was enough to grade his life as successful.

As Anthony began reading through the obituaries and commemorative articles circulating on media outlets around the world, he noticed most were running the same photograph. It appeared that despite his philanthropy and notoriety, there were very few images of the man available to the media. The image showed Lionel Felder at home, seated at his desk. To his left, on the right side of the photo, was a bookcase with a glass front. It looked to be a rather large bookcase, but only a small portion of it was visible, as much of it appeared to be cut off and existed outside the edge of the image. Anthony looked closer at the photo. His attention was drawn to the items displayed inside the case. He used his fingers to spread the digital image, enlarging it to get a better view. On one of the shelves, through the glass, he saw something that startled him. There was no doubt as to what he was seeing because it was something he thought he would never see again - his great grandfather's ring. In that instant, all the doubts that had entered his mind evaporated. There was only one reason his great grandfather's ring could have ended up inside that case. Anthony now knew, conclusively, that all his suspicions were true. Lionel

Felder had isolated him and thwarted any success his God-given abilities may have afforded him.

After the anger he felt, resulting from the proof contained in that photo, subsided a bit, Anthony began perusing the other pieces displayed in the case. There was a small baseball glove with the name "Timmy," signed in purple, which looked as if it may have been scribed using a crayon. Anthony knew that Lionel Felder had a son and a daughter, and his son and daughter had three sons between them, but neither Felder's children nor his grandchildren were named Timothy or Timmy. Whose glove was it? Anthony scrutinized the other items in the case. There were two notices of termination displayed side by side. He couldn't make out the names of the individuals who had lost their jobs, but the letterhead belonged to Lionel Felder's company. Next to those papers was a necklace, and next to the necklace was a theft report from the Philadelphia Police Department. All of these items were in the same display case as his great grandfather's ring. Anthony realized that what he was looking at wasn't a bookcase at all. It was a trophy case. Trophies that had been collected from all the individuals, like Anthony, whose lives had been altered in service to the needs of this egocentric man. The number of those affected was unclear because the size of the trophy case was undeterminable, as the truncated photo hid the furniture's full size. However, the evidence showed that Anthony's life wasn't the only one negatively impacted. This was of no comfort to him.

Anthony's imagination haunted him when projecting how many peoples' lives might have been completely destroyed by Lionel Felder. Anthony surmised that he was probably the fortunate one. Meeting and falling in love with Emily in a moment so brief that Felder couldn't interfere was a miracle. And Anthony's life had been saved on two separate occasions in spite of the man's efforts to cause him harm. All things considered, he had been granted a good life. What about the others? Most, if not all of them must have suffered without even understanding what was happening to them. Without the knowledge that their life's possibilities had been neutered, their path restrained as entertainment for the pleasure of one individual.

Perhaps, just as disturbing as the plight of the victims themselves was the incalculable number of individuals who were drafted into the service of this game, assigned to help surround and aid in the control of the destinies of others. For their 30 pieces of silver, all of these tangential figures had been corrupted. In some cases, they might have been men and women who enjoyed their role in serving Lionel Felder's needs, believing it made them superior to those they oppressed, while in most cases, Anthony presumed they were decent people who turned into ugly participants, and most likely, had minimized their parts in this play of subjugation, in order to not judge themselves too harshly. With the justification of their actions possibly derived from the sentiment that "this is the way the world works." However, this was only evidence of their own fear. Fear that, from one point of view, was understandable, considering the fact that when a man as powerful as Lionel Felder asks something of you, you either follow him blindly and accept your reward or refuse and hope he will not set his sights on you, marking you as his enemy, and inflicting the same lifelong, life altering consequences as he had on his other victims.

It is impossible to speculate as to the cause of all this, the "why" of it. There may have been a trauma in Lionel Felder's early life that created his insatiable ego and merciless heart which spawned an extremely successful individual who, by most accounts, was considered to be a great and benevolent man but whose great wealth subsequently paved the way for him to unleash a destructive energy into the world. Honored philanthropist Lionel Felder, The Isolationist, who controlled and manipulated everyone around him in service to the petty evils of this powerful man.

A DREAM BUSINESS

Story # 2

A DREAM BUSINESS

It's not always governments that carry out assassinations. Sometimes, it's more convenient for a private organization to take care of the problems of those who live above the law.

AGENT NUMBER # 2

(2042 - 2062)

A Dream Business

(2042 – 2062)

Never before had their operatives failed. There had been times, although very few when an operation had been momentarily aborted, where circumstances arose, and the timing and methods of an endeavor required reevaluation. But each mission had always been rescheduled and successfully accomplished without any backlash to those charged with its planning - or their clients. The men and women engaged in these difficult and dangerous tasks were the field's elite, as skillful and effective as the organization that hired them was secretive. For sixty-five years, this privately funded, ghost-like group of seven had authored the assassinations of lives and of character in service of the privileged handful of politicians and citizens who knew of their existence. Seven members of an institution altered lives to benefit those above the law – "The Order of the Black Robes." Never before had their operatives failed, threatening *The Order's* unblemished status. Then came Ecuador.

The news reports posted around the world announcing the assassination of Ecuador's liberal presidential candidate, on their own, failed to illuminate the underlying conditions surrounding the shocking act. Unreported were whispers of a first attempt made on the life of candidate Carlos Guerrero Garcia two weeks prior to his demise. The failure to protect the man so soon after this first attempt was difficult to accept. And simply baffling was the discovery of three men, subsequently deemed responsible for the assassination, found dead in the hills surrounding Tababela International Airport in the city of Quito, with no other evidence uncovered suggesting anyone else's involvement. These three men were the original members of the hit squad hired by *The Order*.

Three men who had failed to complete their assignment and consequently paid the ultimate price.

"The Order of the Black Robes" had been commissioned by the political party in Ecuador opposing Mr. Garcia in their pending presidential election, politicians who had expected a clean elimination of their rival. Although Mr. Garcia's murder would never be traced back to the opposition party or *The Organization*, the series of events was considered a failure by *The Order*, a first in their history. A failure that necessitated the planning of a second mission to clean up the mess left behind by the first. With no room for any additional slip ups, "The Order of the Black Robes" had enticed sixty-two-year-old Francisco Ceballo away from his retired life, living in grand style on the Amalfi Coast of Italy, to eliminate Mr. Garcia and the original hit squad while planting evidence that would satisfy the country of Ecuador and the various authorities' investigation of the crime. However, the need to acquire the services of this legendary assassin would create doubt in the minds of the members of "The Order of the Black Robes." It would cause them to question their methods when, in between the failed assassination and the immaculate work of Francisco Ceballo, the original hit men, on the run and in fear for their lives, had contacted their employer, threatening to expose *The Order* publicly, if a plan was not devised to extract them from their tenuous situation in Ecuador and find them a safe haven elsewhere.

The Order had to consider that the future may hold new risks for the organization, where any professional they employed could be tempted to save themselves by betraying *The Order*. Additionally, there was the cost of hiring a man with Francisco Ceballo's flawless reputation to finish what the original team could not, generating an unexpected expenditure of thirty million dollars. Funds that were withdrawn directly from the coffers of "The Order of the Black Robes." Some in *The Order* believed a new approach was worth exploring.

Eighteen months after the debacle in Ecuador, an advertisement was listed on the website "Jobs at Night." This site, as its name suggests, carried ads for job openings whose working hours would begin any time after 6:00 p.m. and end no later than 8:00 a.m. The ad in question offered a lucrative opportunity for those living in the Cincinnati, Ohio area, boasting the availability of a position for nighttime employment, which would not interfere with those still working nine to five. The ad read:

If you meet our qualifications, a unique opportunity is yours.
Our firm is initiating an extensive,
comprehensive study of dreams.
Come work for "A Dream Business."
And get paid while you sleep.

Richard Vale, at home less than a mile and a half from the address listed in the ad, found the offer appealing. Richard was ex-military. He had been trained in combat and served in the field before receiving two years of experience working in intelligence. Richard had served his country for ten years until pressure from his wife caused him to request an early discharge. He retired from active duty honorably. His wife left him anyway.

Alone and unemployed, Richard had decided to distract himself by writing about his time serving overseas. The ad for a job at night, which would not interfere with his daytime plans to work on his book, presented an extremely desirable option. Although the ad didn't specify what qualifications "A Dream Business" was looking for, Richard's skills and life choices, which made for some interesting and, at times, disturbing dreams, hopefully, would present him as a prime candidate. When his interview concluded, there were no details provided as to why he fit the bill, but the following morning, Richard Vale was notified of his acceptance into the program.

Three weeks later, at eight o'clock in the evening, Richard Vale entered the offices at 20 E. Central Parkway. He followed signs posted on the first floor of the seven-story office building leading to room 106 and the entrance to "A Dream Business." Richard took note of what appeared to be a very sophisticated locking system. He rang the bell and waited until the door opened. He was greeted warmly by a tall, thin man in a white lab coat. The name stitched into the front pocket of the coat was William. The man guided Richard into a small, bare room containing one table and one chair. On the table was a document for Richard to examine and sign: an agreement confirming his willing participation in the program.

The document revealed no specific details about the pending procedure other than the inclusion of a release form granting permission for the use of a pharmaceutical to be administered by a certified physician at the beginning of each session. William assured Richard that the drug was nothing more than a sleep enhancer, equipped with a harmless isotope formulated to aid in the monitoring of his dreams. After signing the forms, Richard was guided through another locked door and into a long corridor. Lining the hallway was a series of rooms equipped with hospital beds and what appeared to be some kind of monitoring equipment. Richard experienced a moment of trepidation, but then another individual in a lab coat entered the room. His name tag read Dr.

David Phelps. Somehow, seeing "doctor" printed on his coat eased Richard's concerns. He relinquished control, laid down on the bed as instructed, and allowed the drug to be administered into his system. This was the last detail Richard remembered, waking up the next morning in the same bed with no deleterious effects from the night before evident. For the next seven days, Richard submitted to the same procedure without feeling any ill effects. Having completed the first week of his ten-week contract, Richard believed he had slept straight through each night soundly, without waking. This was unusual. His regular routine would have him waking up at least once a night to use the bathroom. When Richard inquired about this deviation, he was informed by the attending doctor that the disparity was an intrinsic effect of the drug they were using and that it was vital, for the sake of the study, that his sleep patterns last through the night, undisturbed. Feeling reassured, Richard continued his participation in the study without apprehension.

Eighteen months earlier, following their disappointment in the series of events in Ecuador, "The Order of the Black Robes" had approved a strategy that had been under development for the previous two years. It was a pet project of the head of the organization, the Chief Minister or Vizier of *The Order*, Harmon Shelby. Mr. Shelby was the son of Leland Shelby, the first Chief Minister of *The Order* and CEO of Arcolo Petroleum, the company he inherited from his father, the esteemed Forest Allen Shelby. The project, designated "The Cocktail," was authorized by Harmon Shelby and approved by the remaining six members of *The Order*, all second-generation businessmen and women, each holding the title of Priest Noble. *The Order's* chain of command was modeled after the social structure of ancient Egypt, minus the godlike position of the Pharoah.

The "Cocktail" had been developed by Dr. David Phelps, aided by a small team of chemists. The main ingredient utilized in the mixture was Scopolamine, with just a touch of Xylazine. These two drugs made up approximately seventy percent of the cocktail, with the remaining thirty percent composed of the brain stimulant Modafinil and a small amount of the anabolic steroid, Nandrolone. This mixture of drugs had the capacity to improve the dexterity and physical skills of the subject while, for ten hours, placing them under the complete control of "The Order of the Black Robes."

With no knowledge or memory of what would actually transpire during the time the subjects believed they were sleeping, Richard Vale and the additional four individuals selected for the "Dream Business" study, it was believed, would be rendered malleable enough to be trained as agents for the cause. The subjects could undergo intense physical and operational exercises and eventually be sent out into the field, complete their mission and wake up back in their beds at 20 E. Central Parkway at 8:00 a.m., with no recall of where they had been or what they had done. If captured, they would be incapable of offering any explanation for their actions or, if tortured, would never disclose the identity of those involved or the reason behind their mission. The "Cocktail" would create "perfect assassins."

To improve the likelihood of achieving their goal, each of the five original participants in the program was chosen for their individual and varied abilities and complementary skills to create a formidable team. The "Cocktail" would enhance those skills while removing the impediment of self-preservation, a successful mission their only devotion. The remaining question was where their training would take place. It needed to be somewhere that could be equipped as a private training facility for military type operations while passing as a front for the offices of "A Dream Business." These specific requirements led to the purchase of the building at 20 E. Central Parkway. There was nothing special about the building itself. It was the space beneath the building that held the answer.

Cincinnati, Ohio, is home to the largest unused subway system in the United States, covering two and a half miles of vacated space underground. With one of its stations located directly below the foundation of 20 E. Central Parkway, the perfect solution presented itself. After purchasing this seven-story structure, "The Order of the Black Robes" built elevator access to the empty area below and fortified and redressed the vast site to serve as a military grade training ground. The loading dock and freight elevators had also been addressed, with two elevators transformed into one large and sturdy lift capable of transferring up to forty thousand pounds of equipment to the station below.

Entering daily through the front doors of "A Dream Business," in addition to Richard Vale, were the remaining members of the team: an actress with chameleon-like qualities, Laura Cantrell, a weapons and ordinance specialist, Jayden Reese, a computer geek, Manuel Rogero, with experience in computer programming including AI controlled vehicle systems, and Tia Brown whose physical beauty was disarming - her training in Ninjitsu, deadly.

The abandoned Cincinnati subway system and its two and a half miles underground had been furnished with two gun ranges, one to develop skills for closer encounters with handguns and one capped at eight hundred yards. Richard Vale had the most experience with firearms, but all the team members needed to be prepared to assume anyone else's responsibilities in case of injury or any other unforeseen event. Also, a part of the facility had been redressed to replicate every detail of the mission's environment. By the time the team entered the field to carry out their assignment, they would be well prepared, and "The Cocktail" would eliminate any fear or guilt the team may have felt otherwise. The team was ready after ten weeks of training, the first eight weeks concentrating on improving each member's fitness and skill sets, and the last two spent drilling on specific mission details.

The *Target* of the first assassination to be carried out by the "A Dream Business" hit squad was entrepreneur Samuel Elkins. Mr. Elkins had just completed the merger of his forty-billion-dollar software firm with a company owned by a client of "The Order of the Black Robes," Lyle Sands, whose preference was to run the combined firm all by himself. This led to his hiring of *The Order* to eliminate his new partner a few months after the merger was completed. The time lapse between the merger and the assassination gave *The Order* an opportunity to plant disinformation about Mr. Elkins' Middle East dealings, diverting any blame for the man's murder away from the merger and placing it on international entanglements involving another of Mr. Elkins' businesses, a security company, Lancer, Incorporated.

On October 26th, 2052, the "Dream Team" arrived in Cleveland, Ohio, where thousands of visitors had gathered to celebrate the 59th annual Rock and Roll Hall of Fame induction ceremonies. One of those celebrants was the intended target, Samuel Elkins, who attended the ceremony and after parties every year, always staying in a suite at the Ritz-Carlton on West Third Street. The *hit* was set to take place outside the hotel after the induction ceremony when Mr. Elkins' routine would bring him back to his suite to freshen up for the extensive party scene. By ten-thirty at night, the five members of the hit squad, completely alert but consciously unaware of what they were about to do, assumed their positions.

Tia Brown, dressed in elegant evening attire, sipped a cocktail seated inside the Ritz-Carlton at the Turn Bar & Kitchen while Manuel Rogero and Laura Cantrell sat inside an ambulance two blocks away. Jayden Reese, serving as the team's spotter and immaculately dressed, remained in the hotel lobby, awaiting *The Mark's* return from the Hall of Fame's ceremony. The team's shooter, Richard Vale, held his position on the rooftop of a four-story parking garage across W. Huron Road, with a clear sight line to the front entrance of the hotel.

The limousine chauffeuring Samuel Elkins arrived back at the Ritz-Carlton at 11:40 p.m. Exiting the vehicle first was a bodyguard accompanying Mr. Elkins for the night's events. Once the bodyguard deemed the area secure, he escorted his client through the hotel lobby and up to his suite on the eleventh floor. As they passed Jayden Reese, seated in the lobby, the wheels of the assassination began turning. Reese notified the other members of the team that *The Mark* was in the elevator en route to his suite. Tia Brown paid her check at the Turn Bar & Kitchen and made her way to the lobby, where she sat, waiting, while Reese rode the elevator to the eleventh floor. "The Order of the Black Robes" had secured a room for Reese, situated down the hall from Samuel Elkins' room, where he could keep watch of the eleventh-floor hallway. Thirty minutes later, the *Target* exited his suite with his bodyguard and entered the elevator, as Reese loitered inconspicuously outside his own room until the elevator door closed. Jayden Reese then apprised the rest of the team – it was *Go Time*.

Tia Brown positioned herself near the front entrance of the hotel. She began to exit concurrently with Samuel Elkins' attempt to leave the hotel, creating an awkward but sexually-charged moment before Elkins motioned to Tia to proceed before him in a chivalrous gesture. In that same moment, Laura Cantrell, seated in the passenger seat of the ambulance, repositioned herself to the back of the EMS transport as Manuel Rogero, still in the driver's seat, hacked into the automatic driving system of a Toyota Camry parked nearby. He quickly designed and then activated an AI program, which started the engine on the Camry and guided the car remotely toward West 3rd Street and the front of the Ritz-Carlton. There appeared to be a person sitting in the driver's seat of the Camry.

At the moment Samuel Elkins, his bodyguard, and Tia Brown reached the sidewalk in front of the hotel, the Toyota came racing around the corner and crashed into an SUV parked across the street from where they were standing. The terrible collision distracted *The Mark* and his bodyguard for a second or two, diverting their attention long enough for Tia to attach an infrared transmitter on the *Target's* back, the contact between them seemingly nothing more than a natural reaction to the crash. With the transmitter in place, Manuel Rogero drove the ambulance to the scene of the accident that he himself had caused while Laura remained in the back, both of them dressed as paramedics.

Simultaneously, Richard Vale, looking through the scope of his advanced sniper rifle, took advantage of the confusion on the street. His clear sight line to Mr. Elkins from the rooftop only a half block away, coupled with the infrared transmitter on the *Target's* back and identifying receiver on the military grade weapon of which Richard had been equipped, made failing to achieve the objective almost impossible. Richard fired once, and the bullet hit its mark. The round pierced through Mr. Elkins' chest, the impact of its large caliber causing life-ending injuries as Elkins crumpled to the ground. Tia Brown shrieked in a pose of terror, and the shocked bodyguard checked for vital signs before cradling his dead employer in disbelief. Tia Brown used the opportunity of disarray to run off as Manuel Rogero and Laura Cantrell arrived across the street. They jumped out of the ambulance, opened the driver's side door of the damaged Toyota, and removed what appeared to be an injured man, but what was, in fact, a crash dummy dressed in human clothing. They placed the dressed dummy inside the ambulance and sped off before anyone could flag them down to request that they attend to the actual victim still lying in front of the hotel. Richard Vale picked up the one spent shell casing from the rooftop, dismantled his weapon, bagged it, and carried it with him as he quickly escaped to meet the rest of the team for extraction.

The plan had been executed perfectly, and within two hours of the completion of their assignment, the unit of five was evacuated, flown back to Cincinnati, laid back in their beds at the offices of "A Dream Business," and brought back to consciousness by Dr. Phelps; the five assassins having no recollection of the mission they had successfully carried out, two hundred and fifty miles away.

Having completed their ten-week commitment to "A Dream Business," the five participants returned to the offices at 20 E. Central Parkway, at Dr. Phelps's request, for two additional nights, during which they were sedated but without the use of "The Cocktail." This was done for observational purposes, a sort of debriefing. When no ill effects or memory issues were detected, Richard and the rest of the team were rewarded with a two-week bonus and informed they might possibly be called back at a later date for another round of dream studies. They were then dismissed, as always, one at a time so there would be no contact between them while leaving the premises.

In the days following the completion of their commitments to "A Dream Business," the five unwitting brothers in arms returned to previous routines. Jayden Reese, who was unemployed before joining the dream studies, restarted his search for a new job. Tia Brown continued her training in Ninjitsu while accepting modeling assignments when and where her agent found them. Manuel Rogero had his day job working on computer coding, and the other two participants in the study continued their daily routines: Richard Vale was working on his book about his time in the military, and Laura Cantrell auditioned for work as an actor.

Feeling a bit claustrophobic at home in his small studio at the Fourth and Plumb Apartments, Richard began working on his book at the Starbucks on Walnut Street. From time to time, he would lift his head and take notice of the other patrons. One of those customers, an attractive woman with auburn hair, perhaps in her thirties, appeared familiar to him but without any clear recollection of having met her previously. The woman caught him glancing her way, briefly smiled, but then turned away with no further acknowledgment or recognition. Two days later, Richard noticed that same woman again. And once more, he saw her on the following Tuesday. This time, risking the possibility of a harsh rejection, Richard decided to be brave and introduce himself. In response, the woman was affable if not totally comfortable with the man approaching her, a man who, although handsome enough, was a bit older than she and, of course, a stranger. Then something unusual happened. As the woman, Laura Cantrell, turned back from her casual response to Richard introducing himself, she accidentally pushed the muffin she was eating off the table. As the muffin fell on its way to the floor, Richard did something instinctively, of which even he was shocked. He grabbed a napkin from in front of Laura and used it to snatch the muffin out of the air about six inches from the tiled floor in a display of incredible speed and dexterity. Richard then replaced the unblemished muffin, untouched by his bare hand, back on the table. Richard's actions were incredibly impressive, but there was something else. There was a sense of familiarity felt by Laura at that moment. Somehow, inexplicably, she felt comforted by the act, so Laura Cantrell asked Richard Vale to join her.

Laura Cantrell, now a thirty-four-year-old woman, was once a popular student at the University of Cincinnati. She had starred in many of the school's dramatic productions during her first three years there and had fallen in love for the first time. In her junior year, however, her life appeared to be altered forever when a weekend trip to Red River Gorge in Northern Kentucky turned tragic.

The sun had just set, and Laura and her boyfriend were hiking in the national forest. After walking through one of the forest's natural stone arches, they reached the edge of Chimney Top Rock without the ability to stop themselves from the precipitous fall. In the aftermath, Laura would be considered extremely fortunate as she only shattered her knee and cracked her pelvis while her boyfriend lost his life. Laura was saved by second generation Deputy Chief of the Wolfe County Search and Rescue, Donald May, who was saddled with informing Laura of her boyfriend's demise. Given the circumstances, Laura's physical injuries were considered a miracle, but her recovery still demanded three separate surgeries. She spent months in traction, presenting plenty of time for Laura to grieve her boyfriend's death while the incident replayed in her mind over and over again. To help distract herself, Laura became proficient and eventually masterful in the art of Origami, an art like any other, requiring time and focus. In the years that followed, as Laura restarted her life pursuing a career in acting, whenever her nerves unraveled, it was Origami to which she turned. She never fell in love again, remaining diligent in protecting herself from the risk of commitment. However, as she continued to spend time with Richard Vale, she found herself becoming vulnerable, finally letting go of her fears.

Richard and Laura's first official date continued into the early morning, their affinity towards each other strong and easy, as if they'd known each other from another time. They shared many moments of their lives. Richard spoke freely about his divorce, while Laura, in a surprising reveal, told Richard about her past, the death of her boyfriend, and its lasting effect on her, creating problems with commitment that she hoped to overcome. Neither mentioned their recent employment at 20 E. Central Parkway on that first night, perhaps out of embarrassment, but on their second date, Richard mentioned his ten-week stint at "A Dream Business." When Laura responded that she, too, had taken part in the study during the same time frame, they both looked shocked. Then they burst out laughing. There were no details for them to share, of course, because they were asleep the entire time and never met. The only link that occurred to them was that they both resided near the site of the "A Dream Business" offices, with Laura's apartment located barely a mile away from Richard's residence. This shared but phantom connection had the effect of drawing the couple closer, as if their common, albeit unconscious, experience was a "sign." Their meeting may have been fate, but a month after they began dating, Richard read an online news article that changed everything.

The murder of Samuel Elkins had captured the fascination of much of the world's population, including Richard and Laura. As one of the leaders in advanced artificial intelligence, Elkins' name was prominent, and his flamboyant lifestyle was admired by some and found distasteful by others. The questions concerning his death created continued interest in reports, verified or not, from internet news affiliates, as well as fabricated points of view from conspiracy theorists.

Seated in Laura's living room, Richard had just finished reading one of those news articles online, the latest development in the investigation of the Elkins murder. Immediately, he called out to Laura in a declarative voice that demanded her attention. As she entered from the bedroom, her warm, contented demeanor turned to one of concern. The perplexed look on Richard's face and the aura of his mood, which she could feel, frightened her. Richard showed her the story, updating her on the crime in front of the Ritz-Carlton in Cleveland. It included a fact that had not been reported previously. As Laura read the article, Richard stared at the living room's mantle in front of him. When Laura reached the part of the story that had startled Richard, she raised her eyes to see Richard pointing at the mantle. Laura didn't have to look. She knew what held Richard's attention. The article stated that the police were pursuing the only solid lead they had found thus far. They had located an ambulance, eventually reported stolen and then subsequently abandoned, that they believe had been used in the plot to kill Samuel Elkins. Various witnesses had described the scene from across the street of the murder and those two paramedics who had removed the driver from the crashed vehicle, but that no victim from the accident had ever reached a care facility for treatment. Also, there were no medical supplies missing from the ambulance, and no evidence was uncovered of any accident victim having been treated inside. The only item found that was obviously out of place was an example of Origami, carefully displayed on a shelf in the back of the EMS transport. The Origami was a beautifully crafted dragon situated on top of a coffin, an extremely unusual combination.

On the mantle in front of Richard were many examples of Origami exhibited along the shelf, including a dragon sitting on top of a coffin. Although Richard and Laura knew that the dragon and the coffin were far from definitive proof that Laura had been in that ambulance, the coincidence was too odd to dismiss. As they sat quietly beside each other, they were overwhelmed with questions, and the answers to each inquiry did nothing to appease their fear of what might be true. When had the murder taken place, for instance, and where had the murder been committed? Was it possible to travel back and forth from Cincinnati to Cleveland with enough time to carry out the crime? They couldn't shake the possibility that everything led back to "A Dream Business." And Richard couldn't escape the distinct possibility that if Laura had been there, then he must have been a part of it, as well. However, they were able to alleviate some of what they felt, what they were afraid of, by assuring each other that it wasn't possible. They were asleep.

Richard inquired about the Origami, and Laura replied that a dragon, or Tatsu, was a symbol of power, wisdom and success. She explained that she had created the dragon separately from the coffin. The coffin was one of many she had constructed for Halloween, filling them with candy and handing them out as gifts. The dragon situated on top of the coffin was something she had put together recently, in the past couple of weeks, with no conscious reason of which she was aware, a combination that could be construed as representing the death of wisdom and success. Of course, none of this was proof of their involvement in a crime. Still, the existence of an identical Origami at both Laura's home and at the crime scene began to erode their belief that their connection to the murder of Samuel Elkins was impossible.

Neither Richard nor Laura was prepared to deal with the next series of questions. The fact was, if they were involved, that would mean the pair must have met prior to their introduction at Starbucks. What would that say about their initial attraction to each other? Was it a biological coupling, like true love? Or was it their subconscious minds recognizing a link, memories that their conscious mind did not recall? Either way, the evidence, however weak, when combined with the uneasiness felt by both, demanded verification, one way or the other. But how would they find verification, and how far would they be willing to go to get it? Richard and Laura could just accept the news report and the Origami as a coincidence and continue on, loving each other and enjoying the life they had found together. Maybe they shouldn't be rash in their actions. On the other hand, how could they ignore the strong feelings they shared? The feeling that something was amiss at "A Dream Business." They had to know the truth. Did they actually murder someone or not?

Richard and Laura had learned from the news story that there were no fingerprints to be lifted off the pieces of folded paper found in the ambulance. The speculation was that the person in question had worn medical gloves. Actually, this was true. It had been part of the training for the mission, and the gloves had been destroyed, along with all other evidence connecting the team to the crime. Ironically, even though there would be no identification forthcoming from the authorities, which, at its core, was comforting to them both, Richard and Laura would decide to initiate an investigation of their own.

A DREAM BUSINESS

Once they were determined to find the truth, Richard and Laura began with the only lead they had. Fortunately, it was a strong lead. They would start with the man who had quelled their initial fears when "The Cocktail" was about to be administered. The doctor whose calming demeanor had allowed them to relax and acquiesce to the treatments at "A Dream Business." Someone whom they encountered at the beginning of each session, whose name was stitched into his white lab coat – Dr. David Phelps.

Richard and Laura's new mission was to generate some private time with Dr. Phelps and interrogate him. The first step in their plan, to find out where Dr. Phelps resided, wasn't difficult. Living on the top floor of the *Seven at Broadway* luxury apartment building only a half mile away from the "A Dream Business" offices, the doctor occupied a prime two-bedroom flat overlooking the city. The building's security was formidable, so the more convenient spot to intercept Dr. Phelps would be in the parking garage. The complication that presented itself was that the *Seven at Broadway* apartments were built on top of what had previously been a large parking facility with eight stories of parking spaces. They had no idea on which floor Dr. Phelps kept his vehicle. Richard and Laura began their reconnaissance by carefully scoping out 20 E. Central Parkway from across the street to determine what time Dr. Phelps arrived for work. Next, they retraced the route back to the *Seven at Broadway* apartments to judge the approximate time Dr. Phelps left the garage for the offices of "A Dream Business," only a few minutes away.

The next day, they verified the time the doctor exited the garage in his 2051 Porsche Cayenne, but they still needed to ascertain which floor of the garage he was on and in which space Dr. Phelps parked his car. Incognito, Richard scoped out one floor during the time Dr. Phelps most likely entered his car, while Laura scoped out another. Within two days, they witnessed the doctor entering his vehicle on floor number five.

The following day, Richard and Laura waited for Dr. Phelps to appear and approached him as he opened the driver's side door. Richard, with the service weapon he still possessed from his time in the military, pressed the gun against the doctor's side while Laura demanded his key fob. Laura sat herself down in the driver's seat, and the doctor was directed into the passenger seat. Richard continued to threaten Dr. Phelps with his gun as he settled into the back, sitting behind the doctor. Despite their disguises, Dr. Phelps recognized his captors immediately. Their presence bewildered and frightened him.

Laura drove the doctor's Porsche through the streets and onto Highway 71 as Richard began the interrogation. Instinctively, the curious doctor inquired how the pair discovered that they may have been a part of the assassination before realizing on his own that it must have been Laura's Origami. Threateningly, Richard refocused Dr. Phelps' attention on why he had been seized. Feeling he had no other option, the doctor told Richard and Laura everything they wanted to know. He confirmed their fears concerning their participation in the murder of Samuel Elkins and unmasked the organization that orchestrated it as "The Order of the Black Robes." He divulged the existence of the underground training facility beneath 20 E. Central Parkway and how they had controlled Richard, Laura, and three others through the use of "The Cocktail."

After hearing the doctor's admissions, Laura suddenly felt queasy, momentarily losing control of the vehicle, before regaining her composure. She exited the highway and parked. Dr. Phelps, in an attempt to influence his captors, insisted that they were categorically powerless to do anything about what had occurred. They should forget what they have uncovered and continue to pursue the new life they have found together. He assured them that challenging *The Order* was hubris, a losing proposition, capable of only ending badly for them both. Dr. Phelps implored Richard and Laura not to give up on what they had in order to confront an organization that would most certainly take it all away. Possibly losing their lives in the process.

Richard and Laura sat contemplating their next move. They had received their verification and understood the stakes. But even if they believed their love was real and not the result of their forced beginnings, how could they go on living in silence, knowing they were manipulated into murdering someone without their consent – without choice? Richard and Laura agreed; although they did not have a choice in the act itself, they did have a choice in whatever actions they took next. Burying the truth may be easier in the short run, but they both believed their life together could not flourish for long, with the inevitable growth of guilt that would result from having done nothing.

During the planning stages, when they considered how they might move forward if their worst fears were confirmed by Dr. Phelps, Richard Vale and Laura Cantrell had concluded that the only avenue open to them was to break into the offices at "A Dream Business" and document what was transpiring there, so they could go to the authorities with proof. Now that they were aware of the redressed underground complex, it was clear that photos of the training ground would offer them the strongest opportunity to expose *The Order* and their nefarious operations. They insisted the doctor escort them into the offices and complex below. The doctor agreed, apparently admitting he had no other option. However, because of his abduction, the doctor informed his captors he was going to be late arriving for work, and if he didn't notify his assistant, William, it would raise a red flag. The name William was familiar to Richard and Laura, who was recognized as the other man donned in a lab coat, who had overseen their admission and aided in their participation in the supposed study of dreams at "A Dream Business." Richard warned the doctor they would abide no deception. Nodding that he understood, Dr. Phelps texted William, informing him there was no problem and that he was just running a bit late but was on his way. Laura scrutinized his sending of the text, which appeared unremarkable. Unbeknownst to his captors, the doctor had texted, using a phone number that was utilized only to indicate a protocol breach, signaling a security alert requiring immediate and forceful attention.

Dr. David Phelps stood outside the door to the offices of "A Dream Business," along with Richard and Laura. Richard displayed his weapon and pointed it at Dr. Phelps in clear view of William, who opened the door, stood back, and allowed the doctor, Richard, and Laura to enter. Richard and Laura then began to observe and document the series of rooms equipped with hospital beds and monitoring apparatus using their cell phone cameras. Next, they all proceeded to the elevator at the end of the hallway and rode down to the vacant underground subway system beneath the building. As the elevator door opened to reveal the extensive training facility, the sight of such a vast renovated area was overwhelming to Richard and Laura. They began taking photos, and their intense concentration allowed William and the doctor to take a step back, distancing themselves from the pair, who were so focused on the job at hand that they were unaware of two men appearing suddenly from behind. All they felt was a sudden sting to their backs, the result of being hit by debilitating darts that rendered them unconscious.

Harmon Shelby, the chairman of "The Order of the Black Robes," appeared out of the shadows. He instructed Dr. Phelps that *The Order* had decided not to eliminate Richard and Laura. They admired their ability and courage, having gotten as far as they had, and although it was a calculated risk, they preferred keeping them alive to possibly serve the needs of the organization at a later date. Of course, their awareness of the program would have to be dealt with, and as a result, he was authorizing the doctor to initiate the inaugural trial of another drug they had developed concurrently with "The Cocktail." It was a sister project centered on studies in the use of the pharmaceutical Propranolol. The drug was a proven method for eliminating memories, and with *The Order's* backing and assistance from Dr. Phelps, they discovered that by controlling the doses, they could control how far back memories were eradicated. After three days of treatment, Richard and Laura left the offices of "A Dream Business" separately, with no memory of Dr. Phelps or "The Order of the Black Robes;" without any recollection of their part in the assassination of Samuel Elkins or the Origami found at the scene; with no memory of each other and their time together.

With their problems resolved, Harmon Shelby and the additional six members of *The Order* were free to continue utilizing the "A Dream Business" model to carry out missions, while Richard and Laura returned to their previous activities, with no explanation for the time that was lost to forgotten memories, or knowledge of the love they left behind.

A week later, Richard Vale walked into the Starbucks on Walnut Street and ordered a coffee to go. While waiting, he browsed around the store, gazing innocently at other patrons sitting in the room. One of those customers was an attractive woman with auburn hair, perhaps in her thirties. Richard found himself drawn to her, a tinge of Déjà vu clouding his thoughts, even though he was positive he had never seen the woman before. He considered approaching her but could not summon the courage. When his name was called and his order ready, Richard retrieved his coffee from the counter and exited the store. Once outside, with the image of the woman still present in his mind, he thought to himself – maybe next time.

Story # 3

PRIDE AND PLUTO

"In compiling and then writing this story, I was fortunate to be able to interview every major participant in this story except one. His name was William Forest McKenzie, and he died in 2062, the same year my employment began."

AGENT NUMBER 3

(2062 – 2082)

Pride and Pluto

(2062 - 2082)

In many families, there is one central figure, one relative above all others, whom the family cannot afford to lose. When that person dies suddenly, it can shatter the confidence of the entire clan. That is what happened to the McKenzies and, more poignantly, to Pluto McKenzie when Pluto's grandfather died. It was his grandfather who had given him his unusual name. Pluto was only twelve years old when he realized his mentor-to-be would no longer be there to teach him anything.

William Forest McKenzie was born on October 23rd, 1993. He was fifty-seven years old when his grandson Pluto was born, and most of the experiences of his life would remain a mystery to the boy. William had planned on sharing some of that personal history with Pluto, but as a child, he wouldn't have understood, and then, sadly, William never got the chance. When Pluto was six, however, he asked why he had only one grandmother and his friend Benji had two. The easiest answer, and everyone agreed, was to tell him that his grandmother had gotten very ill and was in heaven. Actually, she was still on Earth, technically, as a resident of Illinois State Prison. Sentenced for life - for murder. And she had been there since 2035, fifteen years before Pluto was born. There's no explaining that to a six-year-old.

The elder McKenzie did share his interest in astronomy with his grandson, particularly his connection to a group pushing for the reinstatement of Pluto as a planet. William was a young teenager when Pluto's status in our solar system was changed. Downgraded to a dwarf planet and a number – 134340. As a young man, he remembered the New Horizons space probe reaching its destination in July of 2015 and the hope that Pluto might be restored as the ninth planet in our solar system. Nine seemed like the right number to William. There was a symmetry to it, he thought. Of course, it never happened, so thirty-five years later, when William's son, Don McKenzie and his wife Patricia had a boy, the boy's grandfather was permitted to name him Pluto.

Don McKenzie was still a young boy when his mother was convicted of murder, and he would absorb more of an emotional impact from this event than anyone else. In his mind, he would always be the son of a murderer. Don gave more weight to the meaning of that phrase than is logical. He allowed it to help define who he became. And his burden manifested not as a debilitating disease but as a lifelong, low grade emotional fever. Don would never lash out. He would turn inward, becoming solemn.

By the time Don met Patricia Garvin, Don's mother had been in jail for five years, but because William had moved with his son to start over in another city after the trial, Don didn't have to contend with any of his current friends knowing about his mother's crime. When he reached the tenth grade, however, one of his classmates searched the internet and found the story. It was inevitable. Although, as it happens sometimes, life can be surprising, and the ridicule this brought to Don was overwhelmed by the empathy and love he found in Patricia's arms. Six years later, he and Patricia married, and they purchased a home in Urbana, Illinois, just a few miles away from where Don's father, William, lived.

As time passed and Don's emotional struggles continued, Patricia, in her attempt to help her husband, came to realize that his mother's incarceration and crime weren't the only problems. More hurtful was that Don had loved his mother dearly through his early childhood, and then suddenly, at ten years old, he began developing a terrible feeling of hatred towards her. Not for the crime she had committed - but for having left him. That feeling of abandonment lingered.

Through the years that followed, Patricia's effort in comforting her husband was unflinching and done lovingly. Unfortunately, when Don's father died, keeping her husband centered became much more difficult, as her maternal instinct forced her son Pluto's needs to the forefront, and the effects of William Forest McKenzie's death hit the foundation of the family like a pick against stone.

Seven years before his grandfather's death, life had been uncomplicated for a five-year-old Pluto. His father's difficulties were being well soothed by his mother's compassion, and Pluto was keeping himself busy playing, inside and outside, as parents had begun re-balancing where their children spent their time, using a phrase that decades before had been a daily cry - "get out in the fresh air!" And Pluto appeared to be happy as a young child. He had many friends, and he felt very close to his grandfather. He loved his mother, of course, but his grandfather was his pal. Pluto's other friends, boys his own age, included his best friend Benji.

When he, Benji, and their other friends were inside, the boys played video games. Games that were appropriate for kids their age. And when they were outside, the games they played at five years old were benign as well, all in fun. As they grew older, however, the games became more combative, as did the kids. When they were five, none of his friends made fun of his name. Pluto was a cool name, and it was fun to say, but when Pluto and his friends turned eight years old, they suddenly began to turn on him. And it appeared it was his best friend who was the instigator. One day, Pluto remembered them playing all together, and it seemed like the next day, Pluto was replaced. First, inside, where Benji and his new best friend, Freddie Vasquez, played video games. And then outside, where Benji created a new game he called "Battle of the Planets." Benji and seven others chose their planets, leaving Pluto out in the cold. They all laughed, but what Pluto heard was, "You don't belong here. And you don't belong with us." It was a cruel thing to do, and it served to help isolate Pluto from all of his other classmates. By the time he was ten years old, it felt to him as if he didn't have a friend in the world except for his pal, his grandfather. Pluto's father would remain a presence in his son's life, but the ebb and flow of their relationship would be complicated by his father's illness.

Following the loss of his friends, Pluto focused on his schoolwork during the day, carefully avoiding those he felt had betrayed him, especially Benji. After dinner and finishing his homework, Pluto's time would be spent developing a reputation online as a skilled gamer for his age, while his after-school time was usually reserved for his grandfather. And part of his weekends were spent with his grandfather as well. Fishing at Rock River or on Clinton Lake. Or throwing a ball around in the backyard of William's home in neighboring Champaign, Illinois, on Harvest Avenue. Pluto's grandfather loved the times they enjoyed together during those years, but it was getting increasingly difficult to ignore the lie they had told Pluto about his grandmother. He would have to be told at some point. He was still too young at ten or eleven years old. He wouldn't be too young for much longer. Even though Pluto's father would eventually tell him about his grandmother's incarceration, William understood elements of the situation that his son, Don, did not. And he found them unsettling. It was apparent that his grandson's anger was intensifying, and it wasn't difficult to figure out why. William understood that even though Pluto would not speak to Benji again, he still had feelings for him. And losing his friends hurt. He was concerned that Pluto's indignation was leading him into a self-absorbed state, with pride being the force that now whispered in his ear. William had seen this before. In his own wife, Pluto's grandmother.

Once again, William wrestled with the limitations of Pluto's age. What can you do when the full measure of something is beyond the ability of a young person to comprehend? This was William's dilemma when dealing with Pluto and his growing issue with pride. And how could William differentiate between pride and confidence in oneself? Confidence is necessary. Pride is insidious. William knew that in the current sociological environment, even adults choose not to see the difference. It had become acceptable. Self-promotion, derived from a self-serving nature, had become the norm. And Pluto was starting young. The chip on his shoulder was bound to get heavier as he got older. He may never stop and question his own behavior. With all this working against him, William still made the effort to reach his grandson. He felt that because Pluto was still young, he would have the time to teach the boy as his maturity allowed, but another power stepped in and would not allow it. So, although Pluto would remember the time they spent together, he would retain relatively little of what his grandfather had tried to teach him.

When the phone call came, Pluto was in class. As his phone rang out loud, a hush fell over the classroom. The teacher stopped speaking. It was the year 2062. No one's phone rang anymore. Ring tones were designated for emergency use only, and it was always terrible news.

The shock of the elder McKenzie's death left the family vulnerable. Pluto was dealing with a loss he couldn't reconcile. Life had narrowed his support team down to three already. And now the nucleus of that team had been taken away, leaving himself and two other human bodies out of orbit. Understandably, Don's depression worsened after his father's death, which left Patricia alone to deal with the parts of life that need to be dealt with, no matter the personal circumstances. And this was in spite of the fact that losing her father-in-law was devastating for Patricia. With Don's health problems and Pluto being awfully young, it was Patricia who had the most complete relationship with William. They were the strong ones. They worked through everything together and leaned on each other when Patricia needed a hand with Pluto or William needed a reassuring word about his son. Unfortunately, Patricia didn't have time to grieve the best friend she ever had. She had to carry on. And for a few months, she did.

Don and Patricia made their living in web design and maintenance, and even though there's some understanding from clients after a tragedy, it doesn't last long. And while Patricia had compensated for her husband and his illness in the past while taking care of the business, it had always felt manageable. This time was different. Before and after the funeral, Patricia was saddled with all the responsibilities. She handled all the notifications: sending out death certificates, closing accounts, dealing with credit card companies, handling business notifications, and rearranging project deadlines where possible. It was too much. Patricia had buried her own needs as long as she could.

Three months after William's death, she finally quelled her frustrations by lashing out at her husband. This was so far out of character that Pluto and his father were stunned. Once Patricia had released this anger from inside her, she broke down and began to cry. Her husband, as if slapped in the face, suddenly felt the shame of not pulling his weight. Pluto moved to his mother's side and held her hand while his father assured the family that he would not be a burden anymore.

Don McKenzie had been taking medication to curb the effects of his illness since he was a teenager. Over time, the medications had improved, but Don would be pulled back down into his own personal rabbit hole despite the medicine at times. Or maybe he was finding his way back down that hole to escape. When it comes to mental illness, we continue to make a noble attempt, and we categorize them as best we can, but it's the brain. Who knows how many forms of mental illness actually exist? In Don's case, whether it was the shock of his wife's despair that caused it is unknowable, but three months after his father's death, Don was able to make the choice to persevere and help take care of his wife and son.

With some of the overwhelming responsibilities of their home and business alleviated by her husband's efforts, Patricia was afforded time to slow down and recharge. The most important contribution Don would make during this time was in parenting Pluto. Patricia was thankful. Pluto had his father to help him now.

Don and Patricia often spoke about Pluto's future, and they shared some concerns about it. As a result of his continuing isolation from his classmates and the loss of his grandfather, Pluto devoted much more time to online gaming than he had before, and he didn't get outside to play at all. Pluto's parents decided to use some of the small inheritance that had been left to them by William to help guide Pluto. Both Don and his father were fit men, each over six feet tall, and at twelve years old, the beginning of a growth spurt was noticeable in Pluto. In response, his parents decided to curb two of their concerns by turning Pluto's attention towards physical fitness. They bought a couple of wall panels connected to an online exercise platform. They bought some adaptable free weights, as well as the latest cardiac training equipment. In order to keep him in the sunshine, or at least in the light, they decided against the basement and set up Pluto's gym in the sunroom, looking out at their small, well-kept garden.

With his father instructing him, Pluto began to establish a routine that would become a commitment that would make him strong physically. However, the exertion of energy didn't curb Pluto's anger. It only covered it like a blanket covering a grave. Still quite easy to fall in. The impetus for the event that put Pluto's pride on display happened two years after his grandfather died and his father began training him when Don's illness exacted a toll. No one could say whether the effort Don had made to control his depression for two years had caught up with him or if it was the cyclical nature of the illness striking another blow. Pluto was in the sunroom when he heard his mother's scream from upstairs. By the time Pluto reached his parent's bedroom, his mother was already on the phone with emergency services. His father was on the bed. Pluto watched as his father's body shook as if chilled for one moment, and then, with his body quiet, his breathing became erratic the next moment. As this cycle continued, Pluto and his mother waited impatiently for the paramedics to arrive.

The attack was severe enough to land Don in the hospital for two weeks. Fortunately, any lasting effects turned out to be mild enough to allow Don to return home after two weeks of care. Exhausted, both physically and mentally, but he was home. As for Pluto, Don's stay in the hospital was particularly difficult for him.

He was afraid for his father's well-being. He was also uncomfortable with, or maybe even ashamed of, his father's condition. Pluto didn't understand it. He couldn't accept the fact that his father had no control over its effects. Although Pluto's anger had started gaining steam years before and had little to do with his father, because one's anger is always one's own, Pluto diverted any responsibility from himself and placed the blame squarely on his father's apparently weak shoulders. This excuse would not last for long.

On the third day after Don returned home from the hospital, Pluto entered the school grounds, keeping his head down as he usually did. A group of students a year older than Pluto appeared to be talking about him as he passed by them. Pluto paused for barely an instant before continuing on, but he'd had trouble with this group previously. When one of the boys shouted something about his father's condition, Pluto no longer controlled his rage. His movement was quick, too quick to allow anyone else to react in time. Pluto attacked the boy, pushing him up against a tree before taking him to the ground. On top of him, Pluto punched the boy in the face. Looking up, he turned his stare toward the boy's shocked friends, turned back, and punched the boy in the face a second time. Then, in a minute, maybe two, Pluto regained a calm demeanor and walked into the school and into his classroom.

The way Pluto was able to stare down those students and then punch the boy a second time made his actions more than an emotional outburst. They became calculated. Pluto chose to throw that second punch. It was excessive and unnecessary. Oblivious to any problem, Pluto felt proud of himself. In his mind, he had stood up for his father and himself, and no one would react thoughtlessly around him anymore. He was still thinking that when the principal entered the classroom with two policemen. They arrested Pluto and took him to the local precinct.

Pluto sat in a barred cell inside the police station, waiting for his mother. She arrived, bringing an attorney with her, which surprised Pluto. Not that this made him rethink his actions. He was still quite proud of himself. An hour later, Pluto was released. However, he was not off the hook. The boy Pluto hit was hurt badly enough to possibly warrant an assault charge and even though he was a minor; any charge that serious could affect his future. Pluto still believed he had done the right thing, although he would have to find a way to stop the incident from hurting him moving forward. The counselor from Child Services, who sat with him for a total of ten minutes, scared him with possible limitations for the rest of his life due to a criminal record. Pluto detested the guy. He was also concerned about how much of what the counselor had said could be true.

Patricia and Pluto arrived home after dark. They had barely entered the vestibule when they heard Don's strained but forceful voice bellow from upstairs, "Pluto!" Pluto looked at his mother. He appeared to actually gulp. Then, he quickly moved up the stairs.

Pluto stood at the foot of his parent's bed. His father was sitting up, supported by a few pillows, as he was still feeling weak, recovering from the mental breakdown that invariably attacked his body as well as his mind. Pluto began to apologize for his behavior at school that day when Don stopped him and told him he had to talk to him about something else first. And it concerned his grandmother. Instantly, Pluto's thoughts turned to his grandma Ann and grandpa Liam, his mother's parents. They lived in Northern California, where Don and Patricia had just taken Pluto to visit six months earlier. Frustrated, Don addressed his son with a stronger tone this time and told Pluto he was not referring to his mother's parents. He was speaking about his grandmother, Rose. It took Pluto a few seconds before he realized who his father was talking about. He hadn't thought about his other grandmother for a long time.

Confused, Pluto asked, "Grandma Rose? She died years before I was born. So?"

By this time, Patricia had entered the room. She guided her son to sit by the bed and urged him to keep quiet and just listen to his father. As Don spoke, the burden of lying to his son for all those years melted away:

"Pluto, there is no other way to begin this discussion other than to just say it. Your grandmother Rose, my mother, is still alive. She didn't die as we told you."

Pluto attempted to interrupt. Don stopped him and continued:

"When you asked us about her, you were six years old. We couldn't tell you your grandmother was in prison."

Pluto can't help himself, "In prison?"

Don added, "For murder."

Pluto was silent. His father would go on to tell him that it was a double murder for which his grandmother was convicted. And that after serving a twenty-six-year sentence, she had been released from prison a couple of years before and had been living approximately twenty-five miles away from them. However, Don insisted that neither he nor Pluto's mother had been to see her. Not during the time she was in prison nor since she had gotten out.

Don continued speaking with the limited strength he had left:

"This brings us to your actions of today, son. Your mother and I have been trying to find the right time to tell you about all this. Today, you forced our hand. Your grandmother was a proud woman, and she thought life had more to offer her than just a wonderful family. So, she left us to chase her dream to be somewhere else. Then, when that somewhere else let her down, she struck out at those she thought wronged her. When I got a little older, I heard that many people considered my mother to be an extremely beautiful woman and that she thought her beauty made her special. Now, before your grandfather died, Pluto, he told your mother and me to watch out for the same self-centered traits in you. Today, we saw them. And if you think you were defending my honor or your family with your actions, you're mistaken. You weren't representing this family with your brutal display. You were thinking of yourself. And how dare those kids disrespect you!"

Don had exhausted himself. It was only his third day home from the hospital. He needed to rest. Patricia led Pluto down the stairs, but before her son could escape to the sunroom and his training equipment, she placed a hand on his shoulder:

"Pluto, we're not finished yet."

Pluto followed his mother into the kitchen, where Patricia asked him to boil some water for a cup of tea while she got in touch with the mother of the boy he had attacked. She scheduled a time for the two of them to go to the boy's home so Pluto could apologize. Pluto was surprised by his mother's plans, and his displeasure showed on his face. However, he was aware he was in a bit of trouble already, so as soon as Pluto realized there was a sour look showing, he changed it. Patricia was grateful for Pluto's apparent awareness, although there was something about his response she didn't love. She just couldn't put her finger on it.

The next day went as smoothly as it could, given the circumstances. Pluto apologized to the boy he attacked with complete sincerity. Seeing the boy's battered face helped him realize that violence would never be an acceptable response. The markings that violence can leave behind can be startling. Serving as evidence of what was done. It was also illegal.

When Pluto returned to school after a three-day suspension, he approached the group of kids who had been stunned by his attack on their friend days before. The group recoiled collectively a bit as Pluto moved closer. Unexpectedly, Pluto calmly apologized to them for his previous behavior and then proceeded to class. The general reception Pluto received from his classmates on his return was mixed. The students were cautious around him. Maybe a bit fearful at first. But fortunately for Pluto, the group he had stood up to, including the boy Pluto had punched, were bullies themselves. From then on, their bullying would no longer be an issue for any of the other students because of Pluto. Pluto began acting friendlier and more accessible to anyone with whom he came in contact, except for his former friend Benji. In time, Pluto and his newly minted, warm demeanor won him many friends.

Pluto would remain popular through his junior and senior years in high school, and it appeared as if he had developed into an honestly caring and giving person. In actuality, this was the beginning of the creation of Pluto's façade. Friendly, helpful, and present. He would always look you in the eye, yet he held a part of himself hidden, disconnected. Pluto wasn't aloof. And he was, in fact, very dependable. However, beneath his outwardly loving demeanor, he was impenetrable.

At eighteen years old, after graduating high school, Pluto began his tenure at the University of Illinois, Urbana-Champaign. Although, at first, he would not be involved with any of the school's sports teams, he developed a small following at the school because of his commitment to basic physical fitness. Pluto had matured into an exceedingly handsome man, and at six feet two and two hundred and eighteen pounds, he stood out on campus. Halfway through his freshman year, Pluto offered informal training classes to students who sought him out. He was eager to share his passion for exercising and for the breathing techniques taught to him by his father. His father had continuously emphasized breathing in their work out sessions. He taught Pluto that breathing was the least talked about part of being alive, and yet it was probably the most vital. By Pluto's junior year, he began assisting the coaches and trainers of the school's football team with individuals with minor injuries who could benefit from the attention of a personal trainer. Pluto had established himself as a solid contributor to the community. Finally, he had grown into his big name. It fit him perfectly now.

Pluto was fortunate to be able to live on campus, even as a freshman. However, the school being located near his family's home gave him the opportunity to visit his parents at least once a month. On one of those visits, Patricia went into her son's room, and on one of Pluto's digital wall posters, there was a picture of someone she believed she recognized as Dean Martin, a singer from the previous century. People still knew who Dean Martin was, but why would Pluto have his picture on the wall?

While having dinner that evening, Patricia asked Pluto about the poster in his room. Reverently, Pluto uttered the name Dean Martin. Patricia said she knew who he was. She was curious about what he meant to him. After dinner, Pluto gathered his parents, and they went online together, where Pluto brought up a website to explain. It read:

Web Maven Leo Landers
The Pop Culture Explorer
Presents

THE COOLEST OF ALL TIME

Pluto's dad chimed in as he always did when he thought he was being told by society's influencers what was hot or chic or "To die for." He would point out that they appeared to be "people with their finger on the pulse of society with barely a pulse in their brain." Pluto assured his dad that web mavens were considered reliable, and anyway, this one was just for fun.

Pluto and his parents continued to explore the website where Leo Landers revealed his "Five Coolest People of All Time." There were also two honorable mentions. They were Miles Davis, trumpeter extraordinaire, who was heard playing his composition, Sketches of Spain and Frank Sinatra, whom Mr. Landers considered more smooth than cool, represented by his recording of "Summer Wind." At number five, Farouk Mahdree was the only contemporary to be recognized, the legendary pop singer with the sexiest scowl since Elvis Presley. Selected at number four was Sean Connery as James Bond, agent 007 in the film Goldfinger. At number three was the smoothest and the coolest, Billie Dee Williams, who had been featured in a long series of Colt 45 Malt Liquor commercials broadcast from 1960 to 1965. Leo Landers' selection for number two was the actor he deemed the coolest in film, Steve McQueen. Two different film clips were seen. The car chase from Bullitt and the "Cooler King" and his motorcycle escape attempt from The Great Escape. Finally, Leo Landers declared that the coolest person of all time was Dean Martin, nicknamed the King of Cool, with the pinnacle being his recording of "Ain't That a Kick in the Head" from the original film version of Oceans 11.

Pluto went on to show his parents the website created in the aftermath of Leo Lander's announcement. It was called Dino's Den. There, they found everything about Dean Martin. There were recordings, articles, photos and a few documentaries. It was one of these documentaries that influenced Pluto. Unfortunately, influences are only helpful when you know how to interpret what you see and hear. And if you don't fill in the gaps with what you want to see and hear. Pluto used part of a documentary on Dean Martin in this way. Some of the included interviews seemed to suggest that even while everyone loved him and felt he was a wonderful and personable guy to be around, Dean Martin may have had a private side that was a mystery. A part that Dino kept hidden while still sharing enough of himself to be admired by virtually everyone. As Pluto spoke about understanding and even sharing the need to keep some of his life to himself, Patricia was reminded of the way Pluto had reversed his reaction that day in the kitchen, when he had been displeased over her insistence that he apologize to the boy he had hurt back in high school. That day, Pluto had been able to quickly mask his true feelings. That's what had troubled her then. And what troubled her still.

After earning his undergraduate degree, Pluto had all the options he needed. He was courted by a couple of the local gyms, who wanted to hire him as a trainer, hoping that he would eventually become a manager and help them expand. Pluto was a minor celebrity in the area and could help their businesses substantially. However, Pluto was honest about his intentions. He would take the job temporarily with the understanding that he had his own plans. Four years after his graduation, his plans were a reality. The first Planet Pluto opened its doors.

The financing for Planet Pluto, a modern gymnasium, was secured easily because of Pluto's reputation. When Pluto wanted a sandwich and juice café attached to the gym, he got it. When he insisted that the gym be closed to members for a few hours every Tuesday, allowing him to open the doors to groups of kids who couldn't afford a membership, there was no opposition from his investors. The only time there was any flack was when Pluto asked for fifteen hundred square feet of space insulated from the rest of the gym. That seemed like a running expense that may not pay for itself. But Pluto had his own unique vision. He asked for a bit of faith. In the end, he got that too.

In eight months, Planet Pluto was established as the top public training facility in the area in and around Champaign, Illinois. The classes held on Tuesdays for the kids in the community were highly regarded, and none of the paying members complained about the few hours that were unavailable to them. And the fifteen hundred square feet of additional space Pluto asked for had proved more than worthwhile. The space was used for stretching and warm-up sessions, and it was available to help everyone train safely. It also served another purpose, where Pluto held sessions with the community's senior citizen population. Twice a week, at his own expense, Pluto hired a bus to bring any senior citizen who was interested into Planet Pluto for Pluto's seminar, "Breathing for Better Balance." His hope was to help minimize the injuries that can come from falling when one gets older. Despite the extra space being costly, the fifteen hundred square feet Pluto had required increased the overall prestige of Planet Pluto.

One day in June, one of Pluto's friends from the gym, Sarah, was having lunch at Pluto's café. She was sitting with her friend Elizabeth, who was in Planet Pluto for the first time. Sarah was giving Elizabeth the lowdown on Pluto McKenzie, a topic that was sort of a hobby for the women members of the gym.

Elizabeth Lindstrom, a beautiful blond-haired woman of Norwegian heritage, lived in Champaign, Illinois, with her cat and her drawing table. She had graduated from the same university as Pluto, two years after him, with a degree in Graphic Design and Studio Art. She was unlike Pluto in many ways. Elizabeth was confident in herself and her abilities, without any need to elevate or exaggerate them or herself. She was a tranquil artist, a rare bird. A self-assured, peaceful soul. From all indications, she was way out of Pluto's league. Her soul aside, Elizabeth was a woman, so when her friend Sarah offered to share what the girls would talk about when they talked about Pluto, she was game.

Sarah started with the stats:

"Alright, let's go through the list. Looks, check. Physique, definitely check. Thoughtful and honest, check. Dependable, warm and desirable. Check, check and double-check."

Elizabeth was waiting for the punchline. Even though "check and double-check" appeared to actually be a punchline. But Elizabeth knew that no one gets all their boxes checked. This was when Sarah introduced the concept of the 80/20 guy. Sarah couldn't claim the idea as her own. It was posed by her friend

Phoebe. However, all the girls agreed that, as well as anyone, it described Pluto.

Phoebe's Theory didn't speculate that an 80/20 guy was nice eighty percent of the time and horrible twenty percent of the time. Sarah explained that an 80/20 guy was someone who gave only eighty percent of himself, holding back twenty. In an 80/20 guy like Pluto, the eighty percent may appear to be more satisfying than one hundred percent of most other men, but that was just an illusion. Eventually, the twenty percent would need to flex its own desires. Consequently, you could never have a completely fulfilling relationship with an 80/20 guy. And it didn't matter how special the eighty percent was; sooner or later, it wouldn't be enough. Pluto was a great guy. A respectful guy. He just wasn't <u>the</u> guy. Sarah continued, telling Elizabeth that if Pluto were sitting at the table with them, she would say the same things in front of him. Of course, that would never happen because Pluto never sat in the café with members of Planet Pluto, and he never dated any of the women who trained there.

Ten minutes later, one of those protocols would be broken when Pluto approached the table, walked around it to face Sarah to say hello and saw Elizabeth for the first time. Without realizing he was having a unique reaction, Pluto asked if Sarah and her friend would mind if he joined them. By the time he was seated, Pluto knew he was in uncharted territory. However, after Sarah's surprised look waned and Pluto was introduced to Elizabeth, any awkwardness soon evaporated. And in spite of what Sarah had said and the warning flags it raised, Elizabeth and Pluto started dating.

For Pluto, his connection to Elizabeth was an attraction of a different kind. He was convinced it was because of Elizabeth and her basic nature and not of his doing at all. One of the traits Pluto recognized in Elizabeth was her basic sense of right and wrong. She was able to see right and wrong without considering any personal attachment to the outcome. Pluto admired her for it, even though that particular trait would never rub off on him. Compared to Elizabeth, Pluto was extremely self-involved. Yet, for a long time, their relationship was strong. Pluto seemed to be drawn to mirror some of Elizabeth's finer qualities, but Elizabeth always knew that any change in Pluto might only be a change to the eighty percent. Regardless, she still fell in love with him. She knew it was a risk. Of course, every relationship is a risk, whether it's an 80/20 guy or no 80/20 guy. So, she followed her heart, and they stayed together for the next two years. During that time, Pluto asked Elizabeth to marry him on two occasions. She had said no, but they stayed together because they loved each other. There was nowhere else to be.

Pluto continued to operate Planet Pluto successfully. His name was used prominently in their advertising, and his face, known from the gym's billboard on Prospect Avenue, reached across the Champaign borderline to Pluto's hometown of Urbana. Many of his former high school classmates knew of Pluto's success, and a few of them had signed up as members of the gym, which was located only nine miles away from home. One of those former classmates was Freddie Vasquez, the boy who had replaced Pluto in Benji's circle of friends. Freddie grew up to be a police officer in their hometown. When he joined Planet Pluto, Freddie was unaware of any lingering, hurt feelings Pluto may have had. Or if he had ever been aware of them, the passing of twenty years had excused them from his memory. However, they had not been excused from Pluto's memory. So, when Freddie brought an unfamiliar guest to the café, Pluto was caught off guard when he found himself face to face with a grown-up Benji Conway. And while our society may not understand mental illness very well, we do know a bit about childhood trauma and how deeply that can run.

Benjamin Conway had started out as a rough kid, although no one could say why. There was no abuse to blame nor evidence that Benji had been driven to be that way. Maybe there was no underlying support for his behavior, which was the reason that, as an adult, Ben Conway no longer had the same issues. He was well-liked and trusted by his friends, including Officer Freddie Vasquez. There was no easy answer for the way he had treated Pluto when they were young boys, but to Ben, just as with Freddie, the event had happened so long ago it was forgotten. Besides, knowing why wouldn't have helped Pluto. They were only eight years old. More importantly, even if Pluto knew the reason for Benji's actions, it wouldn't have mattered to him anyway. The act itself had left its effect. Ultimately, Pluto's reaction to seeing Benji again would be derived from the past and his perceived betrayal.

As Pluto stood in front of Benji for the first time, the control he usually employed over what he showed to others faltered for a moment. He produced a smile quickly enough and shook Benji's hand, but Pluto couldn't mask his feelings immediately. And those feelings were mixed. Pluto was unable to suppress a surprising feeling of affection initially when making the connection with his old friend before hurt feelings reemerged. Quickly, Pluto regained his composure, hid whatever he honestly felt, and presented himself as someone who was happy to see Benji, or Ben, as he was now called, after all the time that had passed.

Ben joined Planet Pluto that day, and although he and Pluto didn't become friends during those first few months, Pluto appeared to be his usual personable self when he saw Ben. Assisting him as he would any other member of the gym. Ben always appreciated his offer of instruction and the two would speak while they trained. Pluto found out that Ben had graduated from Eastern Illinois University's Lumpkin College of Business and that he worked with his father at Conway's Furniture and Appliance Superstore on S. High Cross Road, where many of Pluto's neighbors and their families had been patrons most of their lives.

Pluto and Ben never spoke about what had happened in the past during their time training at the gym. The only time Pluto said anything about it was to Elizabeth after she was introduced to Ben while having lunch with Pluto in the café. When Pluto told Elizabeth about the incident in his childhood with the boy previously known as Benji, he was calm in his claim that it was all in the past, and Elizabeth believed him. The only person in Pluto's life who was alarmed by their reunion was Pluto's mother. Patricia knew her son's reaction and his apparent victory over his past demons couldn't be trusted. When she asked her son how he felt about seeing Benji again, Pluto insisted he was fine:

"After all," he boasted. "He comes into my place. He sees how well I've done."

Pluto then reasoned that he would never allow the past to muddy his present. That sounded quite mature, but Patricia wasn't buying it. In fact, that sounded more like Elizabeth than it did her son. Pluto's façade, she feared, was now firmly in charge. Pluto might not be aware of how his own buried resentments may lash out without warning or logic. Even his mother's pleas to be watchful would be respectfully dismissed.

A few weeks later, Pluto received an email from an old friend of his grandfather's. Pluto thought he recognized the name as someone he met when he was a young boy, but that was all he could recall. He decided to open the email anyway and found what was essentially an advertising campaign for the reinstatement of Pluto as a planet. The note attached read, "Your grandfather would be proud of you." Additionally, in parentheses, the man had written, "But not too proud." Which certainly was a distinction his grandfather would have appreciated.

The man who sent the note represented the group responsible for the reinstatement campaign, and they wanted Pluto to be the face of the effort. The man conceded that Pluto's youth and success were factors in choosing him, as was the idea that Pluto would be fighting for his namesake, which should attract some attention to their cause. Also, they felt Pluto could be a great motivator for others, like his grandfather, whom most of the group had known and respected. Pluto's grandfather had been the group's elder statesman when they held their meetings back in 2062, and Pluto noticed in the email that although his grandfather had died seventeen years before, his name, William Forest McKenzie, was prevalent in all the documentation for the Reinstate Pluto campaign. That meant something to Pluto, and he agreed to consider their proposal. As he reviewed the email, Pluto decided to show the campaign's design to Elizabeth and include her artistic input. Together, they thought that Reinstate Pluto sounded like a directive, and the cause may be better served with a phrase that was more positive, more self-assured, like "Pluto is a Planet."

Once everyone agreed on the new name of the campaign, Elizabeth started designing a logo as well as posters, while Pluto opened a bank account and planned how the fundraising would be handled. An initial check for ten thousand dollars was donated and deposited by Pluto to get the ball rolling. However, there was an issue with the timing of the "Pluto is a Planet" campaign. Pluto's original investors had been attempting to persuade him for over a year to open Planet Pluto II. Pluto had just promised his involvement in the planning of the new gym, and they were ready to proceed. Pluto's partners expressed concern over the amount of time he would be spending on the "Pluto is a Planet" campaign. They conceded that Pluto's image being used or his appearing in commercials for the project was no problem; in fact, it was good publicity for the gym. As a compromise, Pluto was asked to consider delegating some of the day-to-day responsibilities and perhaps the financial obligations for the campaign's funds to someone else. That's when an idea entered Pluto's head that at first came uninvited and then would refuse to be evicted. A thought that fed into Pluto's demons from the past when the words, "like someone who graduated from the Lumpkin College of Business," sparked an idea for revenge in him. And Pluto was eight years old again.

The elements necessary for the set-up would take Pluto a few months to establish. That was a long time to be fueled every day by anger, but after holding on to the scars for twenty years, there was plenty in reserve to fuel Pluto's plans. Pluto never seriously considered the consequences for Ben or whether they might be extreme when compared to the pain of an eight-year-old being abandoned by a friend. In his mind, the past and the present were one moment spilling into the next moment without the years in between.

When pondering his options, Pluto thought it best to keep the setup as simple as possible. When someone who is not a criminal endeavors to commit a crime, many like Pluto tell themselves two things: keep it simple, and it will work. And the biggest lie of all, no one will figure out what they have done.

With his blinders wrapped tightly in place, Pluto believed he had found a workable plan, and he made a list of the articles necessary to follow through with his intentions. Pluto needed to collect these pieces of the puzzle as soon as possible, with no trace of him being the one collecting them.

The items he listed were:
1. One Oak Desk
2. One Additional Oak Board (Size TBD)
3. 16K Nanny Cam "Dots" (Two, one as back-up)
4. A Disposable Burner Pad
5. "Pluto is a Planet" Posters (Three, in identical frames)
6. Cash

Pluto would get twenty-seven thousand dollars of the cash he needed for his scheme from his Ring Fund. This was the money he had put together in the times leading up to one of his proposals to Elizabeth. Pluto didn't present a diamond ring when he proposed because even though when the time came, he would say the words confidently enough, he was far less than confident in her reply. It was implied that if Elizabeth accepted, he would replace the cigar band wrapper with the real thing. Each time she refused him, the fund had grown larger. The money had remained in Pluto's apartment, in his personal wall safe, and no one knew it was there. Not even Elizabeth. That money was a good start, and although Pluto had no exact monetary total that he needed to raise for his plan to succeed, by the time he put his scheme in motion, he had freed up forty-six thousand dollars.

Another of Pluto's decisions to help move his revenge along was to use the adjoining office to his office at Planet Pluto as the headquarters for the "Pluto is a Planet" campaign and as home to Ben Conway's new oak desk. Of course, all of this depended initially on Ben agreeing to assist Pluto in the campaign, which he did without hesitation.

With the money in hand, Pluto then researched desks made of oak, and when he found one that fit his needs, he jotted down all the pertinent information. Make, model number, overall dimensions, and the inner dimensions of the bottom drawers. Pluto had chosen oak for the desk because he knew his parents had a couple of oak boards in the garage, eliminating the need for him to buy the extra board. Pluto did have to purchase the nanny cams, although they could be purchased online, so he wouldn't have to worry about being recognized shopping locally. The "burner pad" presented Pluto with his biggest challenge, and he was forced to take a bit of a risk. He stopped shaving for a few days, and with a ball cap firmly in place, he was hardly recognizable. Then he drove twenty miles south and purchased the "burner pad" from Pete's Electronics in Villa Grove, Illinois, with no detectable issue. The desk itself was a legitimate purchase for the campaign, so there was no problem with it. And Elizabeth would provide the posters. While Pluto waited for the desk to be delivered, he lifted one of the oak boards from his parent's garage and cut it into two carefully measured pieces to fit into the desk's drawers to create two false bottoms.

Three weeks later, when Ben was brought into the temporary office space that Pluto had made available for their project, everything was already in place. Twenty-three thousand dollars had been neatly arranged in the right bottom drawer, and twenty-three thousand dollars in the left drawer. The oak pieces Pluto had prepared fit perfectly on top of the money, and on top of that, he placed a few reams of printing paper on each side, covering the false bottoms. Pluto had positioned one of the framed "Pluto is a Planet" posters directly behind Ben's desk. He had placed a Nanny Cam Dot in the bottom right corner of the poster's frame with its eye focused on the keyboard and computer screen in its field of vision. The location of the camera had to be precise but not perfect for Pluto's purposes. The new Nanny Dots had a wireless adjustment of up to thirty degrees. The only issue was the low whirring sound the camera made when moving. Therefore, Pluto would have to make any adjustments when the office was empty. He also hung one of the remaining two framed posters on the wall behind his own desk, carefully placing it in the same position as he had in Ben's office to present a look of consistency. Subliminally helping to discourage any question about their placement.

One week later, Ben was installed as the financial officer responsible for the contributions raised for the "Pluto is a Planet" campaign. The fundraising was just getting started, but when the Nanny Cam captured the username and password Pluto needed, he picked up the pace in his efforts to raise funds. Seeing Pluto's energy for the project increase suddenly was the first time Elizabeth felt something was wrong. Her concerns carried her to Pluto's family home in Urbana and Patricia. When the discussion between the two women was done, both women were more distressed than they were before.

Once Pluto had retrieved the information he needed from Ben's computer, he took his "burner pad" to a local restaurant where he often had lunch. In a corner, undisturbed, Pluto connected to the restaurant's Wi-Fi and opened a bank account in the name of his chosen nom de guerre, Sammy Waters. It was easy to do. No one wanted to stop him from depositing his money with them. Especially start-up boutique banks. With the account open, his plan was ready to unfold. Still, Pluto showed no sign of questioning his own actions. When the moment came, he didn't hesitate. He waited until the funds in the account managed by Ben totaled fifty-two thousand dollars. Then, in the corner of the same restaurant as before, with Ben's login information, Pluto transferred forty-six thousand dollars out of the campaign's account and deposited the money into the account of the nonexistent Sammy Waters. And since Pluto was the elusive Sammy Waters, as far as facial recognition was concerned, he was able to withdraw the funds, close the account, and lock the money in his safe at home. Pluto knew these transactions might not be that difficult to unravel, but he wasn't worried about the police tracing the transfer. There wasn't going to be any reason for anyone to look for the money. They were going to find the forty-six thousand dollars right where Pluto left it, inside Ben Conway's oak desk.

The last item on Pluto's to-do list was to take down the poster with the Nanny Cam from Ben's office and replace it with the remaining framed poster in his possession. Then, Pluto removed the camera from the frame of the poster he had taken down and erased its software from his computer. After that, he waited. It took less than three weeks for the accounting shortfall to be discovered.

When the authorities accused Ben of having stolen tens of thousands of dollars, he was perplexed. When they uncovered the false bottoms in the desk drawers and removed the forty-six thousand dollars, Ben had tears in his eyes. He locked eyes with Pluto for a second before Pluto stormed out of the office, outraged, as if he were the injured party. Suddenly, Ben understood what was happening to him and why.

With Ben having been taken into custody by the police, a pleased Pluto McKenzie entered his apartment. There, sitting on the couch with a carry bag on the floor beside her, was Elizabeth. She was waiting to say goodbye. Pluto's satisfied demeanor deflated as Elizabeth allowed her disappointment one outburst when she accused Pluto of being an angry, self-serving eight-year-old child!

She had a last request, however, and it wasn't for her own sake but for his. She had written an address down on a piece of paper, which she placed on the table. Her wish was that Pluto go to the address, no questions asked. Then Elizabeth rose off the couch, picked up her bag, and said goodbye. Even though Pluto didn't fully understand why she was leaving, he knew she was leaving him for good. There was nothing he could say. He could feel it.

Twenty-five miles later, Pluto arrived at the Valley Hill Apartments in Paxton, Illinois. It was not a great-looking complex. Pluto made his way to the door of apartment 2G and knocked. A voice from inside the room called out:

"Come in, Pluto."

The elderly woman standing in the kitchen was a complete stranger to Pluto, and yet he knew she was his grandmother, Rose. She noticed that Pluto had an unkind look on his face.

"What's the matter with you?" Rose asked.

"I'd heard how incredibly beautiful you were, that's all," Pluto chided.

Rose had an answer for her rude grandson:

"Well, twenty-six years in prison will knock the sultry right out of a woman, Pluto. And I'm a double murderer. You might want to consider that the next time you insult me." And she smiled.

Then his grandmother consoled Pluto, telling him that she knew if he were there with her, that meant Elizabeth was gone and that he had lost her. She was sorry for that. His grandmother revealed that she had met Elizabeth. Pluto's mother had been to see her on two separate occasions, and the last time, she brought Elizabeth along to see her as well. After hearing this, instead of hyperventilating, Pluto remembered to use his breathing to calm himself. He understood he was there at that moment for a reason. With his grandmother's permission, Pluto sat down at the kitchen table.

"Grandma, he asked, "What happened to you?"

Rose told her grandson that the first thing she did when she got to prison was to accept all the blame for the heartache she had caused. Beginning with her leaving Pluto's grandfather and abandoning her ten-year-old son, Pluto's father, Don. She lamented that leaving a spouse can be understood. Abandoning a child cannot. In Rose's case, the spouse didn't deserve it either. She admitted to Pluto that William was a wonderful husband and father.

Rose confessed, "I wanted out because I wanted more. I liked nice clothes. I had expensive tastes. I loved to travel. So, I found someone who promised me the world I desired. I never considered that this man had made the same promises to other men's wives in the past. Or that he would do it again in the future. The rest is a story I heard many times once I got to prison. I found them both in bed together, and I shot them. I killed them both. I couldn't even recall how many shots I fired. That's how lost I was, bound by my anger and my pride. Just like you, Pluto. Anger and pride."

Pluto still didn't understand what was wrong with pride. In his mind, it helped him to succeed.

Rose asked, "So, what you're saying is, your pride brought you money and notoriety, and spending your time pumping up your own ego and image was a good thing?

Without thinking, Pluto answered in the affirmative. When his grandmother asked him why everything had turned out badly, he had no reply. Rose continued:

"Pride is always hungry, Pluto. And you satisfied your pride with revenge. As a result, you betrayed everyone who believed in you. Just like I did. You included Elizabeth in your scheme, and Elizabeth is not a scheme-type-of-girl. And then you betrayed the memory of your grandfather, using his cause for the reinstatement of Pluto as your weapon to pay back a child's hurt. Your grandfather used to say that Pride and Pluto were foster siblings whose family had forsaken them. They followed the same path. Pluto was ousted as a planet in our solar system, and pride was removed from the seven deadly sins, leaving six for now. The only difference was that while Pluto may not be counted as a planet, it was still out there in all its glory. Even the New Horizons space probe continued to explore farther into space. The sin of pride was gone. Never to be heard from again. Pluto, it's one thing to announce that you are proud of your daughter graduating from college, as an example, and mean, isn't it terrific that she worked hard and finished what she started? But for most people, it's the I in I am proud they are referring to."

Pluto was devastated, especially with his betrayal of his grandfather, and he found himself asking this person he had just met a question he had never asked anyone before. He asked his grandmother what he should do. Rose told him that the biggest regret for most female murderers was not being able to tell their victims that they were sorry for what they had done. She advised Pluto to make amends. And make amends without calculating what he might get out of it for himself. He still had the opportunity to set things straight. And the longer he waited, the harder it would be. Pluto thanked his grandmother and kissed her goodbye, assuring her that they would see each other again soon.

Pluto returned to his car, turned his phone on, and checked his call log. There were no calls from Elizabeth and ten from Freddie Vasquez. Pluto had been avoiding Freddie's texts for hours. Now he called Freddie back, asking him to meet him at his parent's home. And he told him to bring the police cruiser. Then he apologized to Freddie for what he had done and for getting him involved. When Pluto arrived home, he found his mother on the couch streaming the recordings of Dean Martin. By now, Patricia knew everything, of course. She, Elizabeth and Rose had spoken with each other, so everyone was up to date except for Pluto's father. Pluto went upstairs and found his father asleep. He left him a note that read:

Sorry, I was a pain. I love you.

P.S. Go see your mother – I did.

Back downstairs, Pluto sat with his mother, waiting for Freddie to arrive. Pluto asked his mother how she was able to do it. How was she able to put her husband first, sacrificing her own needs? Patricia's answer was that she didn't consider it a sacrifice at all, as she explained:

"Pluto, I didn't marry a weak man. I married a good man with problems. As a result, I had to overcompensate from time to time. It was a small price to pay for a lifetime together. And I believe it's always better to take care of the person you love than have a person you don't love take care of you."

Pluto insisted that he was going to make it up to everyone he could. He just hoped that Elizabeth would hear about how hard he was going to try to change. He knew she wouldn't take him back —

Patricia interrupted him:

"No, she won't take you back, but she will definitely hear about what you do to make things better - and if you finally decide to take responsibility for your own actions."

Officer Freddie Vasquez pulled up to the McKenzie home and parked. Through the home's windows, the police cruiser's lights flashed outside as Pluto asked his mother how she could be certain that Elizabeth would know he had done the right thing.

His mother replied, "Because I'll tell her. After all, I don't see why I should have to give up a wonderful friend like Elizabeth just because you're a selfish bastard."

A bit startled by his mother's candor but resigned, Pluto admitted:

"Ain't that a kick in the head."

Story # 4

FORGED AND FRAMED

"Controlling the future of Energy is a frightening business. Threatening those who believe they control the future is folly."

AGENT NUMBER 4

(2082 - 2102)

Forged and Framed

(2082 - 2102)

Eighteen names inscribed in stone, framed by roses and lilacs on four sides, created a fitting monument for the men, women, and children whose deaths it was meant to honor. All who passed by, paying respect to this commemoration in the gardens fronting the headquarters of the Sunburst Solar Energy Company, believed its origin story. They believed what they had been told. They believed the cautionary tale that surrounded this well-known national tragedy and had adopted it as their own. Eighteen names were forged and framed so we would never forget.

The quaint town of Story, Wyoming, was abuzz. The old Gaines home had been sold, finally, after eight years on the market. The home needed quite a bit of refurbishment, and with most of the townspeople being too concerned with the cost, the home was sold at a very reasonable price considering its possibilities. However, it was the home's new tenant, not its possibilities, that had this small town with a population of just over eleven hundred inhabitants chattering. In the corner grocery store or at the local diner, the only topic of conversation seemed to be gossiping about their new neighbor, Dr. Abigail Paley. The brilliant and infamous Dr. Paley, the sole graduate of M.I.T. to ever grace their town.

Recently released from Bedford Hills Correctional Facility for Women in upstate New York, Dr. Paley's story was well known. Her trial, although cut short by a plea agreement, had been covered by every media outlet in the country, a cautionary tale of greed and hubris, highlighting the actions of a brilliant woman which had resulted in the deaths of eighteen Americans. The trial itself and its sudden cessation had been a disappointment for most of those, who had settled in to watch what they had anticipated would be a long legal battle, expected to contain tales of devious conduct and the vilification and fall from grace of a once-honored high-born, for everyone to enjoy.

As a very young girl, Abigail Paley had been acknowledged as special, gifted, with a curious and capable mind. Born and raised in New York City by her well-to-do parents, Martin Paley, a lawyer and partner in one of the prestigious law firms in Manhattan and her mother, Gloria, a published poet and patron of the arts and the less fortunate, Abigail was far from spoiled while being afforded the freedom to follow her abilities to wherever they could take her. Eventually, that would mean an electronics and electrical engineering degree from the prestigious Massachusetts Institute of Technology and a Doctorate in Science; her main focus is solar energy.

Soon after completing her education at M.I.T., Dr. Abigail Paley would raise a small amount of seed money, with little effort, to further her development of a new solar panel design. Panels more efficient than those currently covering tens of thousands of acres of land and countless rooftops across the country and, for that matter, the world. In her attempt to create a possible overhaul of this trillion dollar a year business, she would attract the attention of those in charge of the solar energy market. Not in a welcoming, "let's see what you're doing sort of way," but in a "fearful of what you're doing sort of way." In business, small advances over time are necessary, while overhaul is viewed as threatening.

After allowing herself a summer vacation staying with friends in the Hamptons, Abigail moved back into her parent's brownstone on the east side of the city to continue her work. Well-acquainted with the technology currently utilized in the field of solar energy, she felt that improvements might be developed in two ways. First, the power emanating from the sun could be captured through much lighter and smaller panels, still capable of absorbing and disseminating the same requisite energy required per square foot of housing or factory space. Second, after the energy is used, there should be a way of recapturing and recycling the energy instead of allowing it to dissipate, which results in the need to capture a new stream of sun power over and over again. The ability to accomplish these two goals would lead to an incredibly inexpensive power source, changing the cost of electricity drastically for everyone. So, as young people do, without understanding the consequences, Dr. Abigail Paley set out to use her God-given gifts to change the world. But what young people never comprehend is that those who are a little older and more established don't want to change the world. They like the world just as it is.

Blissfully unaware of this fact of human nature, Dr. Paley proceeded with her research and experimentation, and when her work began to show promise, she did what all inventors are forced to do: she brought in a business partner. Her partner was thirty-seven-year-old Byron Haskell, a Harvard graduate. Through his firm, Blaisdell Investments, Haskell was anxious to fund the doctor's endeavors, and although it would take almost four years of trial and error after the forming of their partnership for the investment to pay off, eventually, the creation of the Paley Solar Panel would be successful. As were the Paley Plates which were capable of recapturing energy when strategically placed directly under lighting fixtures or suspended and angled nearby. They could then reabsorb the energy coming from the lighting, as well as from heating and cooling units, and feed that power into storage batteries where it could be reused again and again with only a slight loss of energy in the transfer. However, life rarely runs in a straight line.

Long before the doctor's search for a partner became necessary and before the invention of this cheaper energy source could be developed, the work that would achieve it was sidetracked. Two years after Dr. Paley's initial research began, while living in her parents' home, life took a turn, and a different branch of existence ended up consuming most of the doctor's time. Abigail Paley met Alan Bennett, a vascular surgeon and son of one of her father's oldest friends. The two had never met before Abigail's father's fiftieth birthday party, but following their introduction, a few days of continuous companionship revealed true love. Six months later, they were married, and a year and a half after that, while the birth of the Paley Solar Panel would be further delayed, the birth of Abigail and Alan's daughter, Melissa, would be right on time. Whereas Dr. Paley kept her name for professional purposes, her last name sounding more lyrical when applied to her pending discovery, Melissa was given her father's surname, of course, and was baptized Melissa Bennett.

With the responsibility of a daughter, an additional five years would elapse before Abigail returned to work full-time, as her preoccupation with raising a child took precedence until Melissa started attending school. That's when Dr. Paley felt comfortable enough to agree to and accept the aid of a nanny, allowing herself the time to refocus her efforts towards the development of the Paley Panel. Soon after that, the need for assistance would lead her into a partnership with Byron Haskell and Baisdell Investments.

The initial success achieved through Dr. Paley's experiments was dismissed by the Solar Energy community, who were quick to differentiate success in a lab from practical application. Undeterred, the doctor and her newly acquired partner proceeded with the filing of requests for patents. And while patents were pending, a first attempt at utilizing the new technology was tested in a real-life setting by outfitting Abigail and Alan's own residence in Hartsdale, N.Y., a split-level home that the couple had recently purchased, which sat at the end of a cul-de-sac where the work being done was followed closely, appearing at first, to be observed only by their neighbors. The possibilities of the new solar energy equipment were still being ignored by the industry at large, that is, except for one company, Sunburst Solar and their chairman and CEO, Leonard Holstaff, a man as paranoid and as vicious a competitor as could be found. To Holstaff, Dr. Abigail Paley's work was not to be taken lightly.

Regrettably, all new inventions, no matter the strength of their scientific moorings, experience fits-and-starts and the Paley Solar Panels and its accompanying invention, the Paley Plates, would be no different. An additional three and a half years passed with periodic setbacks materializing while the right elements for wiring and assemblage were discovered. Finally, Dr. Paley succeeded, and the project reached the operational flexibility and efficiency necessary to equip and electrically run the home of Alan Bennett and Abigail Paley. No longer could the doctor and her new system of capturing the energy of the sun be disregarded.

With their experimental data limited to the successful provision of electricity for only one home, Dr. Paley and her partner set out to find an appropriate commercial project to further prove their newly tested equipment. They approached Samuel Levenson, owner of Levenson Construction, whose proposed plans for a housing complex had begun advertising in order to secure early contracts for the building of thirty-five homes. Surrounding a man-made lake covering six and a half acres, this series of two-story, medium-priced family dwellings, named "Serene Waters," was to be located in Mamaroneck, New York, approximately thirty minutes from Dr. Paley's Hartsdale residence.

In the hope of securing his support, Dr. Paley invited Samuel Levenson to visit her home, where the builder was impressed, even dazzled when witnessing the Paley Panels and Plates in operation. With the backing of his construction supervisor, Harrison Kramer, he endorsed the installation of the new solar energy equipment for their project. Even though the patents were still awaiting approval, the two men saw nothing alarming in the solar panel's build. The successful feed of electricity to the Paley/Bennett home had continued uninterrupted for more than six months with absolutely no documented issues. Within two weeks, a contract between Levenson Construction and Blaisdell Investments was drawn, and the Paley Panels and Plates were set to furnish the electrical needs of all thirty-five homes at the new site. This beginning and the hope of the possible expansion to follow was a cause for celebration. Dr. Abigail Paley had made good on her promise, creating an effective and affordable source of energy. Her husband and her family were proud of such an important achievement. Even ten-year-old Melissa seemed to feel the excitement in the house without any true understanding of the event itself. Of course, everyone would not be as thrilled as they were.

The agreement between Levenson Construction and Blaisdell Investments, signaling the apparent success of Dr. Paley's invention, reached Leonard Holstaff's desk. With tens of billions of dollars of his company's assets invested in the existing technology, the paranoia of the CEO of Sunburst Solar was stoked. His blood pressure spiked. His devious mind was pushed into overdrive. But he wasn't surprised. In anticipation of this problem surfacing, Holstaff had already begun planning a response months in advance.

One of his main objectives to control the situation had been accomplished by initiating the covert buying of shares of stock in Blaisdell Investments. Surreptitiously, he had accumulated exactly fifty-one percent of the company's total number of outstanding shares, purchased through seven different financial entities, while employing several layers of buffers in the transactions, successfully hiding his name from direct involvement. This would give him significant leverage over Byron Haskell. The leverage necessary to force the head of the investment firm to sell out his own partner and aid in the invalidation of an important invention that Holstaff believed threatened the established conditions for growth within the industry in which he held a prominent position. A position he was willing to do anything to protect.

Seated at his desk in the offices of Blaisdell Investments, comfortable, dreaming of fiscal fairies, Byron Haskell is notified of a phone call requesting his attention. Leaning back in his chair, he gladly takes the call, expecting only good news in a future filled with the promise extending from Dr. Paley's discovery and the fortune that would surely follow. The call, however, would offer the materialization of one of these outcomes while demanding the destruction of the other. When he is made aware of the fact that the man he is speaking with is the person who holds a controlling interest in the company he assumed was his, an unsteady Byron Haskell agrees to meet clandestinely with the man who is now his boss. The future he had dreamed of, his future with Dr. Abigail Paley, was about to become a casualty of corporate war. And CEO Leonard Holstaff's leverage on Mr. Haskell would reveal that when tested, Byron Haskell's view of himself as a strong and independent individual would simply collapse, leaving behind a frightened, self-serving mouse, willing to stoop to any level to retain the appearance of success and save his own skin.

The threats made by Leonard Holstaff towards Byron Haskell were enough to force Haskell's hand. By the time Haskell left their meeting, he was a puppet without the will to question where his actions would lead or what damage they might cause. The plan dictated by Holstaff would culminate in devastating consequences. For his efforts aiding in the ruination of Dr. Paley and the Paley Solar Panels and Plates, Byron Haskell would gain substantial wealth personally, but his treachery in the service of Leonard Holstaff would also, unbearably, result in the deaths of eighteen innocent strangers who would end up being sacrificed for their benefit.

The plan was simple: when you have the resources and, more importantly, the absence of morality available to a megalomaniac like Leonard Holstaff. The scheme called for access to quite a bit of money, which was not an issue, but more specifically, would require a connection to and involvement of one of the more notorious citizens of the world, a man whose skills as a master forger were impeccable, available only to those who had the knowledge of and reach into the most sinister parts of society, and who possessed the desire to tap into its destructive power. Leonard Holstaff had both in spades.

The specifications necessary for the assembling of the Paley Solar Panels and Plates, designated to supply power to the "Serene Waters" housing complex, were being handled solely by Dr. Abigail Paley. This initial commercial use of her invention was too important to entrust to anyone else. Even after providing the documents cataloging the materials and procedure to be employed, Dr. Paley intended to oversee the installation of all of the equipment for the entire project herself. However, her partner insisted that time would eventually become a factor, and they would need to supply the solar equipment for the homes being built more quickly than one person could manage. This is where Leonard Holstaff and his lackey, Byron Haskell, created their opportunity for sabotage. It was suggested that Dr. Paley direct the building and installation of the panels and plates, the most important elements needing her attention, but that she allows the electrical wiring from the plates to the storage batteries and the batteries themselves to be managed by the electrical company, who had been hired by Levenson Construction to install all the internal wiring for the homes. This included the wiring of receptacles and any hard wiring necessary for specialty items, such as hanging chandeliers. Reluctantly, Dr. Paley agreed. Her desire to remain in total control made the decision difficult, but given the time constraints, the request from her partner seemed reasonable. This concession by Dr. Paley would create an opening for Holstaff to exploit. The doctor would draw her signature on the documents containing the specifications for the wiring and batteries that met her standards, but before those plans were passed on to the electrical company, they would be intercepted, rewritten to authorize the usage of supplies inferior to the materials requested by Dr. Paley. Then these altered papers would be sent off to be signed in Dr. Abigail Paley's name, by Antonio Ceballo, the forger.

When the building of the homes located in the "Serene Waters" housing development was set to begin, the Levenson Construction Company's public announcements advertising the availability of the brand new homes included information about the innovative solar equipment being utilized. Samuel Levenson knew that the inclusion of Dr. Paley's invention, connected to the housing complex, would garner the attention of the local media, which would lead to free exposure and could help sales. Immediately, he was contacted by Nancy Mashburn, a reporter working for the Scarsdale Daily Voice, a newsletter serving Scarsdale, New York, as well as Hartsdale, where

Dr. Paley and her husband resided. Ms. Washburn inquired about an interview with Dr. Paley, a request that was met with resistance from the doctor, who was an inherently shy individual. But Samuel Levenson's prodding cut through the doctor's reluctance with a "best for everyone" approach.

One week later, the same day Levenson Construction broke ground to lay the foundation for the first homes in "Serene Waters," Nancy Mashburn sat down with Dr. Abigail Paley for their interview. The reporter took copious notes while listening to Dr. Paley's journey to discovery, and even though it was considered politically incorrect in the advanced sociological times in which they were living, the reporter found herself feeling proud of the fact that a woman had made this scientific breakthrough. However, man or woman, Ms. Mashburn found the person she was interviewing impressive and personally appealing, so in the aftermath of their meeting, while the article she wrote remained objective and factual, the two women would become good friends.

The completed interview, printed and released online on October 2nd 2091, showed Dr. Paley to be a humble scientist but someone extremely confident in her innovative invention while also establishing her direct, hands-on approach to its implementation, which was meant to further a feeling of confidence in her solar design amongst the public. The article, reprinted in the Mamaroneck newsletter, the Daily Voice, appeared to accomplish just that, as the sale of ten of the thirty-five proposed homes found buyers within one month of the article's release.

The sales and the building of residential housing in "Serene Waters" continued at a brisk pace over the next fourteen months. By Christmas of 2092, seven houses had been completed, three others were in various stages of construction, and the first families began moving into their new homes. Nancy Mashburn, in a follow-up article, covered the sense of beginnings felt by the Stuarts, a family of four who were the first to set up residence, alongside the Lynchs and their daughter Kate, whose home sat next to Brad and Meredith Emerson, a family of five, with their twin sons, John and Elton and their daughter Emily. When interviewed, all the parents cited the beautiful lake, visible from their front porches, and the new solar equipment providing a reasonable cost of energy as the main selling points in their decision to choose this particular complex in which to live. In the two months that followed, three additional families began new lives around the lake at "Serene Waters;" a seemingly perfect neighborhood was starting to form.

Continuing to oversee the installation and operation of her solar panels, Dr. Abigail Paley remained excited to wake up every morning, proud of the community she was helping to build. She appeared to be extremely amiable and cheerful when visiting the site daily, and she came to know all of its occupants by name. Her only moments of uneasiness arose during infrequent conversations with her partner, Byron Haskell, whose demeanor seemed suddenly detached. Dr. Paley attributed his behavior to the weight of the financial obligations and other demands associated with the operation of Blaisdell Investments. But the truth of her partner's detachment stemmed from lingering feelings of guilt and the fear that the eventuality of his actions in altering the doctor's material specifications would inevitably prove to be calamitous.

At the beginning of May the following year, almost two years after his complicity in the forging of documents modifying Dr. Paley's original plans, Byron Haskell's fears manifested; his actions were the causation of consequences far worse than he had allowed himself to consider. An event that would damage his psyche irreparably. The same event, whose aftereffects would bring a smile to the face of a real-life villain, a man with no conscience to damage – Leonard Holstaff.

In the middle of the night, January 10th, 2093, the terrifying sounds of a dozen speeding fire engines, their alarms ringing out, bells clanging, are heard echoing through the streets, sparking panic in the neighborhoods as they pass, racing towards a burgeoning pyre lighting up the sky above the homes of the "Serene Waters" housing complex.

It would take more than five hours battling the blaze to extinguish its flames: A catastrophic blaze that would end up engulfing six of the ten homes that had been completed thus far, surrounding that beautiful man-made lake. Losing their lives, tragically, were the Stuarts and the Lynches, as well as all five members of the Emerson family. And the count of those who died didn't end there. Five additional lives belonging to those residing in the two homes next to the Emerson's house were lost. Finally, the death of one firefighter who gave his life trying to save those he attempted, in vain, to reach. Eighteen deaths in total. A devastating number of vibrant human beings were sacrificed in the conflagration. Only to be made worse by the eventual realization of what had caused their untimely and unimaginably horrific demise. The fire was determined by investigators to have resulted from the homes' electrical wiring, tagged as inferior for its intended use and therefore ill-equipped to manage the current. The wiring then caused an overload in the storage batteries, and they exploded, spreading the fire from one home to another within minutes of the initial burst of flames. The fault was due to the solar equipment approved and installed by Dr. Abigail Paley. The equipment was officially labeled inadequate and found solely responsible for the spread of the killer inferno.

The reaction of the population, aided by the media covering the event nationwide and that of the solar energy community as a whole, was swift, condemning Dr. Paley and all those who had supported her disastrous invention. But aside from the families of those lost, no one was more overwhelmed by grief or as perplexed as Abigail.

Samuel Levenson and his construction supervisor quickly tried, unsuccessfully, to separate themselves from the tragedy, admitting their faith in Dr. Paley was misguided, while Leonard Holstaff grabbed the stage to warn of the obvious dangers of legitimizing any endeavor to overhaul a system overnight, whose existing technology was already performing flawlessly, supplying inexpensive and more importantly, safe energy solutions, to satisfy the needs of people everywhere.

In the months leading up to the trial of Dr. Abigail Paley, the "Serene Waters" housing complex would be closed down and placed into bankruptcy by Samuel Levenson, while the assets of Blaidell Investments were sold off by Haskell and Holstaff. The extensive lineup of witnesses willing to testify against Dr. Paley included her partner Byron Haskell, Samuel Levenson and his construction supervisor Harrison Kramer, the fire chief who had investigated the fire and its causation, as well as handwriting specialists engaged to verify Abigail's approving signature found on the construction documents; cursive experts who were prepared to confidently refute the doctor's claim that she had never seen the documents before her lawyers had showed them to her. The forgeries were executed perfectly, so the only person who was positive the signatures were not hers was Dr. Paley, who was shocked to see that the signatures appeared to be authentic, even to her eyes, despite the fact that she had never seen the papers previously and certainly had never signed them. To make matters worse, with all the evidence against her, only her parents had the faith to believe her without question. Abigail's husband, Alan Bennett, quickly abandoned her. And because of the publicity and the hounding of the media, he took their daughter Melissa to North Carolina to escape the notoriety.

Nancy Mashburn, the only reporter granted an interview with Abigail following the incident, wanted to believe her friend's signature had been forged. She wanted to believe Abigail's story of betrayal but was compelled to write her article on the incident at "Serene Waters" based on the accepted facts. Abigail was left isolated, alone, with no viable defense to separate herself from the tragedy that caused so much damage and pain. She fell into a deep depression, and even though the work orders had been falsified, she herself felt that, ultimately, her lack of supervision was at least partially responsible for the equipment that was used and, therefore, the tremendous loss of life. Dr. Paley also came to realize that it must have been her own partner, Byron Haskell, who had set her up. Faced with the possibility of life in prison, Abigail felt she had no other option than to agree to the plea deal her attorneys urged her to accept. With her parents seated behind her and the remainder of the courtroom filled with the victim's families, Dr. Abigail Paley pled guilty to eighteen counts of negligent manslaughter. She received a sentence of fifteen to twenty years in prison, a sentence both harsh in the face of her actual neglect and extremely lenient in the eyes of those who had been directly affected by the tragedy. The latter opinion is shared by the public at large.

While serving her time at Bedford Hills Correctional Facility, Abigail never stopped mourning for the eighteen lives in whose deaths she considered herself, a complicit contributor. She also mourned losing touch with her daughter Melissa, whom she never heard from while imprisoned and whose life growing up had been hidden from her parents, Melissa's grandparents, as well. She had no idea where Melissa was living or how time had treated her. During "free time" in the prison, when Abigail had access to the web, she tried in vain to find any sign of her ex-husband or her daughter. She also attempted to locate her ex-partner, but it appeared that Byron Haskell had completely disappeared, with the last notation, a mention attached to the announcement of the liquidation of Blaisdell Investments. Most of Abigail's time, while serving her sentence in Bedford Hills, was spent reading the books that her life of scientific studies had left no room for, such as classic novels and historical biographies. While the first two years proved difficult as she attempted to get along with the other inmates, she eventually found her way, making a peaceful adjustment and accepting the life that was offered.

As the years passed, Abigail's parents continued to visit her monthly, while the only other person who regularly came to see her was Nancy Mashburn. Since the abrupt end of the trial, Nancy had become a well-known columnist in the New York area. Her reputation began with her reports on Abigail's case and the widely read, exclusive interview Abigail had granted her following the plea deal. However, she never wrote about her visits to the prison. The two women spent their time together, during Abigail's incarceration, chatting as friends.

Then, fourteen years after her initial incarceration, a few months shy of her forty-fifth birthday, Dr. Abigail Paley was released from prison. Her early release was barely opposed by anyone. Nothing could make up for the lives that were lost, but no one believed that Abigail was incarcerated because she was in need of rehabilitation. Her time in prison was purely a matter of punishment. So, with fourteen years determined as sufficient, Abigail began her life as an ex-convict in Story, Wyoming, occupying the old Gaines home purchased for her by her mother and father.

Abigail's life in the small town of Story was quiet and solitary. She spent most days at home except for shopping in town periodically for food supplies. Everything else she required was ordered online and delivered outside her door, mainly by drones, so her contact with the outside world remained minimal. This didn't stop the gossiping of her neighbors, however, many of whom were horrified to be living in close proximity to an ex-con of such infamous regard. As far as her financial situation, Abigail was not employable, of course, not even as a waitress in her new hometown, so it was fortunate her parents had the means to support her. The only positive prospect Abigail allowed herself to cling to was the chance that, as a free woman, she may somehow reconnect with her daughter. Exactly "when" would remain outside her thoughts. Only the possibility of "someday" would fuel her hopes.

Three months after moving into the Gaines home, there was a rare delivery, by hand, brought to Abigail's door. The contents of the package were surprising. Enclosed within the envelope were tickets for transportation designated to take Abigail back and forth from Story, Wyoming, to Raleigh, North Carolina. The accompanying letter explained the tickets as an invitation for Abigail to appear for a job interview with a financial firm, which listed itself as an advisor to many of the executives working in the well-known Research Triangle, six miles from the airport, in Durham, North Carolina. The letter was brief, stating that the CEO of the company felt that Abigail's scientific education would be a welcome asset. The correspondence was signed by Ramsey Baker, a name completely unknown to Abigail. The offer appeared a bit odd to her, but she googled the name Ramsey Baker and found that he was, in fact, a well-respected and long-established financial advisor in the area. Someone with an estimated net worth of fifty-five million dollars. Although initially, Abigail had an uncomfortable reaction to the opportunity presented by the interview, she had to consider that even if she felt unworthy, she owed it to her parents to at least investigate the offer of employment. An opportunity that might alleviate the burden on her mother and father, who alone were providing the funds to keep her alive.

Two weeks later, Abigail exited the airplane and entered the terminal at Raleigh-Durham International Airport. She was greeted by a car service; a limousine was sent to pick her up and take her to the Embassy Suites Hotel, where her room had been prearranged. The driver's instructions were to wait while Abigail checked in and settled comfortably and then eventually take her to the offices of Ramsey Baker's firm located in Research Triangle Park on Alexander Drive.

Seated outside CEO Ramsey Baker's office, dressed in a black M. M. Lafleur wool twill suit, Abigail Paley waited nervously for her interview. Barely five minutes later, Baker's office manager showed her into the CEO's lavish suite. A man in his late fifties stood with his back facing her as he appeared to be gazing through a large picture window out of the fourth floor of the modern, newly constructed office building. Abigail waited patiently, but when the man turned to face her, she involuntarily took two steps backward. Although fourteen years older, the man's face was strikingly familiar. It took a moment for confusion to morph into recognition. The man standing before her was her old partner, Byron Haskell. It took a moment longer for Abigail to conclude the truth that was staring her in the face. Byron Haskell is Ramsey Baker.

"I apologize for inviting you here under a false premise," Haskell began, "but if you allow me to explain, I am hopeful you will find that my motive justifies my deception."

Her old partner began by explaining that he had legally changed his name to Ramsey Baker following her trial. He had done so to allow himself to begin a new life as a different person from the one who was responsible for the injustice imposed on a good woman and a friend. Haskell/Baker continued recounting the machinations that caused Abigail's downfall, including the threats of ruination that prompted his unforgivable participation in the events that led to the tragedy at "Serene Waters," naming the CEO of Sunburst Solar, Leonard Holstaff, as the antagonist who instigated the plot. He told a shocked and physically shaken Abigail Paley everything, including the part played by the forger, Antonio Ceballo.

Before Abigail had an opportunity to respond, her old partner had another admission to share. He revealed that a few hours prior to meeting with her, he had made these same admissions to someone else. Someone who was an employee of his firm. Abigail had no idea who the man was speaking about, so she didn't respond. Then Ramsey Baker reached out to his office manager, instructing her to contact Miss Bennett and ask her to join them. The manager was assured that Melissa was in her office waiting for the call. Abigail's entire body seemed to stiffen at the sound of the name. Her mind would not allow hope to become belief until her daughter, now twenty-six years old, entered the office. After fourteen years of estrangement, the mother and daughter were in the same room. Abigail felt their connection before the facial features of this now-grown woman became clear to her eyes. With the knowledge that her mother had been framed and a feeling of regret, Melissa moved quickly and wrapped her arms around Abigail, who slowly responded, trembling at her daughter's touch. Abigail glanced toward her ex-partner as the two women hugged and wept. It was a look of gratitude and perhaps of forgiveness, in spite of the man's role in the initial injustice that created their separation.

After an appropriate amount of time had passed in the initial reconnection of mother and daughter, Ramsey Baker asked the two women to sit. He then reached into his desk drawer and removed a small stack of papers. He identified the papers as copies of the original documents signed by Dr. Abigail Paley, notating the specifications for the equipment she actually authorized for the installation of solar power at "Serene Waters." He had kept the originals as well, in defiance of Leonard Holstaff's orders to destroy them. Baker informed the women that the originals had been stored in two separate locations. One copy had been uploaded to an account in the cloud overseen by Trustworthy Inc., a legally acceptable and secure method for handling important documents. The original hard copy versions were locked in a physical safe deposit box in the name of Ramsey Baker at his bank. Both files contained a letter of admission recounting the truth behind the tragic fire at the housing complex, which he had signed and notarized.

Baker had done all this out of guilt, a guilt that had plagued him for fourteen years despite his having a stellar reputation for competency in business, the admiration of his colleagues, and financial success. He supplied Abigail with the information necessary to access the documents held by Trustworthy Inc. He showed the women where he kept the key to the safe deposit box hidden in his office safe, supplying them with the combination. However, although it was clear that the files would vindicate Abigail, it was difficult for both women when they considered the ramifications of the release of these documents. Difficult for Melissa, who was troubled by the thought of the devastation the truth would bring to her boss, a man she always viewed as a mentor, a man who had treated her as family. Difficult for Abigail, who, while fearful of how the facts being made public might affect Melissa and her life and career, was especially unsettled thinking about the inevitable effect it would have on the families of the eighteen who died as a result of the plot. And the realization that the elements that led to their tragedy were set in motion intentionally.

Unsure of what their next move should be, mother and daughter left the office, for the moment, somewhat content to spend the day together getting reacquainted. When they exited his office, Ramsey Baker, although afraid of what might come next in his own future, found at least a modicum of peace in having facilitated their reunion.

As Abigail and Melissa walked past the office manager's desk on their way out, Baker's assistant pulled a magazine picture from her top drawer, glanced at it, and then looked up to glimpse Abigail's face one more time to make sure the picture matched her face. Once Melissa and her mother were safely out of view, the assistant grabbed her phone and dialed, quietly informing the person on the other end of the call that Abigail Paley had just left the office with Miss Bennett. Before ending the call, she looked at the picture one more time and reiterated.

"I'm positive."

Ending the call, Baker's assistant ignored the fact that she had just done something devious and returned to her duties.

Ramsey Baker ended his workday that evening at his usual time, got behind the wheel of his Jaguar I-Pace Z and headed home to his twelve-acre estate on Rowena Dr., seven miles away. He took the route he always took, which led him onto Rt. 885. As he approached a bend in the road, he failed to notice a large cement truck following approximately ten car lengths behind on his left. As the highway curved sharply to the right, a quarter mile before the overpass bridge above Angie's Avenue and the railroad tracks below, his view of any vehicles in his rear and side view mirrors was lost. By the time the highway straightened and the road behind him became visible again, the truck and its massive weight were bearing down on his position at a high rate of speed. It was too late to maneuver his Jaguar in time, and as he approached the bridge above the tracks, the cement truck turned hard to the right, crashing into the side of Baker's car. The truck kept pushing to the right until the Jaguar was forced through the barrier and off of the bridge completely. With its front grille leading over the side, the car fell fifty feet, crashing flush onto the railroad tracks below. Despite the deployment of airbags, the impact on Baker's body was brutal. He was pinned inside, his body battered and bleeding. Immediately, his car's emergency system alerted 911, and the paramedics arrived quickly to find Baker barely conscious. They strapped him onto a gurney, moving his broken body carefully, and although he was severely injured, Ramsey Baker managed to mutter two words before passing out.

"Too late."

One of the paramedics urged him to hold on and said that they were going to do everything they could to save him. But Baker's words weren't meant for the paramedics; they were meant for Leonard Holstaff.

On opposite sides of Baker's hospital bed, Melissa and Abigail sat vigilantly with this man who was clinging to life. In spite of his past actions as Byron Haskell, Ramsey Baker, the man he had become, was someone who had been an important and positive influence on Melissa's adult life; so when faced with his now devastating condition, both women put all feelings aside except concern. However, Melissa was so overwhelmed by the man's fate that she, as of yet, had not made the same determination that her mother had made. The timing of the crash, happening so soon after Abigail's arrival at Baker's office, was more than suspicious. Abigail had concluded that the event was no accident. It was intentional. It was attempted murder. And she knew who was responsible. The only question was what to do about it. Abigail left her daughter beside Baker's bed, making her way outside the hospital. Dialing her cell phone, she reached out to someone with whom she could depend. After a brief one-sided conversation, Nancy Mashburn cleared her schedule at work and boarded a flight to Raleigh within a few hours of her friend's request.

By the time Nancy Mashburn arrived in North Carolina, Melissa and Abigail had received some encouraging news from the doctors treating Ramsey Baker. While admitting that his recovery and rehabilitation would be arduous and lengthy, they believed that he would survive and eventually be able to resume his life with only minor lingering physical issues, mainly leg and shoulder problems thought to be manageable. The relief felt by the news was tempered by Abigail's assessment of the events leading up to the crash, its cause and what it may mean, not only for Ramsey Baker's future but for Melissa's future as well. Leonard Holstaff was still a threat. Back in her hotel room, together with her daughter and Nancy Mashburn, Abigail shared her conviction concerning Holstaff's treachery, and how the documents supplied by Baker, holding the truth behind the tragedy at "Serene Waters," might be used for the benefit of everyone involved.

Nancy Mashburn's viewpoint was predictable. As a news reporter, she believed the path was clear. You write the facts and let the results be guided solely by those facts. Melissa agreed. But that was not the way Abigail saw the situation. She was proud of how her daughter could disregard the documents' effect on herself and her own future, but Abigail had a different strategy in mind on how to proceed.

Nancy urged Abigail to let her write the true story of the fire at the housing complex now that they could prove that Abigail's name had been forged and that she had been, in fact, framed. In response, Abigail, while making it clear that releasing that version of the story was not her desired choice, did want her friend to be prepared to compose the factual account that led to her incarceration, but that it would be made public, only if what she had planned, failed. First, she was going to attempt to *reason* with the man who was at the center of the event that imprisoned her, the man responsible for putting the plot in motion that had turned her invention of a cheaper and more efficient energy source into a pariah and heinously caused the eighteen deaths at "Serene Waters" - the CEO of Sunburst Solar, Leonard Holstaff.

When Melissa learned of her mother's intentions, she objected. She had never met the man, but she was familiar with the name. Ramsey Baker had made it clear to her over the years that Holstaff was someone with whom you did not reckon. And even though the firm had dealings with Holstaff from time to time, Melissa had never been allowed to work on those deals. When questioned, Baker would only say that he would occasionally have to do business with him and that he was someone who was difficult to turn down specifically because he was a pernicious foe. In the aftermath of the crash, Melissa now knew just how dangerous Holstaff was, and the thought of her mother confronting him frightened her. Nancy also pleaded with Abigail to just allow her to unveil Holstaff publicly as the criminal behind the whole affair. But Abigail refused. She picked up her phone, dialed the main number for Sunburst Solar and was able to reach Leonard Holstaff, who took her call without hesitation and accepted her request for a meeting.

As Abigail packed a few things for her trip, she told her daughter and Nancy to remain at the hotel until she returned the next day – after *her hand had been played*. By the following morning, Abigail's plane landed in Atlanta, Georgia, where she made her way to the entrance of the headquarters of the Sunburst Solar Energy Company. Once there, her conviction to move forward was momentarily halted, her nerves tested, as she stood in front of the commemorative display forged in stone and framed by flowers honoring the eighteen who died at "Serene Waters." She read each victim's name, most of whom she had known personally, and along with the few she didn't know, imagined their pain and the pain of those who loved them. They had all been a part of her life for more than fifteen years, ever since the tragedy had occurred. Finally finding the strength to continue, she entered the building, rekindling the fortitude necessary for her to confront her adversary.

Realizing that she may find herself emotionally compromised when facing the man responsible for destroying the life she originally had planned for herself, Abigail prepared for the scenario ahead. She must not allow her fourteen years in prison and the weight of eighteen deaths control her actions. However, she also knew, when dealing with a man like Holstaff, that a dignified approach with completely controlled emotions might not be the way to achieve the results she desired.

With Abigail seated on one side of an immense gold inlay walnut desk and Holstaff seated in his vintage Fleming and Howland Chesterfield office chair on the opposite side, Holstaff felt at ease as he began chatting with Abigail as if they were old friends. Abigail could feel the anger building inside her as the sound of Holstaff's chatter began irritating her senses. But instead of governing her anger, her plan was to use it. Abigail allowed the continuing noise of Holstaff's words to trigger the emotions that she believed would lead to her seizing control of the confrontation. Abigail's plan was to allow Holstaff to feel confident in his ability to dominate the conversation; then suddenly, with an unexpected outburst, perhaps with an action that would frighten him, gain the upper hand. Abigail's intention was to stand up and bang her fist on the desk, silence Holstaff and then present him with the papers that documented his criminal involvement in the "Serene Waters" tragedy. Abigail prepared to do just that when something caught her eye. As she bolted from her chair, Holstaff still chatting nonsensically, Abigail grabbed a large letter opener lying in a pen well that appeared to have the presidential seal stamped on it. With a forceful downward motion, she attempted to stab the top of the antique desk, but the letter opener was too brittle to penetrate the walnut desk and splintered, sending shards of thin metal flying in Holstaff's direction. She simultaneously screamed at him.

"Shut up, you despicable bastard!"

Holstaff did just that. Abruptly registering in his mind was the realization that the woman standing in front of him was an ex-convict who had just spent fourteen years behind bars in a maximum security prison and that maybe he had underestimated her intentions.

This was the first time Abigail had unleashed the demeanor she had developed while incarcerated. It was a strength that had virtually eliminated her being victimized by other inmates. It was partially a façade, but it didn't feel like a façade to Holstaff. It struck Holstaff as sincerely threatening and dangerous. Abigail then demanded that he leave Baker, herself, and especially her daughter alone. She laid the copies of the documents on the desk, disclosing to Holstaff the evidence incriminating him as the culprit reprehensibly responsible for the actions of others, actions that led to the event for which she had taken the blame. If he decided not to agree to her demands, Abigail threatened to release the documents to the press, including Baker's signed admissions, which in the wake of the car crash would play publicly as powerfully as a deathbed confession. Abigail made one more demand without waiting for a response. She gave Holstaff two days to comply.

The next day, Abigail arrived back in North Carolina. Nancy and her daughter were anxious to know what had happened, but Abigail answered honestly when she told them that she didn't know, as of yet, what the results of her confrontation with Holstaff would yield. They would find out together by the following day. While they waited, Abigail requested that Nancy write the true story she had been exhorting her to approve, adding that if everything went as she planned, the story would never be published. It would be secured with the other papers held in the safe deposit box. Abigail apologized for asking Nancy to make an effort to write a story that may never be released but assured her that it was necessary because even if Holstaff gave in to her demands, with a man like him, it's never a matter of trust. It's always a matter of leverage. Adding the true story to the other documents would make their package of leverage complete.

One last time, Melissa and Nancy attempted to persuade Abigail to make the truth public. While she waited for Holstaff's response to her demands, Abigail finally explained her resistance to their request.

"Melissa, if it was just you who would be hurt and the families of the eighteen would somehow find solace in what actually transpired, I don't know what I would do. You're my daughter, and I would want to protect you. Although, I do hope that if something might be gained, I would act on behalf of those who continue to suffer over the lives taken that day. But since no one would benefit from the facts being released except me, it makes my choice obvious. Even if we were able to reinstate my reputation, it would not clear the stigma surrounding my solar energy panels, so there would be no benefit for the general population. We will never be able to get past the deaths of those innocent victims. Nor should we. The only caveat is if Holstaff refuses to meet my demands and my daughter's life is in jeopardy. Then, I would have an impossible choice to make. As far as Ramsey Baker is concerned, he has obviously felt the weight of his actions and paid a price for them. As for Leonard Holstaff, he probably never will, but all I need from him is his concession. There is an old saying that states, "The truth shall set you free." The saying isn't the "facts shall set you free." Because sometimes the facts don't tell the whole story. I believe that this is one of those times. But I have my daughter back in my life, and I have my daughter's respect. That is enough for me."

Melissa hugged her mother with understanding, if not complete acceptance of her decision, when Abigail received a notification on her iPad. It was from the Wall Street Journal. They were reporting on a surprising development at the Sunburst Solar Energy Company, announcing the sudden retirement of their longtime CEO, Leonard Holstaff, effective immediately. Holstaff had capitulated and agreed to Abigail's final demand, which was indicative of his acceptance of all her conditions, including the future safety of her daughter and Ramsey Baker.

Convinced she had achieved the best outcome possible, Abigail turned to her daughter, making a simple request.

"Now let's call your grandparents. They've been waiting a long time to hear from you."

THE PAST CAPTURES US FOREVER

THE MURDERERS' PIT

Story # 5

THE MURDERERS' PIT

"What scares a murderer? That was the question we were forced to ask. We could think of only two things. Torture and death.

And we were far too humane for torture."

AGENT NUMBER 5

(2102 – 2122)

The Murderers' Pit

(2102 – 2122)

He writes with an older pen. That's what his agent had to say about his latest effort. It's not quite Shakespearean but closer to Dickens. And being that we have one of those already and the public prefers "A Tale of Two Cities" over an unpublished David Trammel, his agent was sincere when he told him there was nothing he could do. However, if David could write something they could possibly sell, the agency would be happy to look at it. For our unpublished author, it wasn't the "write something in a language we want to read" part that was bothersome. It was the "write something we can sell" part. Writing something that sells will be the eventual downfall of David Trammel, a pretty decent fellow.

By the year 2095, everything in society runs on electricity. Of course, electricity is not foolproof, and the country, depending on an infrastructure that was not yet ready to handle the strain, experienced an increased number of brownouts and blackouts throughout the country. Most are fleeting. Some are more serious. Whereas the blackout of 2103 changed everything, creating a three-day free for all, for criminals from Buffalo, New York, to Raleigh, North Carolina, and from as far east as the Atlantic to as far west as Indiana. In only three days, eleven members of the law enforcement community were murdered, and there were far too many rapes, robberies, and other crimes committed to be counted by the number of police serving an area that represented approximately eighteen percent of the country's entire population. Most of these crimes would remain unsolved, and most of the criminals who were charged with a crime would be set free because of another crisis we were facing at the same time. A lack of available space in the prison system. With four hundred and ninety-two million people living in the United States, we have twenty million convicted offenders in prison and another nine million who were given a much earlier release than they should have, as there was nowhere to hold them. And the officials forced to decide which criminals were to be put back on the street, were resigning at an alarming rate. No one could live with the damage being caused by the convicts they were being forced to set free.

The blackout of 2103 turned out to be the worst of the blackouts. The AEC, an interconnected consortium of electricity providers, discovered it was actually one of the newer safeguards that had been put in place, which created the weakness that allowed such a massive area to be affected. And even though the AEC would improve the protection of their electric grid, the blackout of 2103 still served as a watershed moment for the country. Three days with all the lights off educated the criminals. If they waited and stood ready, they could take advantage of the next blackout when it came, and it always did during this time. Crime is much easier in the pitch dark. Especially when you can plan ahead. In time, the fear that the beginning of a blackout would evoke left no one feeling safe.

It is difficult to understand what this type of fear can do to a society. People from other times who do not live with this pending threat of violence stationed daily above their heads might think our response barbaric. But this was the zeitgeist at the beginning of the twenty-second century. Fear and desperation.

David Trammel started writing the book that would make him famous in 2099, four years before the blackout of 2103. His book would become an immediate best-seller, but when the infamous blackout ended, "The Murderers' Pit" became something else entirely. It became something terrifying. It became the answer.

Edward Trammel, David's father, was an attorney with the law firm of Allen and Hawthorn. He was not a partner or the star of the firm. That honor belonged to Thomas Hawthorn, nicknamed The Law Slayer. However, David's father was a respected and well-compensated member of the firm. This afforded Edward the ability to ensure his son David's education, providing him with the tools he needed to do anything for which he showed talent. David's decision to become an author didn't thrill the more practical-minded attorney and father; however, Edward supported his son's goals and supplied him with the basics of life so David could pursue what mattered most to him. David fully appreciated the fortunate position his father had placed him in, and he never took advantage of it.

Two and a half years after graduating from Northwestern University, David was living outside Denver, Colorado, twelve miles from the center of town where Allen and Hawthorn plied their trade. He had finished his first novel, "Edie's Eden." It would not be published. David's literary agent, a good friend of his father and therefore on David's side, complimented his inventive story writing and David's use of language but concluded that he may not be mature enough to write a "journey for the ultimate truth" type of story just yet. In any case, no one cared about Edie's story. It was no Eden.

Two years later, at the age of twenty-seven, David Trammel completed his second novel, "One Place, One Time." This was the book his agent described as style over substance. As in "too much style and maybe someone else's style at that." "One Place, One

Time" would suffer the same fate as his first novel and would not be published. David appeared to be no closer to finding a voice of his own. As he left his agent's office after his second rejection, rejection with encouragement included, of course, David was angry. He was tired of living off of his father's benevolence, and he was angered by his own failure. From this anger, a voice would emerge, and David would write his third novel, "The Murderers' Pit." After its publication, as sales of the book grew and David's life began to change, he felt an uneasiness he couldn't identify.

In the aftermath of his book's success, David's life became somewhat eventful as he enjoyed a bit of fame and glory for a while. He did not enjoy the endless public appearances he had to make marketing his book, although he understood their necessity. Eventually, David would adapt to his new responsibilities, and it was gratifying to him that he no longer required any financial assistance from his father. Being published had accomplished David's need for independence. It also satisfied his need to prove himself as a writer. Unfortunately, he had proven himself by writing the first words he had ever written that he wasn't sure he wanted anyone else to read. When David started writing "The Murderers' Pit," he convinced himself that he was constructing a satire on the fear of violence in our society, even though the true creative force behind his book stemmed from his own personal anger and frustration. David certainly would have preferred the successful publication and complete admiration of his first novel, "Edie's Eden." But no one wanted to read what David wanted them to read. While millions of people wanted to read "The Murderers' Pit."

David made one fateful choice when writing his ode to anger. He chose a multi-state blackout as the catalyst for change. The same event that would create the conditions for change in reality just a

THE PAST CAPTURES US FOREVER

few years later. It wasn't prescience that led to this choice. In the year 2099, it was just logical. The electrical supply chain was already being tested by the needs of the public, but by the end of the blackout of 2103, David's choice appeared to be more than just logic. And "The Murderers' Pit" became more than just a book. People who read David's book before the blackout claimed to notice the satire and the tongue-in-cheek humor. All those who read the book after the blackout of 2103 believed the book to be serious commentary and predictive, no doubt about it.

Two months after the three-day blackout of 2103, on July 17th, during a brief twelve-hour electrical outage within the tri-state grid servicing Pennsylvania, New Jersey and Delaware, there were twenty-two murders. Including a police captain from Piscataway, New Jersey, that appeared to be a pre-planned assassination. Three days later, on July 20th, 2103, the junior senator from Colorado, Henry "call me Hank" Hathaway, prepared to deliver what would be remembered as the "Speech from Castle Rock." Originating from Castle Rock, Colorado, Senator Hathaway's speech was of special interest to the people of Colorado but would be streamed all over the world. The senator stepped up to the podium. He held a book in his hand as he began to speak:

"My dear friends, throughout the state of Colorado and anywhere my voice can be heard. I would like to open with the writing of David Trammel and the beginning of his book, "The Murderers' Pit."

(The crowd cheers)

"What scares a murderer? That was the question we were forced to ask. We could think of only two things. Torture and

THE MURDERERS' PIT

death. And we were far too humane for torture." The senator proceeded in his own words:

"Fellow citizens, we have reached a threshold where we as a society can either give up and relinquish control of our destiny, or we can start in this moment right here, right now, to take back that control."

Senator Hathaway continued by assaulting the current lack of crime prevention, especially during blackouts, but he was careful not to hold law enforcement officials responsible. Instead, he highlighted the impossible task they had been given. Then, the senator claimed to have the solution they were seeking. It was the same answer that most of the crowd gathered there had in its collective mind. The senator gave them the answer - "The Murderers' Pit."

Continuing his attack on violent lawbreakers, Senator Hank Hathaway whipped the audience into a revengeful fury:

"I return to our favorite author, David Trammel, and repeat these words. Should we, part of the ninety-two percent of the country who respect the law, be swallowed up by the eight percent who refuse to follow the law? And now, my friends, I'd like to ask all of you the initial question from Mr. Trammel's book again. With a slight difference this time.

"I ask you all now, Who scares a murderer?"

(The senator points to a member of the audience)

"You do."

(The senator points to another audience member)

"And you do!"

(He points again)

"And you do! Who scares a murderer? (He yells) We do!"

(He calls out to the crowd)

"Who scares a murderer?"

(The crowd screams)

"We do!"

Senator Hathaway finished his remarks:

"I want you to know, Colorado, this is not something we want to do. It is something we are being forced to do. And to anyone who feels as I do. And everyone else who can hear my voice – please stay safe. And watch your six."

The following day, David Trammel sat with his family, watching Senator Hathaway's speech for the first time. The web counter had the views for the speech at forty-nine million, with the number still climbing. David was emotionally shaken. It was the beginning of a nightmare for him, where his ideas were hijacked, and the book he was already having misgivings about was designated as a how-to book for dealing with the state's most violent criminals.

David never considered that his book could be influential in any way. Now, his effect on current events would be predetermined. He would have nothing to say about it. And it wasn't just Senator Hathaway's quest. A few weeks before the senator's speech, David had been alerted to the possibility that the machinations in his book had been adopted by the criminals. Being thorough in his writing, David had written in his book about a blackout pact, first agreed to by the drug gangs and then by most other criminals who were without any affiliation. The agreement covered conduct acceptable during a blackout in order to maximize the advantage of the dark. The first term agreed to was that gang-related revenge, either internal or between different gangs, would be suspended during blackouts. This was vital. If they couldn't agree on that, then all their time and resources would be wasted protecting themselves from themselves because killing your rival is easier in the dark as well.

While David attempted to find a positive path through his book's unintended consequences, Senator Hathaway's plans were moving ahead. As his staff predicted, the "Speech from Castle Rock" kickstarted the senator's run for governor of Colorado. And because of the fearful condition of the country and the notoriety resulting from his speech, the election in November was no contest. There was only one issue that was important to the public. Crime prevention and The Pit.

Once elected, Governor Hathaway opened his top desk drawer. He withdrew his plans for the construction of the first Murderers' Pit, including the architectural drawings of the support area necessary to make The Pit a self-sufficient and self-financing venture. Also, the governor had documents written that established the extent of the authority of The Pit. Deciding who would be eligible for execution and how they would be ranked. The first murderers disposed of would be the newly convicted, with separate laws needed to consider crimes of the past and the worst of the worst retroactively.

There were still skeptics to be dealt with, even among the supporters of The Murderers' Pit. There were concerns that the selection process itself could not be trusted. Everyone agreed that The Murderers' Pit must not become a corrupt weapon in the hands of politicians and their supporters. In good faith and to satisfy the people's concerns, it was stipulated that if any public official or any member of their family or support staff were to be found guilty of murder, they would be eligible for The Pit automatically.

With his critics won over, Governor Hathaway began building the very first mass grave for murderers, "The Colorado Pit." The governor knew he was operating outside established laws. He knew he was going to have to fight the federal government on the legality of The Murderers' Pit, and the battle would be fierce. His plan was to continue construction while delaying the government's attack, buying time until the operation of The Pit showed positive results. If it did, the governor believed the federal government would leave his state alone.

First, the excavation equipment was brought in to level the land and dig The Pit. When that dirty job was done, a fleet of trucks arrived, hauling enough wood, steel, and other building materials to construct a small town. Then came sewage, lighting, and water lines, all in service of The Pit. Following David's book once more, Governor Hathaway included the building of exhibitions for the public, where murderers and their horrific stories would be recounted to educate and entertain the visitors to The Pit. However, there were also strict limitations on how long any murderer could be prominently placed in an exhibition. Thereby never glorifying any killer, no matter how notorious. Eventually, all murderers were to be relegated to the Permanent Hall of Horrors, where each offender would be represented by a small wall plaque in never-ending rows of wall plaques kept in a basement facility beneath The Colorado Pit's amusement park.

Next, a list of the first murderers to be executed at The Pit had to be compiled. The governor and the panel of lawmakers entrusted with this responsibility chose ten murderers initially to pay the ultimate price for their crimes. The ten murderers were recently convicted and not yet sentenced, which enabled the lawmakers to sentence them under the new guidelines. Scheduling one execution per week, the governor would buy a couple of months in order to accommodate the drafting and, hopefully, the institution of a new law that would allow the state to add any prisoner currently serving a life sentence for murder to the execution list for The Colorado Pit.

When David Trammel realized that The Murderers' Pit, his Murderers' Pit, was actually being built, the responsibility of what he had created dominated his thoughts. He needed to speak out. David's publicist arranged for him to appear on Good Morning Denver in order to voice his concerns. Speaking carefully, David made it clear that he understood that the first ten murderers chosen for The Pit's initial couple of months were all convicted of heinous crimes. Where all sympathy should lie with the families of the victims. David's concern, he explained, was in what might happen after the first ten. He pointed out that in his book, The Murderers' Pit became a thriving business, a small town of proprietors and employees who depended on the drawing power of The Pit for their livelihoods. After the pool of the worst murderers is depleted, who will we feed to The Murderers' Pit next? How will we keep all those people working? And what part of our morality will we overlook to make it happen?

When the governor was confronted with David's remarks, he was very supportive publicly. He acknowledged that as an artist, it is understandable that Mr. Trammel may be sensitive about how his creative work is interpreted. However, the governor added that sometimes the artist may not be the best judge of the potential contained in their own ideas. Privately, Governor Hathaway was not pleased with David. He had his staff contact the law firm of Allen and Hawthorn, the firm where David's father was employed. Colorado was expecting an influx of legal documents coming from the federal government in their bid to stop the Colorado Pit from opening. The state's budget for the legal battle would be substantial, and the governor needed a smart shark to fight the good fight. He needed to meet with The Law Slayer, Thomas Hawthorn. The governor's plan was to hire the only law firm in the state that could silence David, using threats against his father as the deterrent.

Thomas Hawthorn left the governor's office after accepting the responsibility of representing the state in its battle against the federal government. The first call he made was to David Trammel. David had been introduced to his father's boss a couple of times in the past, and although he didn't like him, he was respectful for his father's sake. That protective side of David's feelings for his father was about to be tested when The Law Slayer asked David to meet with him. David wanted to say no, but he couldn't. No matter what his father's boss had to say, he had to listen, at least.

Thomas Hawthorne asked David to meet him for lunch at his private club, the University Club of Denver. It was an attempt to establish a home-field advantage for The Law Slayer. David was nervous about being there but not because of the opulent surroundings. It was a nervousness born out of uncertainty. Hawthorn began the meeting by telling David of the firm's good fortune, which was also his father's good fortune. Once David learned that the governor had hired Allen and Hawthorn, he knew what The Law Slayer wanted from him and why he was there. He wanted his silence. Hawthorn then complimented David on his book. He insisted that David should be proud of what he had created, but now he needed to let the political and legal communities handle things. With his demeanor toughening, Hawthorn told David that no matter what he may think or say publicly, the reason Allen and Hawthorn were hired for this prestigious and lucrative job was his father. Therefore, David's father had more to gain than anyone else. And more to lose. Cold and clear, Hawthorn concluded, stating that either way, from now on, if you speak out against The Pit, you speak against your father.

David knew he was in a tough spot. The governor's true intentions in hiring Allen and Hawthorn would be impossible to prove. People would assume the governor chose them because of David and his father's employment at the firm, but not as a warning in order to muzzle David's objections. Hawthorn's point about his father's reputation being on the line, as well as the veiled threat to his father's livelihood, forced David into a corner. A corner from which David would be expected to remain out of sight and, more importantly, not be heard. The Law Slayer also advised David not to mention their conversation to anyone. And remember that his father was the reason their firm was about to log a very large amount of expensive billable hours to be paid for by The Colorado Pit. David felt he had no choice. He could no longer speak out against the executions.

The construction of The Colorado Pit, twenty-five miles west of Boulder, Colorado, was completed on March 1st, 2104. An additional month was required to test the basic systems of The Pit and to allow the myriad of vendors and support staff to set up shop, stock their shelves and get ready to open their doors.

Excerpt from David Trammel's book –

They came from all over the state. For some, it was a pilgrimage of a thousand miles or more. They paraded around the green grounds, surrounding The Pit in their best attire. Children and grandparents, lawyers, housewives, and carpenters, eating and gawking together as they waited for the historic initiation. Then, the state's officials appeared together on the sturdy oak platform that had been constructed with a perfect view of the newly excavated hole in the ground. Massive in size, it sat empty, waiting for its first tenant.

It was eerie how David's writing of this passage mirrored the first execution, held at the opening of The Colorado Pit on April 7th, 2104. When the moment arrived, all cameras, as agreed beforehand, were trained on the crowd. The large group of enthralled onlookers stopped eating mid-bite. They focused on a trio of uniformed guards walking an imposing figure of a man up a long, steep ramp. Dressed in khaki overalls, with his head veiled in a black mesh material, the first person being judged under Colorado's new law, Lawrence Martin Rigby, murderer of three, including a fourteen-year-old girl, followed the platform towards his end. With Mr. Rigby seated and strapped into a cold iron chair, the crowd grew suddenly silent as a preacher came forward, and one of the guards raised the Helmet of Justice for all to see. As the preacher prayed, the helmet was fastened to Lawrence Martin Rigby's head. When the preacher finished his prayer, a state official rose up and read the charges against the condemned man. Then, three weeks after conclusive eyewitness and DNA evidence had been presented at his trial and Mr. Rigby had been found guilty, he was shot in the head. The sound of the gunshot from the now-smoking Helmet of Justice produced a moment of shock felt throughout the crowd, which led to a truly solemn moment. This

THE MURDERERS' PIT

was followed by the most joyous, jubilant, and celebratory moment that the people of the state had experienced in more than a year. The Colorado Pit had claimed its first prize, and for one moment, revenge was the fear-killer. Lawrence Martin Rigby's body was thrown into The Pit and covered with one toss of a backhoe.

Governor Hathaway spoke briefly in an interview that evening about the success of the state's first execution. He reminded everyone that, regretfully, it would only be the first. A commitment to The Colorado Pit would be necessary for them to achieve their goals. And the people listened. Week after week, the crowds attending the events at The Pit grew larger, showing support for the system as each execution became a national event.

The fifth execution at The Colorado Pit drew forty-eight thousand spectators, and the vendors collected more than two million dollars in one day. The Colorado Pit was a financial success. The man executed that day was Allen Harvey, who brutally murdered a schoolteacher and one of her students. It wasn't surprising that no tears were shed for Mr. Harvey, but there was a noticeable difference in the crowd's reaction to this execution. The initial shock that accompanied the first four executions at The Pit was not present at the fifth. It didn't have anything to do with the person being executed. It was about a feeling of joy felt among the crowd. It was about spending a day out at The Pit, where you could eat, drink, and laugh the day away, anticipating the main event when a bad guy would be shot in the head. Just a few years earlier, it was thought that, in general, parents were overprotecting their children. Fearful, they would discover the horrors in life perpetrated by their fellow citizens. Now, five weeks after the executions began, the people at The Pit were celebrating with their children. Eating ice cream, holding hands and watching justice being served as a family.

The federal government, in its considerable attempt to halt the executions, inundated the state of Colorado with hundreds of legal documents, including a federal injunction. Allen and Hawthorne, with the aid of a few other Colorado law firms acting under the guidance of The Law Slayer, answered them all and were successful in delaying the federal call to close The Pit. Two weeks later, after the eighth execution in Colorado, the federal government's case lost traction.

On May 28th, 2104, Governor Hank Hathaway reported that for the previous two-week period, law enforcement had been called to the scene of only two murders - in the entire state. Both were crimes of passion. The governor stated that there had been very few armed robberies committed during that two-week span, as well, and the few thieves who were caught with guns had used those weapons without ammunition. The death penalty had always been promoted as a deterrent, but when you could be dispensed with two or three weeks after you were sentenced, no one could risk the possibility of an accidental discharge or an unintended reaction. These results, incredible by any standard, reinforced the governor's case to continue with his plans, and the people of Colorado were behind him.

With only two more prisoners from the original ten still awaiting execution, the governor exercised the state's rights under a newly passed state law, which allowed him to compile the next ten murderers from the existing inmates serving a life sentence. It was decided that the executions would proceed chronologically, beginning with the longest-serving murderer going first. The others on the list were to follow according to the length of time they had been confined, waiting to make their final payment to society.

THE MURDERERS' PIT

Excerpt from David Trammel's book —
And next came the exodus.

Violent criminals, who in general had shorter roots dug into their communities than the average citizen, would have little trouble starting over a few hundred miles away. Some would attempt to learn the lay of the land in their new environment before they resumed stealing and killing. Some would impose their will from the start. Either way, it was someone else's problem now.

While The Colorado Pit was being built, there was disbelief throughout the criminal community about the state's intent. By the fifth execution, however, the fear felt by violent offenders escalated, and by the seventh, the migration of the state's worst offenders began. It was this migration of the murderers that was responsible for the sudden drop in the number of capital crimes reported in the state.

As David had written in his book, the criminals' reaction to The Pit was predictable. If the country you live in adopts capital punishment, relocating from one country to another takes documentation, and there's some scrutiny. State to state is easy. Why stay in Colorado when Nebraska is a car ride away? One of the many issues this created was that, in some instances, more violent criminals took hold, where previously, a less brutal offender had been in control. And there were no preparations made ahead of time to combat Colorado's criminals invading neighboring states. To begin with, Wyoming, Nebraska, and Kansas would feel the heat, and the migration would continue to expand as five states, including Nevada and Texas, announced their intention to build their very own Murderers' Pit.

And David failed to object.

It was around this time, as news of the migration of the criminals was being disseminated throughout the media that Edward became concerned for his son. David had not spoken publicly in weeks. With the disturbing development of the migration in the news, his father felt it was surprising that David held his tongue. Also, Edward was concerned that he and his son had seen very little of each other in recent weeks. That wasn't the norm. The two of them, on their own since David's mother's death eleven years before, were very close. David always stayed in touch. At lunch one day at the University Club, Edward found the missing piece that explained David's reluctance to speak out in public and his growing isolation. A waiter at the Club complimented Edward on his son and his son's success. The waiter mentioned that it had been an honor to meet David a few weeks before when he had visited the Club for lunch. The meaning of the waiter's unwitting reveal hit Edward quickly:

He asked, "Was my son here with Mr. Hawthorn?"

The waiter answered, "Mr. Hawthorn, yes, sir. Very impressive."

Edward realized what his boss had done. Hawthorn had silenced his son in order to further the governor's agenda and benefit himself, as well as the firm. Edward no longer cared about his job. He couldn't allow Hawthorn to continue threatening David; he needed to free his son so he could act as his conscience dictated in defense of the principles that were important to him. As an angry and exasperated Edward was leaving the Club, he began experiencing chest palpitations for the first time and a rush of anxiety that made him sweat profusely. He had difficulty pushing the ignition button to start the car. Finally, Edward was able to get on the road, heading home.

Inside the governor's mansion, after The Colorado Pit's ninth execution was behind them, Thomas Hawthorn and Governor Hank sipped an expensive brandy while reviewing their case, battling the federal government. Their defense of The Pit had gained ground because of The Pit's well-documented and well-advertised success. They were no closer to attaining approval, but a stand-off was fine. The governor was pleased. David was under control, and the list of the next ten convicts to be executed was compiled. The plan was to halt the executions temporarily after the last of the first ten was buried in The Pit. The schedule called for a three-week respite before resuming with the state's new list of ten.

Hawthorn and Hathaway continued sipping and celebrating until a knock at the governor's office door interrupted them. The governor's secretary, holding Hathaway's private cell phone, alerted the governor of an urgent call from his wife. The governor took the phone from his secretary, whom he then dismissed while motioning for Hawthorn to remain. As the governor and his wife spoke, The Law Slayer kept his head down respectfully. He could hear the desperation in the nature of the call. The governor appeared shaken. He assured his wife that he would leave his meeting and join her momentarily. When the call ended, the governor turned to Hawthorn and confided:

"My nephew, my wife's sister's boy, was just picked up by the police. And charged with murder."

Hawthorn stood up and showed himself out of the governor's mansion. Both he and the governor knew they would need to speak again as soon as possible about the ramifications of his nephew being charged with an executable offense.

The facts in the case against Michael Simmons, the governor's nephew, were undisputed. Mr. Simmons was buying cocaine from a local drug dealer. There was an argument when Mr. Simmons suspected he was being ripped off, and the dealer brandished a 9mm. When he pointed the gun at the governor's nephew, it induced an unwise reaction where Mr. Simmons apparently panicked and grabbed for the gun and the dealer's wrist. The gun dropped to the ground, and the governor's nephew grabbed it and fired twice into the drug dealer's chest. Then, Mr. Simmons placed the gun by his right foot and dialed 911.

This type of crime would never be deemed a capital offense under normal circumstances. Now, for a relative of the governor, it was mandatory. The only exception to the law was in a clear case of self-defense. The governor's wife and her sister pleaded with him that it was self-defense. His wife reasoned that they both knew Michael and knew he was a good person. Yes, he was buying drugs, but then he was forced to defend himself with the other man's gun. The governor appeared distraught, although he made it clear to his family that he could not interfere with the process. He also comforted his wife and her sister, knowing that his nephew's actions might not be judged as self-defense. Once Michael had the gun in his hand, it could be argued that the threat was over. In the current climate of public opinion, his actions could be judged as manslaughter, which, at this extraordinary moment, would still land his name on the executioner's list because he was a relative of the governor.

After setting the GPS and engaging the auto-drive to navigate his car back to the office, Thomas Hawthorn began reading through the accounts of the crime perpetrated by the governor's nephew. The Law Slayer understood he had inherited a complex situation and that without any knowledge of the governor's intentions, he didn't know where to begin. Would the governor attempt to save his nephew? Would he want to make an example of him? Or would the governor decide to let the process play out on its own? Hawthorn entered the offices of his law firm with his mind swimming, wrestling with all the possibilities, both legal and personal, that might be connected to the outcome of murder charges being brought against the nephew of the governor. And then he ran into Edward Trammel.

The moment the argument began, it drew coworkers out of their offices and into the hallway. Then, the discussion's decibel level grew much louder. No one in the office had ever heard anyone raise their voice to Thomas Hawthorn before, and Hawthorn was never one to back down. Eventually, the two men had to be separated physically, and in front of the people he had worked with for years, Edward quit his job and assured The Law Slayer:

"You won't threaten my son anymore. And you won't control him!"

Edward was still fuming after his intense confrontation. His heart rate was spiking, and as he started the car, the palpitations returned. Edward should have engaged the auto-drive to take him home. Instead, he took off without its assistance. The car was moving at fifty miles per hour when he lost consciousness. Unfortunately, the auto-drive wouldn't engage until it had failed to detect Edward's hands gripping the steering wheel for five consecutive seconds. By that time, the car was headed straight for a guardrail. The best the computer system could manage was to turn the car, causing it to sideswipe the rail. It couldn't stop the car from flipping over on its hood. Emergency Services was contacted by auto-drive and dispatched to the location of the accident.

The car's safety features saved Edward's life. Advances in auto-drive technology have resulted in fewer automobile accidents in general and fatalities in the accidents that did occur are avoided much of the time. When Edward regained consciousness, he saw David waiting at his bedside. Edward was shocked to see that although he was the one who was battered and bruised, it was David's condition that was troubling. Appearing disheveled, David was attended to by two nurses attempting to retrieve a blood sample while urging him to let a doctor examine him. David refused to leave his father's side. Finally, a doctor instructed an orderly to set up a bed next to Edward, and David calmed down and relented. After a few days of observation and care, David's body recovered. However, the reasons behind his self-neglect would not be addressed. When his father asked, David assured him that he was feeling much better and that he didn't want his father worrying about anything. They had enough money, so David needed his father to focus on his recovery, and he was not to spend one more moment worrying about Allen and Hawthorn or the governor. David knew *that was his job*.

The trial of Michael Simmons was about to begin. The governor's decision regarding his role in his nephew's predicament was to show support for his family, publicly and privately, while steering clear of the legalities. Also, the governor instructed Hawthorn to downplay his confrontation with David's father and let that problem fade with a little time. Governor Hank and The

Law Slayer sent balloons and get-well cards to the hospital with their best wishes. David stabbed the balloons and burned the cards in an ashtray. He and his father and a couple of the nurses laughed.

The case against Michael Simmons breezed through pre-trial motions and jury selection, with the trial scheduled to begin one week after Colorado's tenth execution, during The Pit's planned three-week respite. The trial went on for four days, and the instruction given to the jury by the judge included these words:

"The sentencing guidelines for this case cannot be a consideration in your deliberations. The punishment that the state may or may not impose under these unusual circumstances is not part of your responsibility. I believe this is important for you to remember if you are to do your job as the state requires."

The twelve jurors returned with their verdict the following day, pronouncing Mr. Simmons guilty of manslaughter. Michael Simmons, the governor's nephew, was scheduled for justice on July 4th, 2104. His final judgment would precede the executions of the state's new list of ten, and the authorities at The Pit were said to be working on something special for the occasion.

After the verdict was read, the governor spoke briefly on camera about the difficulty of the situation and that in the coming days, aside from taking care of the state's business, he would be spending every other moment by his family's side. Something he hoped the people of Colorado would understand.

When David heard the verdict, he was with his father at the hospital. Edward was recovering nicely from his injuries and would be heading home very soon, although the better he felt, the more he worried about his son. Being present to witness David's reaction to the Simmons verdict intensified his concerns.

Three days later, on June 26th, one week before the executions were to resume, David made his second appearance on Good Morning Denver. It was the first time he would be speaking in public in more than a month. The producers and the hosts of the show were excited to bring him back, and the studio audience greeted David warmly as he walked onto the set. The first question asked of David concerned his father's well-being following his accident. David told the audience that his father's recovery was going well, and they were grateful for all the wonderful messages of hope that had been posted. When the show's host followed up by asking about the rumors of a disagreement between his father and Thomas Hawthorn right before the accident, David minimized The Law Slayer's involvement. He admitted, however, that his father's job was very stressful, so he was happy his father would no longer be working at Allen and Hawthorn. Then enthusiastically, David clapped his hands together one time and revealed to his hosts that he was appearing on their show for another reason.

"I'm throwing myself a birthday party, proclaimed David – and you're all invited!"

The audience erupted, and the hosts of Good Morning Denver prodded David for the details. David announced that he had rented out the Fillmore Denver for the night of June 27th, and the tickets would be free, distributed online through Ticketgate 9000. David continued:

"As many of us in Denver know, the Fillmore Auditorium was given a nice facelift a few years ago, and next year, the Fillmore will celebrate its 200th birthday. So I feel honored to celebrate my 30th in this wonderful venue. I have also made arrangements, with assistance from the mayor's office, for a party outside the Fillmore. The street in front will be closed off, and we're going to host a block party. There'll be a large projection screen set up outside the venue, as well as inside, so no one will miss any of the festivities. Now, I promise you all that this is going to be a celebration, but I don't want any of you to feel ambushed, so I will concede that I plan on saying a few words about Michael Simmons and his pending execution. That aside, we're going to party. And I am very excited to announce that Tio Drage and the Face Craters are going to perform. And joining them onstage, The Meld, featuring my favorite guitarist, Ted Nugent V."

The audience reacted wildly. Then David left the stage, waving his hand high with a "see you there."

David would see them there, indeed, and it was quite a scene in front of 1510 Clarkson Street. David had no idea how many people would show up for his birthday, but by seven o'clock that evening, David saw that there were more than a thousand guests assembled for the party outside and was overwhelmed by the 3500 seated inside. However, there was something quite special about the people's celebration outside the venue. This was the kind of event people had been afraid to attend, but this night, there wouldn't be a single incident involving a pickpocket or a simple assault or robbery reported, even though the size of the crowd outside would peak at 2500 attendees. Evidently, the criminals who were left in Denver were afraid of the crowds and the possible retribution of the mob and a mob's mentality. It appeared that the people had begun shedding their fears, and the criminals were afraid of the consequences.

At 8:00 p.m., the screen outside the Fillmore began projecting the images from inside the auditorium as David walked onto the stage. The crowds, inside and outside, cheered for their host and then everyone sang Happy Birthday. The echo and the sweetness of the sound could be heard three blocks away. When the crowd finished singing, David, tearing up already, thanked everyone for coming to the party. Then he introduced Tio Drage and his band, and as the music played, the people of Denver celebrated. For the first time in a long time, there was dancing in the streets.

The concert ended with Ted Nugent V offering a version of Happy Birthday that would have made Jimi Hendrix cry. Then, the two bands played together, and they performed one of Tio Drage's biggest hit songs, "If I Dare." When the ovation from the audience died down, the lights dimmed. The large screens, both inside and outside the auditorium, began projecting a series of photos of the first ten murderers executed at The Pit. The image would change every forty-five seconds, allowing a prerecorded narrator to encapsulate the lives of each of the criminals and describe their horrendous crimes. Then David appeared on the dimly lit stage. He was carrying a large box that appeared to be a bit heavy. David put the box down on a table that had been placed there at his request; then, he drew the audience's attention to an eleventh photo, which now appeared on the screens. This photo was of Michael Simmons, and there was no accompanying narration of his crime. A spotlight was turned on David as he spoke:

"For a long time, I wasn't happy with what my book helped to create. I had written The Murderers' Pit out of anger. I never considered the responsibilities that might accompany my ideas. Now, I finally believe that I can feel proud of my book and the acceptance of all of you who have supported me. And maybe the

Murderers' Pit and the first ten executions are partially responsible for us recovering some of our courage, shown here tonight, I don't know. But no matter what we do, we cannot stop everyone from being victimized by crime. It's always a matter of how far we are willing to go to retain law and order. The killing of Michael Simmons is going too far. In the same situation, Mr. Simmons was faced with, maybe half of us would have held the gun waiting for the police. Maybe half of us would have pulled the trigger. The buying of drugs was a catalyst, but beside the point, and I don't understand how we can execute someone for something so many of us would do, given the same circumstances. I understand why the law reads the way it does. It attempts to allay our fears of political corruption, but now that we are faced with this boy's imminent death, we cannot proceed. I apologize to those of you who find my position disappointing, but even if you disagree with me, I hope you are encouraged, as I am, by the feeling of freedom amongst the crowd here tonight. My hope is that even if the Murderers' Pit no longer existed, we would choose to remain courageous in spite of the threats."

Inside the governor's mansion, the governor and his family have been watching the stream of David's birthday party. When David had introduced the image of Michael Simmons on the screen, the governor's wife and her sister cried. When David spoke out against the Simmons execution, Governor Hathaway's personal phone vibrated. It was The Law Slayer. The uncertainty of David's next move was unsettling, and they needed to discuss a viable response. The governor looked at his family. There was a palpable feeling of hope alive in the room following David's speech.

"There's nothing we can do tonight, whispered Governor Hank. We'll talk about damage control in the morning."

The governor ended the call and went back to sit with his family.

Onstage, David checked his watch. It was 9:40 p.m.

Inside the hospital, Edward and his two favorite nurses were watching David's party together when an orderly hired by David delivered a nicely wrapped package to his father's room. Edward opened the gift box, and the nurses smiled as he removed a solid gold cross and a handwritten note. As Edward started to read the note, however, his immediate reaction to its contents was disturbing, which caused the nurses to turn off the stream from the Fillmore Denver and leave Edward alone. Feeling horrified and proud simultaneously, Edward clutched the gold cross and the note from his son in his hand and wept.

Standing behind the table onstage, David checked his watch one more time. He saw the orderly's text, confirming that his father was reading the note he had sent him. David accepted; it was time. He took the box from the table in front of him and placed it on the floor. Reaching inside, David announced:

"Now for a little show and tell."

With both hands, David removed the Helmet of Justice from the box and raised it up high. The crowd cheered wildly at first, but when David put the helmet on his head, no one knew what to expect, and it frightened them. David removed the helmet quickly.

"It's scary up close, this Helmet of Justice, isn't it, he asked. But it needs a firing pin to be operational."

David put the helmet down on the table and removed a firing pin from his pocket.

"Like this one."

The crowd was relieved, and David spoke to them:

"Tonight, you are my family. And my father will tell you, if I have something to say to my family, I say it. So here goes. If Michael Simmons is executed, I believe that would be murder. I believe it will make me a murderer. You will all have to decide for yourselves where the responsibilities lie, but the one thing in life I don't want to be is a murderer."

As David lifted the Helmet of Justice and held it above his head, the cameras captured a closer view of the firing pin in David's hand.

Two men from two separate locations in Colorado, miles apart, bolted from their chairs when they noticed the same inconsistency. The man who designed the helmet and the man who manufactured the Helmet of Justice both cried out:

"That's the wrong firing pin!"

Before David placed the helmet back on his head, he confessed.

"I'm sorry for deceiving you. There was no other way."

David touches his phone, producing these words on the screens inside and outside.

I BEQUEATH MY BODY TO THE PIT

HOPING MINE WILL BE THE LAST

And then —

The sound of the firing of the Helmet of Justice echoed through the auditorium. It was a strangely disturbing sound because of the effect of the helmet's Kevlar lining on the impact of the bullet, and terrifying enough to stir your bones. David's body collapsed to the floor of the stage.

As the agent who chose and co-wrote this story, I am permitted to finish the story on my own under extraordinary circumstances such as these.

In the aftermath of David's protest, categorized as a sacrificial suicide, there was no damage control that the governor and The Law Slayer could employ, and the execution of Michael Simmons was postponed indefinitely. Six weeks later, the governor would schedule the resumption of the executions of the next list of ten, but it would never happen. Through a decision released by the Supreme Court, using the Commerce Clause, the federal government finally found its jurisdiction in the case. The migration of the murderers from Colorado to neighboring states was deemed to have a deleterious effect on those states. A substantial and violent effect. The federal courts decided that Colorado would not be permitted to cause pain and suffering for their neighbors by basically frightening the criminals in the state and chasing them next door. At that point, for Governor Hank, the fight was over. David had swayed the people's hearts long enough for the federal government to step in and close the Colorado Pit, as well as shutting down all of the Murderers' Pits being planned in other states.

The governor would eventually return to the private sector, and because of David, his family was still whole. And The Law Slayer was back to his old self-serving ways but without the same frightening mystique.

THE MURDERERS' PIT

A few weeks after David had used the Helmet of Justice for the last time, Edward got in touch with me. We spoke about David's act and its impact on society, and he shared the note David had written him on that day.

Dad,

I just couldn't let them do it
and I'm the only person who may
be able to stop them.
I know this will be hard for you.
I also know you understand.
I love you.

I asked Edward what his thoughts were presently. I felt he should have the final word. And he shared this with me.

"The painful truth that haunts me is that in confronting my boss and quitting my job, I did what I had to do to free my son so he could act bravely. It was absolutely the right thing to do. And I'll regret it for the rest of my life.

THE PAST CAPTURES US FOREVER

Story # 6

A HEART OF GOLD

"I could never understand completely what a beautiful woman like Terry had to go through living in a self-centered society, where she was forced to grow up with a mother who resented her and where she had to deal with the men who desired her, mainly in an attempt to elevate themselves through her."

AGENT NUMBER 6

(2122 – 2142)

A HEART OF GOLD

(2122 – 2142)

She would have loved to have been Florence Nightingale but had no tolerance for blood. She aspired to a life of service but was drawn to the luxuries of life. And she always intended to change, but she had been taught too well from an early age. She is an enigma. A femme fatale with a heart of gold, alluring and unpredictable, as caring as she is vindictive.

You could almost hear a saxophone playing whenever Terry walked into the room. Sweet and expressive but with a sour note placed here and there to see if you were paying attention. She wasn't easy to read because she wanted it that way. She was even harder to leave until she told you to go. But oh, what music if she were in a giving mood? Or a needy one.

My name is Beth Taransky Dunbar, but everyone calls me Plucky. They call my husband Mr. Mick. We run The Retro, a modern version of the city's upscale ballrooms of the past. Beautifully renovated, except for the basement, which still smells of bad cigars from the previous century, the club is located on the ground floor of the old Edison Hotel on 47th Street. A swanky joint mainly patronized by the underworld of New York, where they come to eat, drink, and dance with their girlfriends and sometimes even their wives, on Wive's Night Only, of course. We always feel well protected because of who our patrons are and because the club is an ideal place for them to launder their cash. Money laundering is still as necessary as it has always been, regardless of the fact that almost all of the legitimate parts of society have made the transition to using digital transfers of different kinds to make payments and move funds around. In the underworld, however, cash is still king. Drugs, prostitution and gambling still demand cash for their services. The problem for criminal organizations in the 22nd century is that there are far fewer businesses that can still be used to launder money, which makes The Retro that much more important. So organized crime comes to the club to spend their ill-gotten gains, and then The Boss takes the cash out the back door, clean, with the aid of his man at the bank and the availability of cryptocurrency as the preferred avenue of converting that cash into a legitimate state, where the funds can then be legally withdrawn, to satisfy payroll and payoffs.

I never expected, given our clientele, that I would be tied up and tortured for the combination to our safe, but here I am. Not that I could have done anything to prevent it, but I hadn't considered what The Boss's rivals might do for 3.9 million dollars, which is the average monthly haul for the drugs, girls, and games of chance sold and the protection offered, in our high-end section of New York City. At least that is as much as The Retro could safely launder in one month's time. So here I sit, tied to a chair, bruised and bleeding, watching my husband being beaten until he finally gives up the safe's combination. What our three male thieves don't realize is that their efforts to open the safe will be in vain, and their lives will soon be forfeit. However, their failure will help lay the foundation for three women who would try to exploit what they could not.

It was three months earlier when I saw Terry Grant for the first time. Outside the club, she was hard to miss even through the blinding rain falling that night. I watched as every man outside the entrance to the club fought to have Terry protected under their umbrella. She took out her own and opened it. Its expanse and her demeanor held the men at bay as she entered the club alone. Mr.

Mick had hired her the day before, and while Terry started working in the coat room where most of the women had begun their employment, she was too beautiful to keep off the floor for long. Within two weeks, she became our most popular hostess, the girl all the other women were afraid might steal the attention of their men. I must admit, in the beginning, I was afraid of the same thing.

I watched Terry closely during those first few weeks, mainly to keep her away from my husband. Then I got to know her a bit, and I realized I was blaming the wrong gender. That Terry was just as much a victim of her beauty as she was a beneficiary. Although she would use her guiles to get what she wanted, she was selective. She could use men or hurt men, but in her mind, the men she took advantage of were all deserving of it, according to her own personal scale of sexual justice. It was something I understood, as many women would. For myself and Mick's daughter, my stepdaughter Annette, our experiences from the age of fourteen and even earlier as attractive women were similar in dealing with the attention of men and their expectations. And their frustrations. For a beauty like Terry, these issues were amplified. Of course, it started, for most of us, before we were fourteen years old with the real creeps, but even later on, when we become aware of the power a woman does have, it wouldn't be nearly enough to control men's desires. It would barely be enough to hold them off. And no social engineering could change it, nor could it be softened by the pretense of sophistication.

With some trust established between us, Terry and I would begin confiding in each other, sharing our past experiences and our own desires for the future. To me, those desires were more of a dream, but not for Terry. And although I spoke candidly with my new friend, I didn't speak to her or anyone else about my husband's physical abuse as of yet, out of shame, I guess. However, the two of us being open with each other would lead to Terry's admission concerning her youth and the abuse she endured. Not at the hands of a man but at the hands of her own mother. Her jealous and angry mother. A mother who had always hated her daughter's good looks and the way admiring men gazed past her to compliment Terry even as a young girl. She also reminded her mother of Terry's father, who had died when Terry was nine years old, leaving behind only his handsome features in the form of their beautiful daughter to taunt her. And when her mother remarried, the fear of her inferior looks made living with her daughter unbearable. Then Terry told me what prompted her to leave her home in Pittsburgh, Pennsylvania, and move to New York.

She began by insisting that in the year and a half she had lived with her mother and stepfather, she never encouraged any physical contact between them, and her stepfather had never breached those boundaries. Until Terry had finally swallowed enough of her mother's abuse. Then she seduced and had sex with her stepfather, making sure her mother found out about it before Terry skipped town with her own boyfriend and left her mother completely devastated and her mother's marriage finished. Taken aback, I commiserated with Terry about her home life, if not her methods. Unfortunately, there was more to the story. The boyfriend who had helped her move from her hometown had gotten involved with some bad people in order to make some quick money for the two of them, which had gotten him shot and killed within a month of them moving to the city. I put my own feelings about Terry's beauty aside, and we became good friends.

The hiring of Terry Grant was not the first time the girls working at the club required supervision. Balancing the need to entice our customers into spending their money without causing problems for the female clientele or the men and women who brought them to the club had always been a concern, but it was an issue handled well by the big Boss, Paul, "The Egyptian," Omari. Because while my husband and I operated The Retro, The Egyptian owned the club.

Paul Omari had taken control of the organization two years earlier in a smooth transition after the death, by natural causes, of his mentor. One of the lessons The Egyptian had learned from his predecessor during his ascent to the top was not to mix business with pleasure when it pertained to the female employees of the club. The Egyptian held firm to this belief. He protected the business by protecting the women. The first night The Boss met Terry Grant, he knew she would require special attention, so he assigned his second in command, Aldo Crane, to look after her. Aldo understood what was expected of him, but Terry would test Aldo's commitment to his boss's immutable rule to keep his hands to himself. After all, Terry wasn't just any woman. And she seemed to be attracted to Aldo, as well.

The Retro was open for business six nights a week, and although the club catered to The Egyptian and his criminal organization, it was also open to the public. It was the public's donations to the cause that facilitated the cleansing of so much cash while the bills could still be paid. The old ways of getting the most out of a setup before torching the place for the insurance money were over, and the continuous operation of the business and its laundry service was expected to continue indefinitely.

The favorite draw of customers to The Retro was Showtime. There were two seatings a night at the club, offering dinner, drinks, and a floor show. Currently, because of advances in technology, there is no need to hire musicians or performers of any kind. Recorded music linked to holograms provided a thrilling experience along with the opportunity for patrons to take their dates out onto the spacious, intricately tiled floor for dancing. Sometimes, a comic from the past would open for the band, but every night at 9:00 p.m. and midnight, the holograms hit the stage.

Three weeks before the attempted robbery, everyone was celebrating Paul Omari's birthday at the club. The hologram of his favorite singer, Doris Day, was performing with the big band hologram of Les Brown and his Band of Renown. Suddenly, another voice was heard singing in the room. Barely audible, it caught the attention of the table, especially The Boss. Usually, interrupting Miss Day would be a capital offense, but as one of The Egyptian's top aides rose from the table to take care of it, The Boss stopped him. Listening more carefully, he located the origin of the sound he was hearing. It was Terry Grant, with no self-awareness, singing along. The Egyptian asked Aldo to bring Terry to the table. Not knowing what his boss might do, Aldo looked nervous. Aldo never looked nervous. The Egyptian assured him that it was alright and told him to bring Terry to him. As Terry approached the table, The Egyptian asked her if she had ever sung in public. Terry's response that the only time she remembered singing out loud was in her house back home, before her mother would tell her to shut up, gets a laugh from the birthday celebrants. Amused, The Boss simply said:

"Okay, you've got a nice voice and the looks to match. I'm gonna try something."

Over the next couple of weeks, The Egyptian hired a technician and had him make an alteration to the programming of the club's Showtime system. The option of a live microphone was made available to be set up onstage and synchronized with the existing equipment. It wasn't difficult for a trained technician to temporarily remove the audio stems responsible for the singing voices when desired, so three weeks after The Egyptian's birthday, The Retro introduced a new attraction. For three or four songs a night, the singer's hologram and sound were replaced by the club's new star. Fronting the band's hologram, singing live, was Terry Grant.

There was one problem stemming from the new setup, and that was with the technician chosen to make the adjustments to the system. The Boss had approved the hiring of Louis Farley, the brother of one of the girls working at the club, Sally. The sight of the safe must have been too much of a temptation for Louis, so one month later, Plucky and Mr. Mick are tied up and bleeding, watching three masked intruders fail to open the safe and forced to leave The Retro without pocketing a penny.

Once the masked men have left the scene, Mr. Mick crawls to his desk and pushes the panic button located underneath the outside of the front drawer. Help arrives within fifteen minutes, and although it is 2:30 in the morning, within an hour, everyone in The Egyptian's crew has been notified and is on the scene or outside the club, keeping watch. A concerned Terry Grant arrives an hour later. The doctor on The Egyptian's payroll is still attending to Plucky's wounds when Terry gets there, and Mr. Mick and The Egyptian are in the midst of a serious chat. Aldo notices Terry when she arrives, acknowledges her presence, but doesn't leave The Boss's side. As the doctor examines Plucky, he uncovers the sight of bruises on her upper thigh and the middle of her back, which are black and blue but a bit faded. They are older than the fresh bloody marks of the intruder's attack. The doctor glances at Mr. Mick judgingly before quickly hiding his personal feelings and going back to doing his job. But Terry knows what she is seeing. It's physical abuse placed on Plucky's body, hidden from normal view. Terry masks her disgust just as the doctor had and moves to comfort her one true friend. When Annette arrives and comes to check on her stepmother first before going to see if her father is alright, Terry notices that as well.

The Egyptian knows, even before questioning Mr. Mick, that Plucky's notion that the theft had been perpetrated by a rival gang is not the answer. The reason the combination didn't open the safe was because of the added security measure provided by a timing mechanism that allows the safe to be opened just once a month and only within a specified period of time. Daily, the cash was counted, bundled, and fed through a four-inch slot located on the side of the safe where a mechanical arm would receive and stack the bills neatly inside. His rivals would know that because they all use a similar safe with the same supplemental security feature. It doesn't take long for The Egyptian to figure out that it was Sally's brother who had tried to rob him. Louis Farley is captured quickly and forced to give up his accomplices. All three are found in pieces, hanging as fish bait off the waterfront pier. Sally's body is never found.

Three dead bodies, or partial bodies, found in such a grisly manner brings the investigation of these obvious murders to The Retro's door and The Egyptian's organization. The investigator in charge, Detective Vincent Canale, is well known to The Boss and his men. They know that this detective is not on the take like some other investigators are but that he always remains respectful during any investigation, even when it might involve organized crime. He won't back down, but he won't jump to conclusions either. Detective Canale is an honest and caring man with admirable skills recognized even by his adversaries.

The Egyptian knows the drill, of course. He makes Plucky's office available to Detective Canale so he can proceed with his private interviews, one at a time. All of his employees have been through this procedure before, except for Terry. No one will say anything incriminating or reveal anything about the robbery that had failed two weeks before, which holds the motive for The Egyptian's retaliation. The last person to be called in to be interrogated is Terry. The Egyptian and Aldo look up to see Terry show barely a nod in their direction. Aldo smiles at The Egyptian, confident Terry will play her part.

Detective Canale greets Terry warmly and in a familiar manner as he begins the interview. He inquires as to how she is doing following the killing of her boyfriend. He continues, saying that he is sorry that, as of yet, he has not made any progress in finding the killer. He had heard that she was working at The Retro, and as the detective of record on her boyfriend's case, he wanted to come see her, but he had been waiting until there was something substantial to report. Terry thanked him for his efforts on her boyfriend's behalf, and then the detective moved on to the matter at hand. The detective asks Terry what she knows about the rumors of an attempted robbery at The Retro, which he believes has led to his current investigation of the three murders done in retaliation. Terry denies knowing anything about it, which, in truth, she does not.

Detective Canale informs Terry that the authorities know that The Retro is being used to launder money for The Egyptian, which is why the murders were so gruesome; to send a message. Terry reiterates that she hasn't noticed anything illegal going on at the club. She adds proudly that she is now singing at The Retro, and from her perspective, everything appears to be on the up and up. Detective Canale acknowledges that he has heard she is doing well performing there, but he warns her not to be naïve and to be careful. He assures Terry that he will be in touch when there is a break in her boyfriend's case and that he believes her when she insists she knows nothing about The Egyptian's illegal activities or his way of dealing with those who cross him.

As the detective follows Terry out of the office used for the interrogations, he informs The Egyptian that it appears he is in the clear for now. With no report having been filed after the attempted robbery at The Retro, Detective Canale has nothing that connects the murders to The Egyptian's organization. No robbery, no motive, no case. The Egyptian invites the detective to dine at The Retro one night soon and come enjoy their new star attraction. Detective Canale accepts the invitation but only if he is permitted to pay his own way. As the detective leaves, Terry walks up to The Egyptian and lets him know that she has kept her mouth shut. However, she does share with The Boss her previous connection with Detective Canale and his involvement with her boyfriend's case. The Egyptian is relieved when Terry confides in him because he already knows about her ex-boyfriend and his murder. And Terry - she now knows that The Retro's safe must hold a lot of cash, and she finds that intriguing.

When Detective Canale leaves the club, the Egyptian dismisses most of his men for the night. He instructs Aldo to arrange to get Plucky, Annette and Terry driven home but requires that he and Mr. Mick remain. Aldo tells one of his men to "bring the Caddy around." Aldo loves his Cadillac, but he allows one of The Boss's other men to drive the women home.

With only Mr. Mick, Aldo, and The Egyptian remaining in the club, The Boss admits that there has been something on his mind since the day the doctor examined Mick and Plucky after the failed robbery, and it is time to discuss it. The Egyptian begins by reminding Mick that he has known Plucky for most of her life; that she had been the bookkeeper at The Retro long before Mick married her and before The Egyptian decided to allow the two of them to operate the club. Plucky is, in fact, like his own daughter. If he ever finds out that someone, anyone, is abusing her in any way, there's going to be a heavy price to pay. Mr. Mick starts to sweat profusely. The message is received and understood, but unfortunately, abusers are selfish. They act according to their own unhealthy needs, with no regard for the person they take it out on. And without any self-control. So, The Egyptian is aware that this may not be the end of it. He instructs Aldo to keep an eye on Mr. Mick and keep Plucky safe. He also informs Aldo that his attraction to and possible affair with Terry is troublesome and against the rules. He will let it go for now, but Aldo needs to be careful, especially with her boyfriend's murder still under investigation.

In the aftermath of the failed robbery attempt and the elimination of the three perpetrators and Sally, The Egyptian changes the procedures at The Retro for how the safe and its contents are to be handled. From then on, Mr. Mick will open the safe only when Aldo or himself are present. Plucky will not be involved, and her protection from any threat will be treated as more of a priority. The Egyptian admits that she should never have been directly involved in that part of the business in the first place.

The Egyptian isn't the only person concerned for Plucky's well-being. Terry Grant is also aware that Mr. Mick's basic nature cannot be trusted. Even with The Boss assuring Plucky that if she did have a problem with Mick, he would take care of it, Terry knows it isn't that simple. Plucky would still be embarrassed if Mick hit her, and at the same time, she would be frightened for her husband if The Egyptian should find out. What is obvious from the outside looking in is rarely clear from the inside, where these situations are complicated. So, Terry has a new goal. She needs to devise a plan that will help her friend and also benefit herself. A plan that will reap a substantial financial gain and, at the same time - **revenge**.

A couple of weeks later, Terry is prepared to have a serious discussion with Plucky. She begins by addressing the hidden bruises on Plucky's body, which Terry refers to as the act of a scoundrel. She tells her that anyone who beats their spouse is a coward, but those like Mick, who attempt to conceal their mistreatment in places that are not easily seen, are especially vile. The hiding of the abuse is evidence of a knowing mind, a conscious choice where the abuser knows his or her actions are evil, even as he or she is attacking the person they supposedly love. Terry holds Plucky's hand, telling her that she cares too much about her to let Mick get away with it and that the two of them are going to do something about it.

Terry asks if she can take a closer look at her friend's wounds. The marks resulting from Mick's attack have left behind an odd rectangular-shaped bruise with a very distinct appearance. Plucky discloses that the bruises were made by an old police "slapper," a heavy leather tool that, when slapped against the skin, is very painful and leaves a recognizable impression. That's when Terry admits to her friend that she already knows about Mr. Mick's "slapper." She had seen it, sitting on Mick's desk after witnessing the bruises on Plucky's body the day of the attempted robbery when the doctor had examined her. Terry assures Plucky that the distinctive bruising is, in fact, a good thing and, as it turns out, necessary in order for their plan to succeed. As Terry begins laying out her strategy, the two women realize that someone else is in the room with them. It's Plucky's stepdaughter, Annette.

Seeing Annette standing there causes Terry to abruptly end her discussion with Plucky, and Plucky, realizing that her bruises are still visible, tries to cover up. Annette approaches, saying:

"Don't bother."

She pulls her stepmother's sleeve back up and examines the marks on her arm. Then Annette raises her own skirt and pulls up the sleeve of her own blouse. Plucky and Terry see the same markings. This is the first time Annette reveals to anyone that her own father hit her as well. Plucky is shocked and furious when she sees the marks of "the slapper" on her stepdaughter, but Terry is not. The abuse Terry endured at the hands of her mother had educated her, so the ill-treatment of parents toward their own children comes as no surprise to her. From this moment, the three women would conspire together.

Having Annette on board as an additional ally is welcome and will actually make Terry's plan easier to execute. Terry shares with Annette and Plucky that her idea for revenge had begun to foment following the robbery attempt at The Retro, which meant that Terry had already been working on her plan for more than a month. At that time, she had attempted to locate the one necessary component that would be difficult for them to find. As Terry continues laying out her plan to her new partners, she reaches into her purse, removes a "slapper," and places it on the table. Terry explains to her puzzled friends that this "slapper" is not Mr. Mick's weapon but one she was able to dig up in a pawn shop downtown after weeks of searching. Terry tells her accomplices that she is confident that finding this "slapper" will be the most difficult piece needed in order for them to implement their scheme.

During their discussion, Terry admits that it's important that she keep many of the details of the plan to herself but that her reason for this is to protect them. Her desire is that after their ruse is done, Plucky and Annette will be in the clear. She wants to make sure that Plucky will still be able to run the club and that she remains under the protection of The Egyptian. Terry insists they will just have to trust her. And they do. Plucky and Annette truly believe they have a bond with Terry based on their similar experiences and needs. Terry continues with the details of her plan, telling the women that since timing is going to be everything, they will have to be patient, as well, because the last tumblers that must drop into place have to do with the specifics of when the safe will be opened and who will be there to open it.

The Retro is closed on Mondays, and the women know that the contents of the safe are always removed on the last Monday of each month. So that is one consideration. The other is making sure The Egyptian is otherwise engaged when the safe is set to be emptied so the women are positive that it will be Mr. Mick and Aldo who'll be taking care of it. Both of these elements are vital for the plan to succeed.

For three months, the three conspirators bided their time while Terry continued singing at The Retro, drawing huge crowds.

Detective Canale, true to his word, stopped by to catch Terry performing, although he still had nothing to report on Terry's boyfriend's murder. During this same period of time, Annette and Plucky had each endured a beating at the hands of Mr. Mick without saying a word to The Egyptian, and while making sure they kept the evidence of the beatings hidden from Aldo. However, the women were not idle over those three months, as many of the details of Terry's plan were accomplished. One of Annette's responsibilities was to purchase two canvas bags, one that was extra-large and one that was of medium size. Annette also visited the Port Authority Bus Terminal, where she had secured a bus locker, taken the key, and then hid it in her apartment. And Plucky, she had done her job. Garnering some cloth she found at home; Plucky had cut the material into a size appropriate to use as a gag; then she located a length of rope adequate for their needs in the basement of The Retro, where she hid the gag and the rope out of sight. Terry's initial responsibility would be to prep Aldo.

Lying in bed one night, Terry voiced her concern for Plucky. The marks on Plucky's body were strange-looking and frightened her. They appeared to be the result of an especially brutal and painful attack. Aldo told Terry that he knew exactly what Mick had used. It was a police "slapper." When Terry acted as if she had no idea what that was, Aldo assured her that her friend was protected. The Boss addressed the situation and put him in charge of looking out for Plucky. Terry acted relieved for a moment and then seemed uneasy again. When Aldo asked her what was wrong, Terry appeared reluctant to say anything further, but when prodded, she confessed that Mick made her uncomfortable. She didn't like the way he looked at her at times. It was creepy. Aldo's demeanor suddenly turned dark. He reached for his 9mm, offered it to Terry, and told her that he would show her how to use it just in case.

When Terry turned him down, expressing an abject fear of guns, Aldo comforted her and told her that if it became necessary, he would take care of Mr. Mick. Terry felt confident that everything was now in place to put her plan in motion.

On the last Monday of the month, November 30th, 2131, The Egyptian is set to celebrate his 25th wedding anniversary with his family at their home on Long Island, while Mr. Mick and Aldo would be responsible for the safe and its contents. Terry, Plucky, and Annette are ready.

Early in the afternoon, four hours before the safe at The Retro is to be accessed, Terry Grant is in bed with Aldo. She gets up, telling Aldo that Plucky is going to meet her at the club to unlock the doors so she can rehearse a couple of new songs with the holograms. She expects to spend a couple of hours there, at most and should make it back to the apartment before he has to leave for the evening. Terry knows that Aldo will wait at home for any last-minute instructions from The Egyptian. Important conversations are still held on a landline, when possible, to avoid any information being dropped, misunderstood or intercepted. Also, he will want to wish The Boss well on his anniversary. Terry tells Aldo to give The Boss her best and kisses him goodbye before heading out. At the same time, with Annette making her way to the club, Plucky, at home, excuses herself, telling Mick that she's leaving to meet Terry. She's going to open the doors of the club so Terry can rehearse for an hour or so, and then she's going to pick up Annette so they can go shopping. Mick reminds Plucky that he may not be home when she gets back because he and Aldo have to take care of the safe. Plucky responds with an, "I know, dear," before kissing her husband goodbye and heading to The Retro to meet up with Terry and Annette.

The three women enter the club with the conviction to proceed. They've gone over the specifics of Terry's plan enough times to begin without discussion. First, Annette hands the key to the bus locker to Terry, who puts it in the side pocket of her purse. Then, Plucky walks down the stairs to the basement, followed by Annette, who is carrying the two canvas bags she had purchased. Annette hides the bags out of sight while Plucky makes sure the rope and the gag are still in the basement, where she had left them. Which they are. When the two women return upstairs, they see Terry holding the "slapper." Annette and Plucky hesitate when Terry asks which one of them is less squeamish. She reminds them that the marks they leave on her body will have to look ugly enough to be believable, to appear as if Mick had caused them. Annette steps forward, takes the "slapper" in her hand, and turns to Terry for guidance as she asks:

"Where?"

Terry pulls up her skirt and points to her upper thigh:

"Here."

Annette's initial attempt is tentative. Terry raises her voice:

"HARDER!"

Annette strikes Terry again, this time drawing blood and leaving a deep impression that is definitely reminiscent of Mick's handiwork. Terry bites her lip and, through clenched teeth, insists:

"AND HERE," pointing just below her kneecap.

Annette complies. Next, Terry points to the upper part of her other thigh:

"AND HERE."

Annette hits her again, hard. Finally, as per Terry's instructions, Annette uses the "slapper" on both of Terry's arms, leaving terrible welts and, again, drawing blood. Terry has bitten her own lip hard enough for it to be bleeding, as well. Finally, Terry calls Plucky to her. She assures Plucky that she is okay and coaxes her to slap her across the face. She does.

"Again, and harder," cries Terry.

Plucky hits her one last time. Annette and Plucky are very upset, as sorry as they can be, but Terry hugs them both warmly, and with tears falling down her face, she says:

"Let's go."

Annette and Plucky support Terry's body, assisting her as they move down the stairs back to the basement. Once there, Annette leaves her accomplices and heads back up the stairs to the office. Annette walks back and forth in front of the safe and stamps her feet a couple of times. The footsteps on the office floor could be heard clearly from downstairs. Then Annette returns to the basement and helps Plucky move Terry into a position directly below the safe's location, so Terry will be able to hear when Mick is above her, opening the safe. Plucky retrieves the gag and the rope. The rope she cuts into two pieces. With one piece, the two women tie Terry's hands behind her back tightly enough to be believable but not enough to be unbearable and place her on the floor, which is a bit cold but is mostly ameliorated by the carpeting that must be a hundred years old. Then, they bind her legs with the second piece of rope. Last, they grab a couple of old paint buckets they knew were there and place them near enough to Terry so that when she tips herself over, she will fall into them, and their preparations are complete. One at a time, Annette and Plucky kiss Terry on the forehead. They tie the gag around Terry's mouth before the three women share a last-knowing look, and Plucky and Annette leave the club, locking the doors behind them. Tied and gagged, Terry waits.

Whether Mr. Mick or Aldo arrives at the club first will make no meaningful difference to Terry's plan, but by the time Aldo makes it to The Retro, Mick is already in the office. Aldo acts a bit concerned, telling Mick that he is having trouble reaching Terry. Mick's response is he hasn't seen her.

At 5:10 p.m., it is time to open the safe. Hearing footsteps above her, Terry is patient until she hears what she believes is the door of the safe swinging open. To be sure, she lies still for a few minutes more; then, rocking back and forth to gain momentum, Terry throws herself over, falling on top of the paint cans, which bounce and hit against each other. The sound is clearly heard in the office and unmistakably comes from the basement. The unknown sound startles both men and prompts Aldo to draw his gun. He puts his finger to his lips to indicate to Mick that he should stay silent. Aldo makes his way down the stairs carefully, with his 9mm pointed in front of him. When he discovers the origin of the disturbance, he is shocked. He puts his gun away and rushes to Terry's side. She gazes up at him as if terrified. When Aldo removes the gag and unties her, she grabs him, holding on tight. Terry doesn't have to say a word. Her blouse and skirt were in a disheveled state, in a position where the marks of the "slapper" were uncovered and plainly visible.

All Aldo asks is:

"Mick?"

Terry, with her lips and body still bleeding, replied with a single word:

"Mick."

Aldo's concern for Terry turns to rage. He asks Terry not to move and to wait there, and then he storms up the stairs, drawing his 9mm with focused intent this time. When he reaches the office and sees the man, whom he believes has beaten his girl, the only words to escape Mick's lips are:

"What was -," before the shots ring out in rapid succession. Five shots in all, and Mr. Mick, a lifelong abuser and a man utterly confused in his last seconds of life, is dead.

By the time the fifth shot has jettisoned from the 9mm in Aldo's hand, Terry is standing at the top of the stairs, staring at him. When Aldo sees her, his reflex is to holster his weapon to somehow keep Terry from understanding the true meaning of the scene. As ridiculous as it is foolish. Terry rushes to him, but she isn't going to end up in his arms. Terry has a 357 snub nose at her side, a gun she had hidden in the basement without anyone's knowledge. When she's a few feet away from Aldo, she raises the gun and fires into the unarmed man's chest. Maybe, when Aldo sees the 357 in Terry's hand, he thinks, "That's a lot of gun for a woman." Or maybe he is thinking what Terry is thinking. That he killed her boyfriend.

As Aldo drops to the floor with a stunned look on his face, in the flash of a few seconds, Terry is back in her old apartment, reliving the past as her hometown boyfriend comes through the door in a panic. He is terrified. Something has gone terribly wrong with the job he had taken, and the only thing Terry knows is that it involves some guys connected to this club from midtown called The Retro. Her boyfriend forces her into the bedroom closet. He tells her to hide and, no matter what, to not make a sound. There's a knock at the door, and when the men enter, Terry can hear a brief argument before she hears the gunshots that will kill her boyfriend, the boyfriend who had taken her away from her awful home life and abusive mother. Terry relives how it felt to clasp her hands over her mouth so not even a whimper would escape her lips. And the last thing she would hear before the intruders leave the apartment is someone saying:

"Bring the Caddy around."

Then, months later, on the night of the failed robbery attempt at the club, when The Egyptian had told Aldo to arrange to have her and the other women taken home in his Cadillac, she had heard that same phrase again. That's when she knew.

Terry stands over Aldo as he is bleeding out at her feet, and she repeats the words out loud:

"Bring the Caddy around."

Then she fires once more directly into Aldo's chest, and it is done.

After killing Aldo, Terry turns her attention to the open safe. She moves down the stairs to the basement and returns with the two canvas bags. Terry acts quickly. The less time she spends emptying the safe, the more time she will have to get away. She isn't concerned about the sounds of the gunshots. The club's soundproofing will take care of that. And it is New York City. There's always a lot of competing noise on the street.

The bundles of cash in the safe hold twenty thousand dollars each, and there are close to two hundred of them. Terry counts out fifty bundles in a matter of a couple of minutes and stuffs them in the smaller bag. The rest she places in the larger bag. And before leaving the club, Terry closes the safe. Then she grabs the 357 snub nose, which has cooled down, and places it inside her purse, picks up the two canvas bags, and hurries out onto 47th Street. Terry's hope is that closing the safe may buy her an additional hour or more; that until The Boss, who is still on Long Island and is the only person who can override the system's timing mechanism, reopens the safe, he won't know if the money has been stolen or if the two men had killed each other before it had been opened. The Boss may assume it, but he won't know for sure.

The two bags of cash are heavy in Terry's arms, but desire and adrenaline help her as she walks two blocks west before hailing a cab. She informs the cab driver of her destination, the Port Authority Bus Terminal, which is only about fifteen blocks away. Once inside the terminal, Terry locates the locker number on the key Annette had given her, opens it, puts the smaller bag holding a million in cash inside and locks it. She removes the key and takes it with her as she proceeds to the ticket counter and pays cash for her ticket out of town. She has plenty of time to make her bus to Cincinnati, leaving at 8 p.m.

At 6:30 p.m., Aldo is an hour late getting to the bank to make the deposit. When The Egyptian's man at the bank, a Vice President on The Egyptian's payroll, tries and fails to reach Aldo a number of times, he is forced to call The Boss. Still on Long Island preparing to go to dinner with his wife, The Boss attempts to reach Aldo, but when he cannot, he arranges for a couple of his most trusted men to check out the club. When his men relay the picture of the grisly scene they find there, The Boss apologizes to his wife and heads back to the city. While in the car, The Egyptian calls 911. He knows the incident at the club can't be whitewashed and the police need to be notified. The Egyptian tells the authorities what he knows of the crime, gets in touch with Plucky, informs her of her husband's fate, and asks her to call Annette. Next, he contacts the doctor, summoning him to the club, as his services may be needed for the sake of Mick's wife and daughter. Regrettably, The Egyptian realizes he won't be able to check the safe to see if his money is gone until after the police clear the scene.

When The Boss arrives at The Retro, Detective Canale and a crew of investigators are already on the job. Plucky and Annette are consoling each other, crying uncontrollably. Although the women are not completely surprised by the outcome of Terry's plan, they haven't anticipated the violent sight in front of them, and it still shocks them. The doctor administers a mild sedative to both women to quiet them as Detective Canale approaches The Egyptian. As procedure dictates, Detective Canale must ask The Egyptian a couple of questions first, but once he is satisfied that The Boss has no knowledge of what transpired at the club, that, in fact, he was a couple of hours away at the time, he shares some initial information with him. The detective tells The Boss that he believes Aldo killed Mick but that Mick hadn't killed Aldo in an exchange of gunfire. He knows this because Mick had been shot by a 9mm, and the bullet casings appear to have come from Aldo's gun, but Mick's Glock had not been fired at all. He also informs The Egyptian that the shell casings they found around Aldo's body were 125 grain, too heavy to have come from a Glock, and they think they came from something closer to a 357. In the Egyptian's mind, this information confirms there must have been a third party involved, and therefore, the money in the safe must be gone. The next thought that pops into The Boss's head is a name, Terry Grant. The connection is tenuous, but he can't shake the feeling that this whole affair might be revenge for the killing of Terry's boyfriend and that just as Aldo had dated Terry while knowing he had killed her boyfriend, Terry could have dated Aldo while knowing the same thing. And then killed him.

The Egyptian couldn't help feeling a tinge of respect for a woman who would be able to play such a game, if it was her, but any feeling of admiration is fleeting. The first chance he gets, he attempts to reach Terry, but when he cannot, he sends his men after her. Then he goes to comfort Plucky and Annette, and when he shares his thoughts about Terry and her connection to the murders with them, they are convincing in their reaction that the idea is crazy, however, they add that if she is responsible for the murder of their father and husband, they want her head. By all indications, The Boss appears to buy it.

Fortunately for Terry, by the time The Egyptian sends his men out to look for her, it is well after eight o'clock, and she is already on the bus heading for Cincinnati. The rest of Terry's plan is simple. It begins with the fact that Terry Grant isn't her real name. When she moved to the city with her boyfriend, they both decided to change their names as part of making a fresh start. Neither of them needed a driver's license to live in New York City, and they paid cash for the dump they stayed in when first arriving. A month later, her boyfriend died, and so using the name Terry Grant, she went to work at The Retro, where identification papers weren't a necessity, especially for a woman as beautiful as she. The club was paying quite a few vendors and employees in cash, so paying her in cash wasn't a problem. What Terry has, from before her move to the big city is a driver's license, passport, and credit cards in her real name, documents she never used once she moved to New York. So, when she gets to Cincinnati, she wipes the gun clean, ditches it in a dumpster outside a convenience store and rents a car under her real name, Linda Gordon. She makes sure she gets the car from a major rental company so she can return it easily in another state. She keeps the "slapper" in her purse for some protection, given the two and a half million dollars in her possession, then takes the key belonging to the locker that holds Annette and Plucky's share and sends it to Annette overnight with instructions to destroy the package the key arrives in, thereby eliminating any evidence of where the package is mailed from including the note she wraps around the key advising them to wait a month or so in order to make sure they're in the clear before retrieving their share. Then, before continuing on, she stops in one salon in Cincinnati to have her hair cut, a second salon to change her hair color and finally, a local shop to buy some new clothes. She changes the clothes she's wearing and places a couple of additional outfits in the canvas bag, covering the cash. With her looks transformed, Terry Grant disappears while Linda Gordon drives on. She changes cars in Illinois, outside Chicago, where she buys a used car for cash.

Linda knows she will have to stay on the run, at least for a while. But looking back, it seems like she's always been on the run from something. From men, from her mother, and now on the run from The Egyptian and the law. And so, what if she isn't able to settle down in any one place for long? There's a difference this time. This time, she's on the run with two and a half million in cash, so she'll just have to keep running from one five-star life to another. And that's just fine with her.

The following day, The Egyptian meets with Plucky to discuss the future of the club, asking Plucky to continue with her responsibilities while The Boss trains one of his other top employees to replace Mr. Mick. Plucky suggests Annette help out in the meantime, and The Boss agrees. When The Boss adds that he is happy that he won't have to worry about Mick beating her anymore, Plucky shows him the recent marks, still fresh on her body, which seems to confirm, in The Egyptian's mind, that Aldo had shot Mr. Mick Dunbar because of his abuse.

Following the meeting with Plucky, The Egyptian is driven to the bank, where he deposits two and a half million dollars of his own money to cover the funds Terry Grant had taken from the safe. The remaining million taken was The Boss's monthly cut, so that wasn't an issue for anyone except The Boss himself, of course. It's a lot of money, there's no doubting that, but The Egyptian always takes the long view and, in a few months, with the right mindset, his losses will feel like they're in the past. And after all, it isn't enough to alter The Egyptian's lifestyle, and this way, no one in the organization or outside the organization will have to know that any money was stolen.

That night, a party is thrown at The Retro in honor of their fallen comrades. The Egyptian announced that the club would close for one week and then reopen while all of their other operations would continue undisturbed. And no one will lose even a week's pay. Everyone is satisfied that the night before didn't have anything to do with money, and rumors started making the rounds about Aldo's killing being personal. Terry Grant's personal revenge for the killing of her boyfriend.

As for Detective Canale, the only evidence he had of Aldo's murder was the fact that Terry Grant had vanished the same night. Again, there was no robbery reported, and a person leaving town without any other evidence would never be enough to warrant hundreds of man hours of combing through an unknown amount of video surveillance across an undeterminable number of states in order to find someone who is barely a person of interest in the killing of a member of the underworld.

Beth Taransky Dunbar, now Beth Taransky minus the Dunbar, who is still known to everyone as Plucky, had this to say about her friend and ex-ally, whom she never heard from again.

"The woman I knew as Terry Grant wasn't perfect. She had the capacity and the desire to be good, but the world around her made it difficult. This may not absolve her of all responsibilities or excuse her actions; however, from my point of view, if she loved you and cared about you like she did her hometown boyfriend or even myself - she really did have a heart of gold."

Story # 7
THE INVASION OF BRAZIL

One of the responsibilities in choosing and writing these stories is to highlight some social relevance or human condition worth telling but without preaching. Although I have attempted to adhere to this mandate, I admit that the nature and implications of this story may have me showing a somewhat more liberal approach in this regard.

AGENT NUMBER 7

(2142 – 2162)

THE PAST CAPTURES US FOREVER

THE INVASION OF BRAZIL

(2142 – 2162)

Some thought it was a story whose time had come. Some thought it was a story that had come too late. While others thought it was a story, like most, whose time would be short-lived, no matter the importance of its content. Although there is truth in all three of these statements, the novelty of this particular story being released by four fifteen-year-olds would prove fascinating, making it newsworthy. Because that's the way human beings are. They require something more than the facts to stand up and take notice. So, when these courageous high school sophomores posted their story of local corruption and its connection to the continuing exploitation of the Amazon Rainforest in Brazil, many began paying attention, and the students gained fame, known globally as "The Forest 4," a name truncated from their original moniker, "The Forest 4 The Trees." The content of their webcast, "A Matter of Life and Breath," would ripple through the consciousness of the entire world.

Paulo Ribeiro grew up in Rio Branco, Brazil, near enough to the Amazon Rainforest to afford his father the opportunity to take him exploring from the time he was eight years old. They would travel by boat or by raft, and even travel down narrower tributaries by way of canoe to see a world that most people only catch a glimpse of when viewing pictures on the internet. Fortunately, despite the deterioration of the Rainforest, which had continued unabated for well over a century, there were still wonders to be enjoyed. At ten years old, Paulo's father bought him his first camera, and by twelve years old, Paulo had developed a keen interest in Drone Photography. He quickly became adept at flying his equipment over and through the vegetation and wildlife inhabiting what was easily his favorite place on Earth. To him, the sights and sounds of its lushness and unfathomable beauty were as exciting as a sporting event as if experienced from inside the solemn ambiance of a church.

But Paulo Ribeiro was also a witness to the undermining events affecting the Amazon, watching them unfold firsthand. Eventually, Paulo, along with his three young comrades, would find their place in assisting many others in educating people about the greed and carelessness that was changing all of their lives without much fanfare. It would still take a very long time for the world's governments to act, but eventually, military forces from every industrialized country began moving in from all sides in an attempt to put a stranglehold on the illegal and, in some cases, legally sanctioned activities that were creating a crisis for the entire planet. Counterintuitively, much of the Brazilian populace was not resentful of the military surrounding their country. They were grateful.

The majority of the population was just as concerned with their government and the blind eye it had turned toward the deterioration of the Rainforest as the rest of the world had become. Even more so. Just because the land was being decimated in order to raise cattle, plant soy, and unearth minerals didn't mean it was being done for their benefit. It was the same for them as it had been for all people throughout history. The thoughtless mining and deforestation were being perpetrated by, and their land used up, to benefit the very few. Perhaps the top 1%. Maybe the top 2% of their countrymen, with the wealth trickling down to a fortunate 10%. But as in the past, outside of revolution, there are no options. Even a revolution is similar to a new election in the end. It only creates a changing of the guard and, ultimately, does not bring about a change of political philosophy. In the case of the Amazon, nothing aside from threats or aid from the outside world could stop the ravaging of the land. Without it, the justification selfishly adopted by those who grab power always exists when there is so much wealth to be had. But Paulo Ribeiro also believed something else. That the rest of the world was just as much to blame as Brazil; all leaders and their benefactors operate about the same. If they were to act only on principles designed for the betterment of all people, they would be ousted from office.

But now, with the tipping point in the destruction of the Amazon agreed by many as being at least twenty years in the past, possibly placing the entire planet at risk, the basic concept of a country's borders was being brought into question; not the borders of the United States, Russia, nor Great Britain, but just the borders of Brazil, because the Rainforest affects life on the planet beyond any borders established by Man. A fact that should have been understandable to everyone. Yet, human beings, for the most part, believe only what they need to believe. When those beliefs are shattered and their safety is threatened, they will turn to blame before accepting responsibility. For decades, tens of thousands of species were becoming extinct in the Rainforest and very few cared about them. In the more than one hundred years following the Paris Agreement of 2016, as the situation in the Amazon was allowed to become more and more dire, while everyone talked about change, very little was accomplished. The proverbial apple cart would remain intact. However, when the Manaus Fever Pandemic in the year 2153, caused by the deterioration of the Rainforest, began threatening the health of the entire world, fear took hold, and the world invaded Brazil. However, the invasion never had to fire a shot.

THE INVASION OF BRAZIL

Brazil has a border with every country in South America except Chile and Ecuador. It is the third largest country on the planet, and it includes 4600 miles of coastline bordering the Atlantic Ocean to the east. There were far too many fronts on land and sea to defend, so when the world descended on their country, Brazil was indefensible. Despite the military presence, this invasion was never meant to start a war. It was meant to create a standoff in order to cease all harmful activities in the Amazon while swarms of satellites and drones from different countries identified and marked all those who still attempted to continue profiting from the land. These poachers, newly designated as criminals by the world's leaders, were rounded up quickly, so the problem at hand, the deterioration of the Rainforest, was arrested where it stood, and the threat staged around Brazil's borders created the peaceful standoff that was intended. Consequently, everyone had hope that maybe the Amazon Rainforest would be able to heal itself. The story of how the world finally responded to this global calamity is, in part, the story of Paulo Ribeiro, Juliana Matos, Samuel Freitas, and Lila Cardosa, "The Forest 4."

It begins years earlier, when at the age of fourteen, Paulo and his friends, at first just to entertain themselves, create an online cartoon. Taking advantage of Paulo's affinity for and skill with drones equipped with audio/video recording capabilities, they start by establishing a main character for their web stories, whom they name Detective Artemis Drone.

Aside from Detective Drone, all the other characters they create are animated, with the artistic duties handled by Juliana Matos and Samuel Freitas and the scripts written by Lila Cardosa. Detective Drone's adversary in their stories is the king of the Amazon, Jaguar Jake, aided by a pack of Mane Wolves, serving as his enforcers. Assisting the Detective is a Harpy Eagle, capable of flying up to fifty miles an hour named Flo, whose job is that of an advanced scout and infiltrator. Also enlisted by Detective Drone to lend a hand as his eyes and ears in the trees is a Giant Leaf Frog named Sebastian, who can bark in Morse Code.

Paulo and his friends use the live footage shot by Detective Artemis Drone, interspersed with the animated sections they create. With a second and third drone, Paulo films the main drone, which he uses to play the role of the Detective. Fashioning his flying video and audio recorder with a mustache, a goatee, and a black Windsor-knotted tie, which at times trails behind him like a tail blowing in the wind, Detective Drone flies fearlessly through the jungle as the area's only investigator and peacekeeper. Every other month, the four friends release their web stories centering on Jaguar Jake and his rule over the community at large, where he overcharges for the treehouse slums he claims to own and where he establishes tolls at all river crossings. Jaguar Jake also demands exorbitant fees for swimming and fishing rights. He makes the lives of the creatures at his mercy difficult to endure, such as the Toucan and the Three-Toed Sloth, the Caimans, and the sea otters. Even snakes live under the thumb of Jaguar Jake and his henchmen. Their only assistance is provided by Detective Artemis Drone, alongside his two trusted allies.

The stories cover the despair of the animals being taken advantage of, with the most popular titles, "This River Is Closed For Repairs" and "Someone Buried My Hutch." When the hope of the Amazon's animal community wears thin, Detective Drone steps in to accept the case, always promising one thing to those who depend on him:

THE INVASION OF BRAZIL

"If I can see it, you'll see it too."

The stories of Detective Artemis Drone find its fan base continue to increase across Brazil with every new release. By the time their most popular title to date, "Jaguar Jake Raises The Rent," premieres, the web stories of Paulo, Juliana, Samuel, and Lila were attracting over thirty-five thousand followers per story. The number of comments that are posted in reply to their animated tales grows handsomely with each new issue as well, but one posting catches the eye of the creators. It is a comment that's extremely complimentary, as most of the comments are, but this person adds something that they think is missing. Of all the animals included in their depiction of the Amazon, one animal is being left out – Human Beings.

When discussing the inclusion of human beings in their next story, Lila brings up two possibilities for them to consider. The first has the potential to be a lot of fun. The introduction of human beings into the mix, threatening the status quo, might force the animals to band together in at least a temporary truce. The second possibility, on the other hand, might be dangerous. Introducing humans would invariably center on the damage they were causing to the Amazon rainforest, having the potential of turning their little comedies into threatening commentary. However, with a small amount of faith and quite a bit of naivety, the four friends, guided by Paulo, who is secretly thrilled with the idea of pushing their project into more controversial territory, decide to see where it takes them.

Their next web story has Detective Artemis Drone arranging a parlay with Jaguar Jake after two bulldozers clear enough of the forest in two days to displace eight hundred residents of the area

Jake controls. At their meeting, Detective Drone takes the position that this latest impingement on their land is going to continue, with humans moving farther into the jungle. So, the members of their community will be forced to relocate continually because human beings tend to forge ahead in order to claim what they want, rarely backing down for the sake of the welfare of others. Although the development of this tale, which they call "Encroachment," includes humor and adventure, Paulo's friends realize it does not fall into the first category they had discussed: just being fun. This story falls squarely into the category of being dangerous and risky. But Paulo is very convincing when he urges his co-creators to consider that the concepts they are exploring are nothing new while conversely posing the idea that since the four of them represent a new generation, maybe it is their responsibility to reveal these ideas through younger eyes.

When "Encroachment" is released to the public, it becomes a sensation, with more than ninety thousand views in the first week, and the four fifteen-year-olds become satisfied with the direction they have taken, as the backlash to their story's content turns out to be minimal. However, this doesn't console their parents. They feel very proud, of course, but they are also experiencing normal parental concerns.

Emboldened by the success of their latest release, one week later, Paulo decides to fly his drones farther into the jungle than they had flown previously to record some advance footage in hopes of cultivating some new ideas for their next story. As his drones record what they see and hear, they see and hear something that isn't supposed to be seen or heard. Paulo's drones accidentally record a conversation that's meant to remain private but a discussion that, once captured, cannot be ignored.

Paulo keeps his three drones airborne and well hidden as he continues filming the scene, even after he realizes the possible implications of what is happening in this small clearing in the jungle. He knows one thing for sure. He would not be welcome if discovered. There are two jeeps and two large pieces of equipment visible, surrounding a couple of men holding powerful rifles while a few additional men stand in conversation. Adjusting Detective Drone's camera, Paulo pans closer to achieve a tighter shot and recognizes one of the men as the mayor of Rio Branco, the honorable Eduardo Nuñes. The other men are unknown to Paulo, but he captures the business name printed on the side of one of the large vehicles, which reads, "Excavation by Teixeira – Supplier Of Exotic Hardwoods."

Paulo calms his nerves, and with a firm hand, he moves his other two drones carefully into position, close enough to record the conversation between the men clearly. He holds the drones in place, keeping himself out of sight until the conversation ends. Then, the mayor and an associate leave in one of the jeeps, followed by the other men, including the men holding the rifles, leaving in the other. Paulo keeps his nerves under control until everyone else has left the area, but once he's alone, he is barely able to keep his hands from shaking in order to control his drones, retrieve them quickly, and get his equipment back home where he can review the footage, under safer conditions.

Alone in his bedroom, Paulo Ribeiro reviews the audio and video recording, capturing the conversation in the forest. Although its content frightens him, there is a clear sense of responsibility realized by him, as well. The recording reveals the mayor of Rio Branco in negotiations with Antonio Teixeira, the area's largest supplier of exotic hardwoods. The mayor is offering to grant Mr.

Teixeira's company the rights to excavate thirty-two square miles, the equivalent of twenty thousand square acres of the Rainforest over a two-year period. The honorable mayor is recorded laying out the terms of the agreement that will cost Mr. Teixeira fifteen percent of the total proceeds, based on wholesale pricing, generated by the sale of all the lumber he cuts down, with an initial payment of 1.25 million Reals, the equivalent of two hundred and fifty thousand U.S. dollars to close the deal. The mayor continues, instructing Mr. Teixeira that following a three-month hiatus, he would then be responsible for monthly installments based on the lumber harvested. Mayor Nuñes also suggests that "Teixeira Hardwoods" attempt to limit their harvesting to the different species of Ipe trees, the forest's most valuable commodity, leaving other less valuable trees standing, which will make their venture more difficult for any spying satellites to detect.

When Mr. Teixeira is heard trying to renegotiate, the mayor stands firm, insisting that the percentage he is demanding is necessary to ensure that all the participants needed to solidify the agreement are on board. However, no other names are mentioned, and it is made clear that Mr. Teixeira will be dealing only with *His Honor*, the mayor. Mayor Nuñes adds that the fifteen percent being charged is the same rate the cattle company will pay for grazing rights when they move in to develop the land once it is cleared. The mayor closes the meeting with his assurance that the terms he has laid out are non-negotiable. Paulo is a witness, as Mr. Teixeira agrees. The two men then shake hands, and the recording ends with everyone at the scene getting into their vehicles and driving away.

Paulo sits in his room, stricken with fear. He has absolute proof of corruption. Even at fifteen years old, he knows how dangerous that could be. He decides that he cannot tell his parents, putting them at risk. But what about his partners? Before deciding whether or not to share the recording with his friends, Paulo distracts himself by doing a little research. With the understanding that the calculations he's attempting are too complex for him to evaluate with complete accuracy, he judges that it is fair to estimate that within three or four years, between the sale of the hardwood and the cattle, the deal the mayor was making, had to be worth more than forty million Real or approximately eight million U.S. dollars, with fifteen percent, or around 1.2 million U.S. dollars going directly to the mayor and his cronies. The money from the grazing rights, and additional cattle sales, would continue after that. Of course, replacing the Ipe trees takes eighty to a hundred years, so that was never going to happen.

Paulo Ribeiro is unable to sleep that night. He spends his time planning. How does he share what he knows? His two major concerns are protecting his friends and family while reaching as many people as possible in the smallest amount of time. He understands that protecting himself will be tricky, a risk no matter how clever his preparations are for the information's release. And time is a factor because he must consider that the mayor will probably move in quickly and attempt to have his website shut down. When he believes he is as prepared as he can be, Paulo meets with his friends and partners, Juliana, Samuel, and Lila.

Usually, in their creative sessions, the four friends work openly, making their decisions as a team. This time has to be different. Paulo has concluded that he cannot involve his friends until after the recording is made public. It is the only way to protect them. So, he asks his friends for some latitude. He asks them to fulfill his requests for what he needs for this next story without any input, or questions. He informs Lila that no script is necessary while informing Juliana and Samuel that the animated sections will be limited. All he will require of them is that they create the images he instructs them to create. It is a difficult moment for the four partners, as their past endeavors have always been completely collaborative. Paulo assures them that he is not trying to seize control of their stories, but not wanting to say too much, he asks sincerely that, just this once, they grant him their trust. And that is what Juliana, Samuel, and Lila decide to do. To trust their friend and comply with his requests.

The story is released to the public one week later. The webcast begins with an animated scene in the jungle. Some of the members of Jaguar Jake's community are seen setting up a large projection screen as a plethora of representatives of the animal kingdom arrive. At first, the scene is filled with hijinks. Spider Monkeys, hanging from surrounding trees, throw popcorn at the screen. A Caiman pulls the chair out from under a cougar, attempting to sit down. There is a lot of bantering noise throughout the crowd, but the animals are getting along, all in good fun. Even Jaguar Jake and the Mane Wolves are present, taking their seats in the front row, as Detective Drone enters and asks everyone to quiet down. Then, he introduces someone he calls a friend, someone to whom they need to listen. He introduces Paulo Ribeiro. This is the first time Paulo or any of the show's co-creators appear in one of their webcasts. He speaks directly into the camera.

"First, let me introduce myself. My name is Paulo Ribeiro. I want to thank all of you for allowing me to speak to you. I am happy to see Jaguar Jake and the rest of the members of the Rainforest community who have come here today."

A short animation of the animals greeting Paulo is seen before he continues.

"What I am about to show you is important for all of you, but it is even more important that the audio and video captured by Detective Drone a little more than a week ago be seen by the people of my home, Rio Branco, and all the people of Brazil. I know you will find it as disturbing as I do. And the fact that we are jaded to the point that we may not be shocked by what I am about to show you is, indeed, shocking. To anyone with the capability of recording this webcast, I urge you to do so, and if you know anyone in the media, either in Brazil or abroad, I ask you to share what you are about to see. Also, I want to state that I have done this on my own without the knowledge of my family or the knowledge of Juliana Matos, Samuel Freitas, or Lila Cardosa, who have been my partners on these webcasts previously. Any contribution they have made was made without any context presented to them. I want to be clear about being solely responsible for this release because I expect two things to happen within a short period of time. I expect our website will be shut down and that I will undoubtedly be arrested. Not because I am doing anything wrong. The footage you will see was recorded in public and, thankfully, for once, not from behind closed doors. Regardless, I am doing this because I have to, despite the consequences. However, your support will be appreciated. Without it, the powers that be will probably bury me. When you see the footage, you will understand. So now, here is Detective Artemis Drone, bringing you a story of corruption that I call "With Your Pants Down."

During the scene of the mayor's meeting with Antonio Teixeira, there are several animated pieces intercut throughout the scene highlighting the animals' responses to the plans being made and the deal being struck. Some of the animals are shocked, and some, like Jaguar Jake, show anger. Others are confused or perplexed by the blatant lack of decency on display.

The story is posted on the Detective Drone website, at one o'clock in the afternoon, on March 21st, 2149. Also included by Paulo within the release is a link leading to the raw footage of the scene between the mayor and Mr. Teixeira, making it easy for anyone to repost or share the video without the animation.

Before the story is uploaded, Paulo sends out the usual pre-announcement about a new Detective Drone story being released to everyone on their extensive email list. Right after posting the story, Paulo contacts his three partners to let them know, inviting them to his home to watch the webcast together. After they do, Paulo reiterates his reasoning for keeping them in the dark, something they now understand completely. By the time Paulo's mother arrives home an hour later, everyone's cell phone is already starting to ring. While Paulo shows his mother the webcast, he realizes he needs to get in touch with his father. Juliana, Samuel, and Lila call their parents to notify them. But each of their parents was already receiving phone calls from friends, congratulating them for something of which they were unaware. Paulo's father is on his way home; his boss, having seen the webcast, had slapped him gleefully on the back before sending him off to be with his son.

Within two hours of "With Your Pants Down" going live, over sixty thousand views are counted, and the story seems to catch the attention of the entire country. By five o'clock that same day, the story receives over five hundred thousand views with the sharing and reposting of the story, a number difficult to calculate. When Antonio Teixeira, enlightened by his two teenage sons, finally finds out what is happening, he contacts the mayor, but the mayor already knows. Countrywide, television newscasts were already preparing segments that included some or all of Paulo's raw footage, and the information provided by the footage was featured in practically every news blog in Brazil. This does not deter the mayor from acting. Without thinking it through carefully enough, Mayor Eduardo Nuñes sends the state's military police to Paulo Ribeiro's front door to arrest him and bring him in for questioning.

At home, Paulo and his friends have replayed the webcast of "With Your Pants Down" for their parents, who are speechless. There is a mixed sense of pride and fear palpable in the room when they hear a sturdy and obviously unfriendly knock at the door. It produces an uneasy feeling in everyone's gut. The police, with a warrant to take Paulo in, warn everyone to stand back and not interfere. Paulo's mother and father, along with Paulo's friends and their parents, are shocked, frozen in place, as they watch fifteen-year-old Paulo Ribeiro being manhandled, then roughly tossed into a police vehicle and taken away.

Inside the police station, seated in an interrogation room, Paulo is handcuffed to a table. The mayor and Antonio Teixeira watch from behind the one-way mirror that allows access to the proceedings in the room behind the glass. As an investigator begins questioning Paulo, the boy speaks bluntly, telling the detective that he has done nothing wrong. No one with a conscience will support a man who thinks that the Amazon Rainforest belongs to one man to do with as he pleases in order to profit from the land he doesn't own and doesn't legally control. No one. When the interrogator presses Paulo in defense of the mayor, he actually slaps Paulo across the face out of frustration. The fifteen-year-old boy, with a tear escaping his eye, calls the detective a disgrace, and then he asks to see an attorney. The mayor, unable to control himself, enters the room. He threatens Paulo, screaming at the boy, claiming that he will be sorry and that he has put his family and his friends in jeopardy. But these threats are a fantasy. What the mayor has yet to realize is that his power is already coming to an end.

The chief of police, appearing distressed, rushes into the room, interrupting the mayor, who is still berating the boy. He whispers in the mayor's ear, and Paulo Ribeiro's interrogation stops abruptly. Outside the building, hundreds of protesters have gathered, their numbers growing by the minute. Paulo's friends posted an update on the Detective Drone website, sending out notifications and informing everyone on their list of Paulo's arrest. By the time Juliana, Samuel, Lila, and their parents arrived with Paulo's mother and father, the crowd of supporters had stopped traffic in front of the precinct filling the street. The mayor, Antonio Teixeiro, along with the entire staff of policemen inside the building, looked out at the scene, which now included news crews filming the protesters and broadcasting the event live. The mayor, still believing that he is in control, orders the police chief to go out with his men to break up the demonstration. The police, some of whom were on Paulo's side to begin with, realize that the event has reached the point of being unmanageable. Any orders from the mayor are now moot.

The police chief returns to the interrogation room, removes the cuffs from Paulo's wrists, and escorts him out of the building into the waiting arms of his parents, his friends, and the massive crowd of supporters who cheer for him as he joins them. All of it is captured by the cameras of those present and the film crews who report the story throughout the entire country. The reign of the honorable Mayor Eduardo Nuñes is over. In no time at all, the mayor's associates in the government who were involved in his extortion plans were rooted out, as well; brought down by a fifteen-year-old boy and his drones. The story wouldn't end there, however. The images of the mayor's devious plan and the subsequent protest would find an international audience, with the accompanying notoriety shared by Paulo, giving credit to his friends Juliana, Samuel, and Lila. In the aftermath, their website's influence increased, reaching more than four million followers worldwide.

In the weeks that followed, the four friends decided to drop the Detective Drone webcasts in exchange for a new, more serious forum to tell the stories they believed needed to be told. They call their new website "A Matter of Life and Breath," with the reporting done by four friends who call themselves "The Forest 4 the Trees" but who eventually become known simply as "The Forest 4."

For the next two and a half years, the webcasts posted on their new website dealt with a number of issues, including the disturbing spread of Malaria due to tens of millions of mosquitoes carrying the disease, after being forced from the environment they inhabited, because of the continued deterioration of Brazilian swamplands. Other stories discussed problems caused by flooding, as well as the wildfires that were exacerbating the issues of deforestation.

Although "The Forest 4" no longer attracts the four million viewers that their famous story of corruption had garnered, they remain very popular. They regularly draw an audience of over a million followers to each webcast. These loyal viewers would begin contacting "The Forest 4," providing them with the initial details for many of the stories on which they would report by relating local issues of concern for them to expose.

When Paulo and his friends turn eighteen, they begin attending the same college, the Federal University of Acre, the top school in

Rio Branco, while continuing to post their webcasts monthly. The new format for "A Matter of Life and Breath," established after the dropping of Detective Drone and the animated sections, evolves slightly, maturing with a clear attempt to avoid drawing premature conclusions, now a priority. Instead, the show concentrates on offering a venue for open and frank discussions that attract pertinent authorities and scientists to share and debate their opinions. This is considered particularly important when discussing issues such as global warming and the Rainforest's role in absorbing carbon dioxide. However, there is one point of view the "The Forest 4" does cite, continually, by posing a question: Why would society play Russian Roulette with the environment just because there is no absolute proof that the destruction of the Amazon Rainforest would mean planetary suicide? Then, in the year 2152, whispers of a distressing situation were brought to the attention of the "The Forest 4," emanating from the city of Manaus, on the banks of the Negro River in Northwestern Brazil; the capital city of Amazonas and home to over two million people.

Paulo volunteers to take his cameras to Manaus for a first look at the situation brought to their attention by one of the viewers of their webcast. The city of Manaus is located eight hundred and sixty-eight miles from Rio Branco. A direct flight would take just over four hours, but with layovers, which cannot be avoided, the trip takes at least nine hours. On Friday, November 3rd, 2152, Paulo sets off to investigate these reports of something new.

When he arrives, Paulo bundles his equipment and personal belongings into a hired car and heads directly to the Fiocruz Amazônia Biobank in the heart of Manaus. It is a famous institution that has been the center of viral and parasitic studies since early in the previous century. Although still a part of Brazil's Ministry of

Health, their reputation has afforded them total freedom in investigating whatever conditions they deem important. Continually exploring the possibility of infectious diseases dangerous to primates, they direct some of their work on parasitic worms, causing diseases like Filariasis. The institute's other main interests are the study of monkeys, rodents, and bats, which may produce a wealth of possible threats to the health of the population, including deadly viral fevers. What has brought Paulo to the Fiocruz Biobank on this occasion are rumors of a new virus spreading very slowly but causing a deadly scare because of its unknown origin.

Paulo Ribeiro, a minor celebrity throughout Brazil, is welcomed warmly inside the Biobank. He is then asked to don protective gear, covering his entire body, before being allowed to enter the lab's facilities, where he meets Dr. Alexandre Alves. Having received authorization to bring his recording equipment into the lab, Paulo begins filming this area of scientific study, and although he does not understand everything he is filming, it is overwhelmingly impressive to the sight, despite its ominous feel. Paulo photographs the walls of frozen chambers safely guarding the animal specimens being studied. He also photographs Dr. Alves standing in front of the tables of microscopes and other instruments, which he has no way of identifying. As he does, his camera peeks around the doctor and records someone else. Someone who forces his camera to linger. Unaware, Paulo cannot help but continue focusing on a young woman whose intense concentration on her work gives her an almost angelic appearance. From behind his camera, he is entranced. Dr. Alves interrupts:

"She's one of our lab assistants. Would you like to meet her?"

Paulo is embarrassed, having paid so much attention to the girl caught in his camera's eye, and as Dr. Alves touches the young woman on the shoulder, breaking her focus, Paulo is a bit awkward, certainly less than suave when the doctor introduces him to Elena Mendes, a student from the University of Amazonas, Manaus. Elena's eyes meet his, and the angelic look on her face that had appealed to him appears to remain; she is immediately attracted to the boy. Even when Dr. Alves begins educating Paulo on the seriousness of the disease that had been recently uncovered, Paulo seems to be lost in something more personal before he regains his composure along with his ability to, at least, feign professionalism.

After Dr. Alves's orientation, the doctor asks Elena if she would escort Paulo to the two hospitals where patients suffering from the new virus have been isolated. After checking into his hotel, Paulo meets Elena at the first hospital, the Universitario Getulio Vargas. Then they move on to film at the Hospital Rio Amazonas. Elena explains what is known about the cause of the suffering of these patients and the manifestation of their intense fevers. She shares her concerns about a rapidly increasing contamination and the possible outlook for its effect as Paulo films an overview of the scene while being sensitive to the privacy of the individual patients. And he films Elena caring for them. After tending to their needs, Elena begins sharing some of the lab's thoughts on what might be the root cause of this new virus but admits that those thoughts are germinal. However, they believe the culprit may be a species of bat. Brazil is home to approximately twelve percent of the almost fourteen hundred species of bats found in the world. It is feared that these bats are flying from their homes because their homes are being decimated by humans, and they could spread the virus over long distances, causing a serious outbreak or maybe even the next pandemic. And although there are no deaths cataloged as of yet, it is probably just a matter of time.

Being early in the lab's investigation, Elena has nothing more to report, allowing her and Paulo to spend the rest of the weekend getting to know each other. Their relationship progresses as Paulo returns every weekend that follows, while he is also kept up to date with the progress being made on the disease that, alarmingly, is beginning to spread quickly. In between his third and fourth visit to see Elena, Paulo and "The Forest 4" post their first webcast highlighting the new viral fever in Manaus. Paulo's interviews, featuring the footage of Dr. Alves and Elena, filmed in the lab and at the hospitals, draw more attention than any of the other "Matter of Life and Breath" web stories since the establishment of their new format. Thereafter, an update of the Manaus virus is included in all subsequent episodes.

Paulo continues visiting Elena weekly, even when there is nothing new to report because, amidst the increasing number of people contracting the disease and its possible implications, Paulo and Elena are falling in love. Then, on December 21st, 2152, seven weeks after Paulo's initial visit, the first patient suffering from the Manaus virus dies. Then, the second. Suddenly, over the course of the next two weeks, there were twenty-two deaths, with two hundred new cases diagnosed. It is the beginning of an epidemic.

Once the outbreak of the Manaus Fever begins, it is impossible to contain. Thousands begin dying, and tens of thousands contract the illness. Even with the discovery of the disease's carrier confirmed as a species of bat, the research to find a cure had just begun. While the contagion spreads quickly, well beyond the city of

Manaus, those who are ill begin occupying most of the beds in the hospitals throughout Northwestern Brazil.

During this time, "The Forest 4" became a major voice urging the government and people of their country that while the protection of their own population is of utmost importance, they must also acknowledge a responsibility to the rest of the world. With Elena and Dr. Alves on the front lines of research, Paulo is kept up to date on the worsening situation that politicians are claiming is still containable but which "The Forest 4" relates to their followers as dire. Followers, whose numbers are now increasing with every new report. "The Forest 4" rose up against their government's positions, urging anyone listening to fight for a ban on any travel from one area of the country to another, as well as an immediate ban on all air travel leaving Brazil. For this stance, "The Forest 4" are attacked by the forces in the country who, unlike Paulo and his friends, have the real power. "The Forest 4" are marked as naïve sensationalists whose rallying cry is ignorant of the country's needs and the responsibilities of its leaders.

To battle back, in their next webcast, Paulo, Juliana, Samuel, and Lila return to Detective Drone in an episode entitled "Outbreak, There It Goes." The story ends with Paulo and his friends, intercut with footage of Dr. Alves and Elena all looking up to the sky as a plane flies overhead. Inside the plane, aside from pilots and frantic flight attendants, there are no other human beings. The plane's seats are filled with celebrating bats, laughing, drinking and joyously flapping their wings. It is a disturbing image. The next day, the "Matter of Life and Breath" website is shut down by the government. Three weeks later, the first cases of the Manaus Fever were detected in the United States.

At the same time, as the bravery of "The Forest 4" is being recognized and a movement to have their website reinstated begins, Paulo Ribeiro is struck by fear. He is still in love with Elena, but she is battling a crippling disease from the inside. Exposed to possible contamination daily. Uncontrollably, this fear poisons his desire to visit Elena. He is afraid of losing her but selfishly fearful of being too close to the disease himself. With a worldwide Pandemic blooming, he starts to pull back while Elena's responsibilities and involvement in finding a vaccine continue to grow. Paulo abandons her, consumed by a concern for his own well-being.

When a few weeks pass without Paulo returning to Manaus to visit Elena, his friends and family question him. Paulo tells them that he and Elena are taking a break. His excuse is that with Elena extremely busy working on the Manaus Fever, he has decided to focus on his schoolwork, concentrating on his first year of finals. No one believes this to be plausible, but no one interferes.

Paulo does continue to contact Dr. Alves, and although it is a bit awkward, the doctor recognizes the value of keeping "The Forest 4" in the loop, as the pressure of the group's followers has, very publicly, forced the reinstatement of their website. Aside from input from the Fiocruz Biobank, "The Forest 4" has been able to establish many other contacts during the escalation of the Manaus Fever. They continue to fight against ignorance and misinformation with their reports, as the viral disease is now spreading to all corners of the Earth and is declared a Pandemic.

A major development in the way the world's leaders react to the Pandemic changes, as the number of deaths surpasses two million citizens and people begin to panic. Also, it has been discovered definitively that the virus had originated in Manaus as a result of damage done to the Amazon Rainforest. And there is outrage when it is widely reported, after being featured in a "Forest 4" web story in the summer of 2153, that Brazil had continued deforestation with 460,000 square acres being harvested, sanctioned by the government in the first four months of 2153, in spite of the focus of the world's attention and the possibility of the creation of new threats. Fortunately, in October of 2153, a vaccine for Manaus Fever is successfully developed in cooperation with many of the world's scientists and drug companies, including the important work done at the Fiocruz Biobank. However, even with a vaccine ready for implementation, the future is a recognized concern.

In an emergency session of the United Nations Security Council, alongside political discussions amongst leaders of all countries, it is determined that allowing the Rainforest to be ravaged any further without a comprehensive reassessment of any possible detrimental effects is a problem for everyone. In a vote that is unanimous, except for the isolated objection of the representative of the country at the center of the controversy, an unprecedented decision is made. At the beginning of the year 2154, the world invades Brazil.

Modern battleships cover the entire eastern coast of Brazil from miles offshore in the Atlantic Ocean, while the cooperation of every other country in South America makes it easy to surround Brazil on all land fronts. Satellites begin identifying problem areas in the Rainforest while drones patrol the designated regions. Within two weeks, there is capitulation by the leaders of Brazil. Their disagreement with the rest of the world becomes a cooperative effort to gain control of the future of the Amazon Rainforest and its possible effect on the world's environment.

Three months later, the Manaus Fever Pandemic is declining. The cooperation of Brazil and all of its neighbors, with smaller areas of the Rainforest inside their borders, halt the destruction of any additional land while considerable aid begins to flow into and throughout the continent. This includes financial compensation and donations of needed commodities, especially much needed food supplies. No one knows how long it will last, but for this one moment in time, there is worldwide cooperation, a shared responsibility. And the forces that had invaded Brazil began their return home.

As the Manaus Fever is waning, "The Forest 4" is recognized as one of the important private contributors to the cause. But there has been a devastating personal loss felt deeply by one of the four. Elena Mendez contracted the Manaus Fever during her work on the vaccine, and on April 3rd, 2154, she succumbed. She will be one of the last to die of the disease. Paulo is devastated. He had never reconciled with Elena. As a result, the same selfish, misguided need for self-preservation that dictated his previous actions leads Paulo into a state of denial, while his friends and parents are deeply concerned that his true feelings will unavoidably surface and catch up with him.

Two months after Elena's death, with the Pandemic contained, the United Nations promoted a gathering in New York City at its headquarters to pay homage to the victims of the Manaus Fever and to recognize the world's commitment to acting responsibly. "The Forest 4" are invited to the convention that is entitled "A Matter of Life and Breath" in their honor, with Paulo Ribeiro chosen to speak last to close the proceedings. However, for Paulo, the denial of his feelings for Elena, which formed the defense protecting him, abandons him now and turns into shame. He feels completely unworthy of the honor being bestowed upon him. His friends, Juliana, Samuel, and Lila, present a different point of view. They insist that Paulo reclaiming his courage and speaking at the conference is an opportunity he must embrace, a chance to be the man he should have been. A way to honor Elena, his lost love, and eventually, the path to forgiving himself.

When the day arrives, the convention at the United Nations, broadcast and streamed throughout the world, welcomes speeches by scientists, scholars, agriculturalists, and environmentalists. Then, the last person to speak is introduced, Paulo Ribeiro. Seated with his colleagues, Juliana Matos, Samuel Freitas, and Lila Cardosa, Paulo rises and approaches the podium. He begins by giving credit to his friends, "The Forest 4," making it clear that his words are their words.

"In the past, one of the issues my friends and I have spoken about is whether there is a measure of exaggeration in the position taken by those who warn of the consequences resulting from the deterioration of the Amazon Rainforest. One of these eventualities, amongst other claims of doom, concerns the Rainforest's ability to absorb carbon dioxide in order to keep our air breathable and how important that may be. But even if we accept, for the moment, that these claims are an exaggeration, does that mean we can just ignore the possibility of their truth so we can continue our current course? It is still akin to playing Russian Roulette. What's the difference if there is only one bullet in the gun or four? Or whether the first bullet is not loaded into the chamber for another two hundred years. It is still irresponsible, isn't it? From this overview, one of the realities that becomes clear, and one we must address moving forward, is that the drawn borders of man are, in some cases, an illusion.

'These borders, which were drawn five hundred years ago or more, could not possibly account for the needs that would eventually cross those borders in the future. We need to recognize that if the Wyoming grasslands, as one example, require the filtration of carbon dioxide and the rainfall kept intact by the health of the Rainforest of Brazil and its neighbors, then Brazil cannot be expected to assume that enormous responsibility to the rest of the world, alone. All of us who assumed complete independence before interdependence became an understood reality must share in the responsibilities that arise from that interdependence. A country's established borders can still be respected for the sake of the safety and peace of its citizens, as long as there is an agreement allowing for the possibility that under certain circumstances, all borders created by human beings are ultimately an illusion when we view the planet as a whole and attempt to assure the continuation and welfare of life everywhere."

Paulo takes a moment before continuing:

"We have all suffered losses in the last couple of years because of the Manaus Pandemic. I have suffered the loss of Elena Mendez. But I lost her long before she died. Elena was a member of one of the teams credited with the development of the vaccine that is eliminating the Pandemic. She sacrificed her life, fighting to save ours. I stopped seeing Elena, whom I loved, because I was afraid of the consequences to my own life. I want to use what that has taught me to end my speech today. I have learned that sacrifice is hard, and its results can be frightening. That's why we don't commit to change even when we know it's right. But somehow, we have to find the courage. For the sake of each other and for those to whom we owe the future."

As the applause died down, no one could predict whether Paulo's speech would remain in the minds of those who were listening. And there was no redemption for Paulo in the admission of his own shortcomings. All he could hope for was that it would become one personal step forward. Regardless, he had taken the opportunity given him, representing himself and "The Forest 4" quite well. As far as the content of his speech, whether it be five hundred years from the present or a thousand years, the truth of what a twenty-year-old boy had to say that day, eventually, will be inescapable as long as the Earth remains our home.

THE WATCHMAKER'S FAMILY

Story # 8

THE WATCHMAKER'S FAMILY

"Sometimes decisions made in the past promote unintended consequences that can take decades to emerge."

AGENT NUMBER 8

(2162 - 2182)

THE PAST CAPTURES US FOREVER

THE WATCHMAKER'S FAMILY

(2162-2182)

Initial conversation between the local Denver Military Police and their superiors at The Pentagon, August 14th, 2172.

"How many bombs did he say there are?"

"Six, Sir. That is if it was a male. The voice was electronic."

"Assuming it was a man, how much time did he say we have?"

"Twenty-four hours. For all six bombs."

"Did he say where the bombs are located, soldier?"

"We only know where the first one is, Sir. It's here in Denver. Whoever made the call said they wouldn't reveal the location of the second bomb until we diffuse the first. He also said that the design of each of the bombs will be different."

"Did this person say anything else?"

"Yes, don't cut any wires until after we are able to stop the timer. Or the bomb will detonate."

"What does that mean? How do you diffuse a bomb without cutting any wires?"

"I don't know, Sir, he didn't say. Colonel, could this be a game?"

"I don't know, son, but if it is, it's a very serious game. We'll be sending out a team of demolition experts, so just man your post until they get there."

"Copy that, Sir. And Colonel, there is one more thing. I don't know why, but he also requested my personal cell phone number."

"Stand by soldier. I'm going to send someone to pick up that phone."

Timothy Perot sits down to have dinner with only a picture of his wife and two children to keep him company. The setting is far from a happy one and is a far cry from the elegance of Timothy's past or, to be more accurate, the past of his lineage. Whereas his wife and children are content living a few miles away, Timothy is alone, harboring feelings of resentment and anger. He can't help the lingering horror that he blames society for bringing upon him, which contributed to his divorce and his station in life. A horror resulting from an arbitrary political choice that had adopted a law pointing the finger at his birthright, all to satisfy a mob in need of a bone tossed their way. This internal venom had plagued Timothy, growing inside him his entire adult life. Even as a thirteen-or fourteen-year-old, it began to consume him. For the last five years, it has guided his every thought and movement until this present moment, when the resentment that fueled him now steadies his very capable hand. It had taken five years to devise his revenge on those who had selected to end what should have remained intact. Five years to trade for and accumulate the materials he would need and to make all the arrangements necessary while designing his complex plan to make *them* pay.

Beginning at the end of the 18th century, Timothy Perot's ancestors began their journey from simple metalworkers, ascending by way of the intricate design of watch pieces. By the beginning of the 19th century, the members of Timothy's family were establishing themselves as fine artists, and by the middle of the century, his family had become one of the artistic dynasties of their time. Their pieces of functional art were treasured by the upper echelon of society, a favorite of kings and queens. They created timepieces that were recognized as capturing mankind's most intricate form of beauty, and were admired all over the world. It would remain this way and, in fact, steadily grow until the Perot pedigree became legendary, and their family members were scions. A family whose reputation was royalty in its own right. This should have been Timothy Perot's legacy. Instead, three hundred years later, Timothy's status was that of a laborer, his intricate mind undervalued and his pedigree not forgotten, but which, along with his family's reputation, was viewed as villainous to aid in a political dilemma that had occurred fifty years earlier. When the politicians at the time, in order to gain the time needed for a crisis to pass, appeased and simultaneously took advantage of what should have been a loud but insignificant band of dissidents, whose violent actions afforded them a voice and leverage within a time of pain and sorrow.

During most periods of ebb and flow in the economy, wages and inflation have a way of balancing out over a few months or maybe a year or so, but as it is with many elements of life, sometimes these cycles can encompass an unusually extended period of time. This was the case between the years 2133 and 2142 when inflation completely overwhelmed wages, and tens of millions of middle-class citizens began suffering as they had never suffered before. The backlash from this downturn took many forms, with one of the most egregious, a result of the ultra-rich continuing to flaunt their wealth in the face of millions in pain.

Up until the year 2132, Perot timepieces remained a premium brand recognized in the same category as a Patek Philippe or a

Vacheron Constantin. The prices of their watches ranged from the least expensive, selling for ten thousand dollars, to the Limited Edition masterpieces collected by society's wealthiest, which could cost millions of dollars, with the Perot Star-Face Titanium, Caliber 57-T, a collector's dream at ten million dollars apiece. These rare items were sought after just as a Monet or Van Gogh might be coveted, but as beautiful as these timepieces were, the heart of this desire was grounded in something far more mundane. Billionaires impressing other billionaires. From the point of view of functionality, these exorbitantly expensive items that told time were unnecessary. A person's cell phone could exhibit the exact time. And a five-hundred-dollar watch could take your temperature, perform an EEG, start your car, feed 3D video to your AI glasses and do hundreds of other tasks.

However, under normal circumstances, in spite of function alone, capitalism allowed for individual desires to flourish without much criticism. Of course, at any point, it could be argued that money spent on a million-dollar watch would be better off being used to feed the hungry. But it took an economic downturn, where the normally comfortable began suffering, to create the vulnerability necessary to place a target on these excesses and those who purchased them. The group that would rise up to take advantage of this disconnection between the fortunate and the unfortunate was called *The Decadencia*. And since gaining access to and doing damage to a hundred-million-dollar home is difficult and excessive physical violence against an individual is problematic, *The Decadencia* chose something that offered easier accessibility with less direct physical contact – expensive timepieces.

The Decadencia began by confronting the ultra-rich and their wrists on the street. Then, in their offices, they enlisted temp workers to carry out their attacks. They also showed up at fundraising galas, disguising their members as waiters and busboys, where they would remove and destroy million-dollar watches in front of the other guests, as well as in front of the watch owners' partners and children. With the numbers in their membership rapidly growing, *The Decadencia* gained the strength to overwhelm the trained forces that these rich men and women hired to protect themselves from these assaults. In desperation, the political arena stepped in to appease *The Decadencia* and to aid the men and women on whose donations they depended to support their own ambitions. It was certainly arbitrary to pick on expensive watch pieces and maybe even ridiculous when viewed from another point in time, but it served a purpose. It pacified *The Decadencia*. Giving in to this small demand and ending the wearing of art on the wrists of the wealthy was a small price for them to pay to regain their safety. After all, billionaires could find other ways to impress each other. So, the Luxury Watch Act of 2136 was quickly adopted, and any watch with a price tag of over five thousand dollars was outlawed.

Originally, it was thought to be just a beginning with other excesses to be considered for elimination, but seven years later, in 2143, when the economy turned around, the pursuit and flaunting of a luxurious lifestyle slowly became acceptable again, and *The Decadencia* was dismantled. Unfortunately, the damage to the once famous, and then infamous, families who were manufacturing luxury timepieces was complete. Because of the expense of changing legislation and the fact that no one was willing to risk championing their cause, the Luxury Watch Act was never repealed. With their manufacturing shuttered and no hope for the reinstatement of their businesses, eventually, the four-hundred-year-old art of watchmaking was abandoned. The old stock of expensive wristwear whose numbers were unknown remained hidden, and the families that created them would garner no further attention until almost forty years later when the forgotten sociological give-and-take that had ended the industry produced unintended consequences. Instilling a strong purpose in one individual to strike back with the planting of six bombs. One individual who would respond to the arbitrary actions of the past. A past that decades later created Timothy Perot and his personal quest for revenge.

Forty-five minutes after the threatening call was made to the military police in Denver, a team of local experts in bomb disposal, briefed by Washington, arrives at the Cherry Creek Apple Store in Denver, Colorado. The store has already been cleared, quietly, by the local police under the pretense of their having received advanced knowledge of an impending robbery. This mega store, with a footprint of over one hundred thousand square feet, houses more than one hundred clocks on the walls and thousands of watches in its display cases. With no specifics to guide them, the team begins hunting for the bomb. A moment after their search is initiated, the cell phone belonging to the soldier who had originally called in the threat, which is now in the possession of the team's lead investigator, beeps, indicating an incoming text. It reads:

"In twelve minutes at 6:00 p.m. Denver time, the timer will start ticking. Remember, do not cut any wires, or I will detonate the bomb, and the three two-pound blocks of C-4 it controls will take out the store. Now that I have your attention, I will provide you with a tip to save you time. The bomb is attached to one of the wall clocks. A wall clock whose face will show a more intricate design than the others. And this timepiece is able to do something that no other can. This timepiece can tell you when to pray. And major, one more thing. To stop me, you will need outside help. I recommend Professor Joseph Graves from the University of Missouri, St. Louis. Enlisting his aid is the only way that you will have any chance of disarming these devices. Remember, Professor Joseph Graves. In fact, I insist."

Major John Edwards informs his men of the information he has just received, and their search, narrowed down to a specific wall clock, is underway. Then, thinking out loud and speaking to no one in particular, he asks, "How did they know they were texting a major?" However, with the need to prioritize, Major Edwards begins giving orders to the two captains assigned to assist him. While finding the bomb is clearly the most pressing issue, following close behind will be trying to trace the bomber's text to ascertain its point of origin, as well as locating Professor Joseph Graves to enlist his assistance. Then, they will need to check the professor's background for any clues as to why the bomber demanded his involvement. Once the bomb is located, the major's men will have to scour the area for DNA and fingerprints. Also, they will have to try to determine how the bomber was able to plant the device. How did they access the store? How could the bomb be set up without anyone noticing? The major must consider that although it appears as if contact has been made by one person, it is possible that a group of people may be involved, including a terrorist cell, so the activity of any active cell they are aware of must be investigated. Finally, with the clock ticking, the major knows that even though they have been granted twenty-four hours to locate and diffuse six bombs, they still need to stop each bomb as soon as possible. They may have four hours before each detonation, which will be difficult enough, but saving time, even minutes, on any one device may buy them time as the threat continues.

While his men search for the wall clock with a different face, Professor Joseph Graves is reached at his home in St. Louis and brought to a local police precinct where a connection to the major by way of video conferencing is set up. When apprised of the situation, the professor does not offer any initial answers for why the bomber had asked for him, other than the fact that he is known for having extensive knowledge in the history of the art of watchmaking or Horology because of personal interest and appreciation. When pressed further, however, he admits that his fascination stems from his family's past, specifically his grandfather, Byron Henry Graves. The professor reveals that his grandfather had been the head of an organization that existed from the year 2134 until the year 2143 called *The Decadencia.* The major, having no prior knowledge of the group, has one of his captains search for all the information that can be found on Byron Henry Graves and the group with which he was affiliated. After retrieving the group's history, although considering that there may be a connection to their bomber, the major cannot rule out the possibility that the bomber may just be a dangerous maniac playing a game; a maniac who knows Professor Graves as someone with the knowledge for him to play the game with or against. On the other hand, after the major informs him that the bomber had asked for him personally, the professor shares his belief that it is more likely this could be revenge. That it might be a plot being perpetrated by a descendant of one of the families his grandfather helped to destroy. But which family and which descendant? There are hundreds of men and women, sons and daughters, grandsons and granddaughters of the families of watchmakers who had suffered at the hands of the Watch Act of 2136. It could be any one of them. For Professor Graves, the realization that there may be personal culpability attached to the crisis they face is disturbing. Then, they hear the shout of one of the men in the room. The wall clock they are looking for is found. Discovered in the same room where they are standing. A moment later, a second text from Timothy is delivered to the major, which reads:

"I assume you have located the first bomb, so now is a good time to inform you of my demands. I require two hundred million dollars in cash for the information necessary to diffuse all six bombs. This number will remain the same no matter how many of the bombs you are able to dismantle unless you are fortunate enough to get to them all in time, which isn't something you should count on. I will also need the professor's cell phone number so I can contact him directly if I choose."

After receiving the professor's number, Timothy instructs the major to send a picture of the clock to Professor Graves along with a copy of the first text he had sent, in which he had so graciously provided them with the tip about the timepiece and its ability to let them know when to pray. Then Timothy destroys the burner phone. He had purchased twelve burner phones to be used for no more than two hours each.

When Professor Graves sees the text, then examines the picture of the timepiece and sees the manufacturer of the piece printed on its face, designating it as made by the *Zenith Watch Company*, he recognizes it immediately. A bit stunned, he says:

"I know this timepiece, major. It is unmistakable. It's a replica of the timepiece owned by Mahatma Gandhi."

The professor tells the major to have him taken back to his home immediately. Major Edwards reminds him that they are pressed

THE WATCHMAKER'S FAMILY

for time and that he can get him anything he needs. The professor's response is curt, as his demeanor appears suddenly enthusiastic.

"No, major, not everything I need. But for now, you need to take a picture of the clock from a side view for me, with the sharpest angle you can manage."

The major complies, sends the picture to the professor, and when he sees the photo, the professor continues:

"Alright. While your men take me home, it will be necessary for you to acquire a few pairs of needle nose pliers of different sizes. To be safe, acquire a pair that a jeweler may use up to a pair that may be used to pull on a half-inch screw. We will also need a firm piece of plastic, about eight inches by four inches, that is approximately one-eighth inch thick."

Major Edwards can't help noticing a bit of admiration for their newly discovered nemesis seeping into the professor's tone. When confronted with this observation, the professor shares the point of view that if you cannot appreciate the knowledge and ability of whoever is involved in this seemingly insane act, you will have a much more difficult time stopping them. Then he adds some optimism:

"I have an idea, major, but I have to get to my library to be sure. The book I need to refer to has been out of print for at least seventy-five years. In the meantime, you need to find out the daily prayer times practiced by Hindus and if they differ from those practiced in the part of India where Gandhi lived most of his life. We will also need to know the time difference between that region in India and Denver, Colorado. I think I know how to stop this bomb."

Fifteen minutes later, with the aid of a military escort, Professor Graves arrives home. He locates the book he is looking for, where he finds a picture of the watch owned by Mahatma Gandhi and verifies the quote attributed to him, which the professor believes is the key to the bomb's construction.

"I hate it if I am late for prayers, even for a minute."

The professor is brought back to the police precinct, where he continues his video conference with the major to oversee the diffusing of the first bomb. He instructs the major and his men to carefully cut the wall surrounding the clock to allow the clock to be pulled away from the wall and placed on a flat surface. Since the C-4 is there, the major is cautious. They have to cut out as much of the wall as necessary so they don't disturb the explosive material or the attached wiring. When the entirety of the bomb is in view, the major's men lift the clock, the wiring and the C-4 from the wall and place it on a table with the clock laid on its back, face up. They can now see four red L.E.D. lights attached to four of the seven wires that are connected from the clock to the C-4. One of the wires has an additional L.E.D. connected to it. It is also lit and green in color. The major clears the store of everyone except himself and his two captains. The professor has them remove the bevel and the glass piece covering the face of the clock. His further instructions are followed with great caution. The heart rates of the three men left in the store begin rising as the professor guides their movements:

"We need to remove the *seconds* hand first. It is located in the sub-dial at six o'clock."

When Professor Graves is sure that the men understand he is referring to the separate circular dial located at the bottom of the clock's face, he tells them confidently that this part should be easy.

However, the professor's assurance does nothing to remove the tension or the sweat from the men's faces. The professor continues with his instructions.

"Place the eighth-inch plastic piece against the stem in between the face of the clock and the clock's hand, then placing pressure upward, grab the *seconds* hand with the needle nose pliers that best fits, and lift the hand free. Don't worry about bending the hand. Just remove it."

When the *seconds* hand is freed, one of the red L.E.D. lights turns off. Experiencing an initial feeling of hope, the professor continues:

"Next, we are going to remove the *minute* hand to free up access to the *hour* hand underneath. Be careful not to bend the *minute* hand. We are going to replace it once we remove the *hour* hand, so steady yourself."

Carefully, with one of his captains mopping his brow, the major, with nervous hands, places the plastic piece in between the *minute* hand and the *hour* hand. He is able to lift the *minute* hand from its stem, but no L.E.D. reacts. The professor tells them not to worry about that and continue by removing the *hour* hand. Slightly more confident in his handling of the procedure, Major Edwards removes the *hour* hand, and a second red L.E.D. light turns off. Next, they proceed with the most delicate part of the operation, placing the minute hand back on its stem and pushing it into place. A third red L.E.D. light turns off. Two lights remain lit, mounted on the same wire. One red, one green. The last action requires the information about the daily prayers and the time differential the professor had asked for, which informs the professor's final instructions:

"This clock's design replicates a pocket watch, so there is a winding crown at the top. Wind the crown from right to left to power the alarm's striking mechanism. Then, use the button on the top and to the right of the crown and turn it to adjust the alarm time. It will adjust the sub-dial at twelve o'clock. Using the information you have supplied, the daily prayer time closest to the bomb's detonation is called Dhurh. It begins at 12:38 local time in the Sabarmati Ashram in India, which equates to eight minutes after midnight in Denver. Adjust the alarm time slowly, especially when you get close to ten minutes after twelve."

The major carefully twists the button, adjusting the alarm's timer. Just before the hand reaches the 12:10 mark, the last red L.E.D. light turns off. The green L.E.D., however, remains lit, causing the men's heart rates to spike again. However, three seconds later, the green L.E.D. turns off as well. The bomb is diffused. There is a momentary relief felt by the major and his two captains, and when word of the bomb being neutralized reaches the men who had been evacuated from the store, there is a loud celebratory cheer on the street until they all realize that there are five more bombs out there and this is just the beginning. The time is 8:30 p.m. The first bomb has been neutralized in just two and a half hours. They await further instructions.

At home, in his basement, Timothy Perot has been watching everything unfold at the scene on a monitor. With the bomb diffused, as per Timothy's instructions, the major begins cutting the wires away from the C-4. When he cuts one of the three wires that is not equipped with an L.E.D., Timothy's monitor goes dark. All the excitement of the last few hours brings a smile to his face, and he sends a text directly to Professor Graves. He congratulates him on their success neutralizing the first bomb so quickly but adds:

"You are going to need that hour and a half to offset some of your travel time. The next two bombs are in New York City, so I suggest you get moving. And let's not break up the team. I've become fond of the major, so let's inform Washington that I prefer to work with people I trust. You know, too many cooks spoil the broth and all that."

Then Timothy destroys this second burner phone as he did the first.

Back in Denver, the major has secured the two-pound blocks of C-4 and is having it dispatched to the Hawthorne Army Base in Hawthorne, Nevada, to be placed in storage when he receives a copy of Timothy's text revealing the location of the next two bombs. The major calls his superiors in Washington to arrange swift transportation for himself and Professor Graves. Both need to get to New York City as soon as possible.

While the St. Louis police escort the professor back home to retrieve anything else he can think of that may help them diffuse the next five bombs, Major Edwards leaves the Apple store in Denver on his way to Buckley Air Force Base, which, fortunately, is only eighteen miles away. In the car, while reviewing the last few hours, the major realizes he may have missed something. They never checked inside the back part of the clock. Quickly, he contacts his men, who are still at the store. They follow his instructions to open the back of the clock and attached to one of the remnants of one of the wires the major had cut, they find a digital calendar display that tells them the bomb could have been set months in advance. Next to that, attached to another wire, is an audio/video transmitter. Then, on closer inspection of the clock's face, specifically searching for the eye of a camera, they locate one, cleverly hidden at nine o'clock. That is how the bomber knew he was a *major* when they first made contact. He had been watching everything unfold live. And that is why their instructions included a warning not to cut any wires.

Of course, knowing this would not have changed anything because of Timothy's threat to detonate the bomb if they did cut the wires, but this knowledge may help them in the future. At least, the video feed was something else they could attempt to trace. So far, everything else they had tried, such as tracing the burner phones or how the store may have been accessed to plant the bomb, had turned out to be dead ends. And there was no recoverable DNA or fingerprints found other than the store's employees. The major had also received word by this time that there was no chatter about, or any link to, a terrorist cell's involvement. He was now entertaining the possibility that they could be dealing with just one person and that the event was, more likely, as the professor had thought, revenge against those responsible for the creation of the Watch Act of 2136.

The professor, back home, has gathered a number of books on Horology, a notebook owned by his grandfather, and an antique watch repair kit and is on his way to Scott Air Force Base outside St. Louis. The base is approximately twenty minutes from the professor's home which will get him there around the same time as the major's projected arrival at the Buckley Air Force Base in Colorado. With the major flying by way of a Quesst LRX7, he will easily make up the difference in mileage between St. Louis and Denver, so he will reach their destination at Teterboro Airport in New Jersey even before the professor, traveling more than twice the speed of the Gulfstream GX9 the professor will take.

During the flights, the two men communicate directly, with the major updating the professor about the discovery of the camera located inside the timepiece in Denver. The major concedes that he now believes the professor is probably correct in his assessment that these acts are about revenge, and their investigation will proceed accordingly. After the major receives an additional text from Timothy, providing the specific location of the second bomb, he details their immediate plans. He tells Professor Graves that they will meet at Teterboro Airport, take a helicopter to the 34th Street helipad in Manhattan, nine miles away, and then be driven by motorcade to 230 Park Avenue on the corner of 45th Street and Park Avenue.

Their estimated time of arrival is 10:30 p.m., one-half hour after the timer starts ticking. In advance of their arrival on the scene, however, a demolition team will precede them and attempt to find the bomb. In the meantime, the major sends a list of the occupants of 230 Park Avenue to Professor Graves, hoping to narrow the search. As soon as the professor begins perusing the list of law firms and corporate offices of all sorts, both foreign and domestic, located in the building, one name immediately stands out – The Arlington Post, one of the largest web news providers in the country.

The professor grabs his grandfather's notebook, which contains contact information, and what appears to be scheduling plans and other notations on *The Decadencia*. On page three, he finds the first mention of Frederick Arlington, with further notations revealing him to be a close friend of his grandfather's and a main proponent of *The Decadencia's* cause. The Arlington Post appears to have been a fledgling business at the point of these initial notes, which begin in the year 2133, but when Professor Graves cross-references this with further information available about the Post, he can see that by the year 2143, the size and financials of the Arlington Post had increased exponentially. Its growth is obviously tied to *The Decadencia's* years of power and influence. He informs the major of his findings so his men can concentrate their efforts on the offices of the Arlington Post. This leaves three separate floors to search. Also, the building needed to be evacuated and the entire block secured. The time was approaching 10:00 p.m., so it was mostly the janitorial staff and the few midnight oil-burners who were working except for the Arlington Post, which ran shifts twenty-four hours a day. Outside, pedestrian traffic was light, but Park Avenue supported a constant stream of cars traveling at night, so the cordoning off of the area and the rerouting of traffic needed the attention of the NYPD. With the building being cleared and the outside situation handled, under the guise of a water main break, the search for the bomb began.

At 10:30 p.m., the major and the professor, face to face for the first time, are in the car a few minutes from their destination when the major gets word from a lieutenant who has been researching the family descendants of watch companies put out of business by the actions of *The Decadencia*. Unfortunately, when checking the top twenty manufacturers affected, the results yielded over one hundred family members over the age of twenty-one. Trying to find their suspect in this way would be impossible, at least until they had more information about the bomber and some way to tie him or her, personally, to the bomb sites.

The search for the bomb was proceeding floor to floor, starting at the lower floor of the Arlington Post's offices. With nothing found as of yet, they were now scouring the executive offices with their sensitive instrumentation on the 33rd floor, where the major and the professor joined them. Finally, in one of the senior vice president's offices, their instruments indicate a presence. Not in the walls but emanating from under a large ornate wood desk. When the desk is removed, it is obvious that the wood panels on the floor underneath the desk have been replaced, their newer condition hidden by the desk situated on top. They have found the second bomb.

Removing the wood flooring reveals another six pounds of C-4, the same as the first bomb, along with a digital calendar, a timepiece and an audio/video transmitter flanking either side of a beautifully painted clock face. The professor needs no book to identify what he is seeing this time. It is a replica of a Rolex Oyster and one of the most important and recognizable timepieces ever made. Originally a watch face in Cloisonné enamel, created by the great artist Marguerite Koch, it depicts a whale and a frigate battling the high seas. Its numerals are mostly star-shaped but placed at six o'clock is a Rolex cornet, which is an unusual inclusion. This intricately painted surface is a recreation of one of the most coveted watches in the history of watchmaking. This version, however, has no hands on its face to cover the image. The timer for the bomb is being kept by a digital timer placed beside it. Even in its enlarged state and obviously being the work of an amateur painter, the men in the room are taken back by its beauty before a feeling of alarm returns when reawakened to its true purpose.

Timothy Perot watches the scene on his monitor at home, eating a sandwich and sipping a soft drink as if he were watching a documentary being made just for him. He unwraps a new burner phone and sends another text directly to Professor Graves:

"The face of this clock is quite beautiful, don't you think? And even though I did my best and spent weeks creating it, it would appear primitive if we could compare it to the original, which, of course, is impossible because your grandfather had it destroyed. My version of this masterpiece has only twenty-two different pieces, as well as the twelve numerals, but every piece is important, so you will have to remove them all to uncover the ability to diffuse the bomb. I am hopeful that this will teach you to appreciate the permanent damage that can be done when something that is truly valuable is so easily eliminated by a few individuals serving their own insignificant agendas, causing the end of my family's fortune and artistic contribution. The end of time as I knew it. Throughout history, art has been stolen, and it has been degraded by weather and time. Art has even been lost at sea on sinking ships, but rarely has art been purposefully destroyed. Be thankful this replication is not as delicate as the work of Marguerite Koch. If it were, your hands would never be steady enough, nor your mind capable of the concentration necessary for the task at hand. It is now 11:00 p.m. You should get started. Your time is short."

Timothy throws what is left of his sandwich in the trash, places the burner phone on the ground, crushes it with his foot, and then grinds it with his heel, displaying his anger over the lost Rolex masterpiece.

Before proceeding, Professor Graves must decide what instruments to use. The watch repair tools he brought with him were too small, but the demolition team that had been sent ahead by the major brought a large toolbox with them. While studying the clock's face, he explains to the major how Cloisonné enamel is applied. Marguerite Koch would have used ribbon or gold thread to outline the spaces where each color would then be filled and fired in a kiln individually. In the case of this replication, the bomber has used some sort of metal wiring to separate each block of color. Fearful that the metal may be conductive and actually part of the bomb, the professor requests a small ball peen hammer and a set of rubber-tipped, flat-head screwdrivers to be safe. The twelve numerals of the clock, including the Rolex crown, sit above the surface of the face of the clock so they are easy to access without touching the wiring, but when those are removed, and the professor begins loosening the individual painted pieces surrounded by metal, the caution necessary to lift each one free becomes tedious and time-consuming. Removing twenty-two of these pieces will take time. And then, they will have to figure out how to diffuse the bomb.

At first, each piece takes so long that the projection of the time it will take puts them past their deadline at 2:00 a.m. As with the first bomb, the major clears the room while remaining alone with the professor. As each piece is lifted free by the professor and the major carefully grabs and removes them from the clock, the rhythm and speed of their work increase. At 1:40 a.m., there are only two pieces left. They are part of the frigate design and very small, however, so it takes seventeen minutes to remove them. At 1:57 a.m., with the building and the street outside cleared of traffic and pedestrians, the professor and the major view the inner workings of the timing mechanism. There are twelve toggle switches labeled one through twelve. Twelve wires from those twelve positions all connect to four red L.E.D. lights at positions three, six, nine, and twelve, and four wires from those red L.E.D.s connect to a single green L.E.D. positioned dead center where the hands of the clock would usually be mounted. The professor believes that the four L.E.D.s indicate a four-digit code. Now, they just have to figure out the code. With one minute remaining, he asks the major to reread the bomber's text.

The odd phrase that strikes him as the key is "the end of time as I knew it." Both men react. The Watch Act of 2136, 2-1-3-6. Professor Graves pushes the toggle at two o'clock. A red L.E.D. turns off. He pushes the toggle at one o'clock. Another red light turns off. The same happens when he pushes the toggle at three o'clock. One to go. The timer shows thirty seconds left. The professor touches the toggle at six o'clock – but he hesitates. The major counts down the timer out loud, now at twenty-five seconds. The professor asks why the Rolex Oyster. Why this timepiece? The Watch Act is too obvious. When was this watch destroyed? He consults his grandfather's notebook as the major announces the count – fifteen seconds. Then, the professor finds what he is looking for. The Rolex Oyster was destroyed in front of a room full of people during a fundraiser on November 4th, 2135. The major insists, five seconds. With two seconds remaining, the professor pushes the toggle at five o'clock. The final red L.E.D. turns off, and then, so does the green. They have succeeded with one second to spare.

A text from Timothy, using another new burner phone, comes through less than a minute later.

"That was very exciting. Good job, but I still want my two hundred million dollars! So think about it on your way to the location of the next bomb at 1 East 97th Street and the home of Senator John Keeley. And I hope you don't mind but I took the liberty of clearing up the deceptions you used to keep the media in the dark. I don't think they believe your cover story in Denver anymore about the incident being a robbery or your contention that the activity on Park Avenue was a water main break. Also, they know about the senator's home, so I hope you don't mind an audience. Further instructions will follow if you find the bomb in time."

The professor answers the first question on the major's mind. Senator John Keeley's father, the Honorable Edward Keeley, who himself served in the United States Senate for over twenty years, gained his popularity and influence by championing the Watch Act of 2136.

Given that the planting of this bomb is at the residence of a United States senator, the major knows he will need all the help he can get. He contacts his superiors in Washington, and the coordination of agencies begins. The residential buildings close to 1 East 97th Street at the corner of Fifth Avenue will have to be evacuated. Traffic will have to be diverted, and because the press has been notified, they must anticipate their attempts to surround the premises. And even though it is the middle of the night, word will spread quickly in the city that never sleeps, and the number of onlookers will grow. Also, all this will divert time and resources that the major might have used to help figure out the identity of the bomber, although they now know they are looking for one person because of the phrase, "…the end of time as I knew it," from Timothy's last text.

By the time the major and the professor make their way from Park Avenue and 45th Street to 97th Street and Fifth Avenue, Senator Keeley and his wife, in Washington D.C., had been alerted and are on their way toward boarding a helicopter back to New York. At the same time, the wealthy residents of Fifth Avenue living next to the senator are being rousted from their comfortable beds and put out on the street while Major Edwards, his team, and the professor fight through the gathering crowd and the media's inquiries to gain entrance to the senator's home. The report of a serial bomber, shared with the media by Timothy Perot a half hour before, has attracted hundreds of New Yorkers to the scene already. While they watch from across the street at the edge of Central Park, Timothy watches from his home as live remote broadcasts appear on virtually all media outlets nationwide.

Major Edwards and his team enter the building on the Northeast corner of the block. A six-story residence that was once made up of seventy separate apartments, it had been bought in 2145 and completely reconditioned. It now accommodated twelve apartments on the first three floors, with the upper three floors serving as Senator Keeley's New York City home; his residence alone worth over one hundred and fifty million dollars. The major's team concentrated their search on the three floors belonging to the senator. The building itself was too large to completely cover in the three hours they had left before the 6:00 a.m. deadline and the bomb's projected detonation. Two hours later, they still had not located the device. There was one possibility that remained.

Senator John Keeley arrived in New York City an hour before, and he and his wife were sitting in their limousine blocks away from their home. The major is able to contact the senator through channels and give him an update. The only place left for them to look is in the senator's safe, on the wall behind the original Matisse painting hanging in his bedroom. When the major, with one hour remaining before detonation, requests the safe's combination, a terrified Senator Keeley insists on opening the safe himself. The senator is driven to his home and emerges from his limo, leaving his wife behind. Fighting through the media aided by security,

Senator Keeley enters the building. When he reaches his bedroom, the major and the professor turn away from the safe, as the senator's shaking hand is barely able to grip the dial and enter the combination. But it isn't the possibility of finding a bomb that is making the senator's hand shake. It is the possibility of finding only the bomb; which is all that they find. The bomb and one small manilla envelope. Everything else that had been kept in the safe is gone. And whatever is missing must be damning indeed because Senator John Keeley sinks to his knees. The major has the senator escorted from the room and out of the building, where he rejoins his wife in the limousine. They drive off.

With thirty minutes to detonation, Major Edwards removes the bomb from the safe. He sees that this device is more simplistic, compared to the others, and smaller, with only one two-pound block of C-4 attached and no timing mechanism. He places everything on the bed and then takes the manilla envelope and empties its contents, revealing a watch that does not appear to be working and a letter that is unsigned.

"To whom it may concern. This timepiece is an F.P. Journe. It was capable of keeping time through the use of a very complex system called a resonance chronometer. Based on the physics of two pendulums working in tandem, it took fifteen years to perfect. It remains an example of humankind's attempt to evolve even when a satisfactory system is already in place because curiosity and commitment to exploration can lead to advancements that we haven't yet considered. This particular commitment to discovery died with the Watch Act of 2136. This amazing timepiece, which needs repairing, will never work again because there is no one left who can repair it. The physics of this watch is too complex for any of us, including myself, to fully understand, so I will explain it this way. Whereas many inexpensive watches made today can measure your heartbeat, this watch cannot. This watch, however, has a heartbeat all its own. Two sets of connected wheels and springs that move independently but also work as one. When one-wheel speeds up, the other compensates to stay on course. Like two hearts that need each other to move through time. Two hearts beating as one that are now broken.

'Antithetical to the complex nature of the watch, the bomb you find here is a simple one. I am sure you will be able to diffuse it easily. I am not watching you, so you don't have to worry about my detonating the bomb if you cut the wiring. I have already taken everything I need from this location."

The major and the professor do not yet know what to make of this note. For the moment, they must proceed with the diffusing of the bomb. A few minutes later, with five minutes to spare, they succeed. At 6:00 a.m., Timothy Perot unwraps another burner phone and sends his last text to Major Edwards and Professor Graves.

"The last three bombs have been placed in three different locations in the same residence: the Long Island mansion and family compound of the billionaire Laurence Milford on Meadow Lane in Southampton. It is one of the most beautiful homes this man has ever seen. Unfortunately, it may not be beautiful for much longer. Since I must now assume that I will not be receiving the money I have asked for, I will not be able to vouch for the reliability of the last three timers and their control of the eighteen pounds of C-4 placed in three different locations throughout the home."

The major reacts quickly. The ominous threat of this last text has alerted him to the likelihood that the four-hour timeframe afforded them to diffuse each bomb no longer applies. Again, he contacts his superiors, notifying them of the need to evacuate the Milford compound immediately while he and the professor make their way back to the 34th Street Heliport. During the ride, Professor Graves reviews the events of the last twelve hours, attempting to unravel the bomber's true goal. He begins questioning whether money is this man's motive.

The first bomb at the Apple Store doesn't appear to have any connection to *The Decadencia*. However, there is a connection to Mahatma Gandhi. A man who had virtually no possessions, no desire to own anything. Yet, he loved his timepiece. And in a world where possessions dictate status and respect and are of premium importance, it was this timepiece, his only possession, and others of its kind that were outlawed in a seemingly arbitrary act. The second bomb involved a work of art, disposed of forever, to serve *The Decadencia*, as well as turning the Arlington Post into a thriving enterprise, and establishing its reputation. Next, the politician who jump-started his career by supporting the Watch Act, whose son was targeted. And finally, the billionaire who funded it all. The major asks the professor how he knows about Laurence Milford's involvement, and the professor answers:

"Because Laurence Milford's name is all over my grandfather's notebook. And none of this happens without the influence of financial support: The money to build a business like the Arlington Post, the money to fund a cause like *The Decadencia*, and the money to support the decades of political campaigns run by Senator Edward Keeley and his son John. Everything leads back to the Milford fortune. Whoever the bomber is, this is personal. Even the two hundred million dollars requested by the bomber was not enough of a focal point in his communications. I don't believe he ever expected his demands to be met."

From this perspective, as they board the helicopter that will take them to Long Island, the professor and the major reread the letter found at Senator John Keeley's home, stopping with the phrase, "Two hearts beating as one that is now broken." The professor asks the major to check the list of possible suspects compiled from the descendants of the families destroyed by *The Decadencia*'s campaign and look for males who have been divorced. The professor continues:

"I believe we will find that one of those men is familiar with the Milford compound. The bomber said it was the most beautiful home he had ever seen. He spent time there. He worked there."

The major begins checking the list of suspects for men who had been divorced while tracking down the employee history for the Milford Estate as their helicopter takes off, and they begin the thirty-minute flight to Southampton and the coast off of Long Island, New York. It is 6:45 a.m.

Timothy Perot is making his final plans. First, he tips off the media about the three bombs planted at the Milford Estate. Then, since he knows he doesn't have much time before his identity is discovered, he reveals it himself. That he, Timothy Perot, is the person responsible for all six of the bombs that have dominated the news and the efforts of the authorities in Denver and in New York. Furthermore, he promises that he is preparing to release the story behind the bombs and why they were planted, and he will also release documentation supporting his claims. Those claims will begin with a forgotten group called *The Decadencia* and the law they assisted in creating, the Watch Act of 2136.

More importantly, Timothy promises that the supporting documents he will provide, found inside the safe at Senator John Keeley's home, will uncover the actual reasons behind the adoption of the law. Documents that will show that the true nature of the events was to aid in the ascendance of the Arlington Post and the gaining of riches for their publisher, Frederick Arlington, that the purpose of these actions was to also promote the careers of a powerful political family, the Keeleys. And that these previously hidden papers will uncover the purely personal reasons behind a billionaire's manipulation of our country to assist in his acquiring more wealth, but incredibly, in his acquiring the ability to use that wealth and the accompanying influence to exact revenge on two good people who inadvertently and without malice deprived him of something that he believed should belong to him. As a result, hundreds of others were destroyed for no good reason, and their families were forced to suffer.

As the major and the professor review a report that lists Timothy Perot as an employee who worked as a carpenter at the Milford estate for four months the year before, they receive word of Timothy's pronouncements to the media. Simultaneously, the local police were dispatched to arrest Timothy at his residence in Queens, New York. However, before they can, Timothy posts his story of The Watchmaker's Family along with its supporting documentation on the web, with copies sent to most of the country's prominent news outlets, including the Arlington Post. The story begins:

"Once, there were two college friends who loved the same girl. The girl, by all accounts, loved the better person of the two, the better man, but the other became the more powerful. In the end, my grandmother, Lillian and grandfather, Henry, never had a chance, and our family and many others paid the price. Because there is no perspective when it comes to a megalomaniac and the revenge of the heart."

Timothy Perot calls his father, who is already awake and watching the news. Timothy tells his father that he has done what he has done for the Perot family and the others like them. He also claims that he believes his actions will result in a tremendous opportunity for his wife and children. He hopes his father will help them exploit this opportunity. He explains that a large collection of high-end timepieces, some of which he previously owned and many of which he had recently acquired, were being held in three safe deposit boxes registered in his wife's name. He had hidden the keys for the boxes, having taped them on the underside of his wife's dresser with a letter of apology for the grief he had caused them due to his obsession with *The Decadencia* and the damage they had done. Timothy asks his father to wait a month or so before he begins selling the watches. He adds that he believes that his actions and subsequent notoriety will make the collection worth tens of millions of dollars. As history teaches us, fame or infamy will always spark demand and make something far more precious and much more valuable.

Inside the Milford estate, the evacuation is almost complete when those in the compound get word of who is behind the attack. Hearing the name Perot stuns the ninety-three-year-old Laurence Milford, sitting in his wheelchair. He suddenly turns to reenter the mansion. When his son tries to stop him, the patriarch of the Milford family assures his son that he will only be a few minutes, and it is his job, as his son, to make sure everyone remains at a safe distance, free from harm. The elderly man then makes his way to his library, and hidden behind a book on a lower shelf is a button that he pushes to reveal a private room. This room, unknown to anyone else in the family, should have contained one of the most exclusive collections of timepieces owned by any man. A collection belonging to this self-serving hypocrite, which had included the only remaining Perot Starface 57T, valued in the year 2133 at ten million dollars and assumed lost or destroyed by *The Decadencia*.

As Laurence Milford gazes around the room, he can see that his entire collection is gone. The only item visible is a picture standing on a table at the room's center. The elderly man wheels himself to the table to view the picture. It is a photo taken at Dartmouth College from the year 2099. In the photo are three young people. One of them is twenty-year-old Laurence Milford. There is a note taped to the table that reads:

"For my grandmother Lillian and my grandfather Henry."

Flying in from a quarter mile away, the helicopter with its passengers, Major Edwards and Professor Graves, is approaching the Milford compound when all three bombs explode violently, without warning, one after the other. Laurence Milford feels the full impact of the third bomb, which had been placed in the secret room where he is still sitting in his wheelchair, clutching the picture of himself with Timothy's grandparents, Lillian and Henry, his oldest friends.

Timothy Perot, watching the explosions at the Milford Estate being broadcast live, sees his pursuit, five years in the planning, finally brought to fruition. And the raging fire of the lifelong obsession that had paralyzed him was extinguished. As the police break down his door and place him in handcuffs, a look of contentment appears on his face for the first time since he was a very young boy when Timothy was too young to understand the terrible consequences that can evolve when one friend becomes envious of another.

LIVING ON MARS

Story # 9

LIVING ON MARS

The ever-expanding universe may end somewhere, but our exploration of space never will. As long as the human race lives, we will continue to take baby steps in order to gain knowledge of and insight into ourselves and the wondrous, unfathomable experiment that surrounds us.

AGENT NUMBER 9

(2182 - 2202)

Living On Mars

(2182 – 2202)

Olivia Ellen Manning dreamed she saw a McDonald's on the moon last night. The light from its Golden Arches extended through space and reached the surface of the Earth. She could feel its comforting glow warm her body. However, the strangeness of this picture in her mind wasn't that the restaurant's neon sign could illuminate the sky brightly enough to travel 256,000 miles and be visible on Earth. It was that Olivia was having this dream while asleep in her bed on Mars.

In the year 2078, during the final years of the existence of the privately run space exploration company known as SpaceX, its founder, Elon Musk, finally accomplished his dream of placing human beings on the planet Mars. Although he had not fulfilled his original hope of creating the first city on the far-off landscape, Mr. Musk's significant achievement was lauded as revolutionary. He completed the mission with the aid of many great scientists and advances in robotics, succeeding not only in putting two men and one woman on the Mars surface but also in bringing them back home. Elon Musk and his team were celebrated for their ability to facilitate solutions pertaining to a myriad of complex problems and capturing the fascination of the hundreds of millions of people worldwide who followed his ship's journey in awe.

Unfortunately, after Mr. Musk's death in 2082 at the age of 110, SpaceX was dismantled. Without Mr. Musk's commitment to exploration, the board of directors who were put in charge of the company could not justify the continued outlay of capital. There was no clear avenue towards profit that they could see and the idea of merely advancing the minds of men was not enough of an incentive for their stockholders. It would take an additional eighty years for others to resume Mr. Musk's dream, the goal being the establishment of a base that would support a colony of forty human beings living 140 million miles away. During the eighty-year interval void of space travel, the governments of the planet focused on the issues at home, from the cessation of burning all fossil fuels and the development of a safe way of disposing of lithium batteries to the compensation of Brazil and its neighbors in order to allow the rainforest to replenish itself in an accord starting in 2154. A process that would spread to other countries where rainforests existed, slowing extinctions and even allowing for the appearance of new species. Once we believed we had mitigated and, in some ways, reversed conditions that were damaging our planet, the thirst for space travel was reignited. In the year 2165, extensive plans were initiated to rekindle our journey to the surface of Mars.

The actual distance between the Earth and Mars varies greatly, as the two planets revolve around our sun at different speeds and distances. Earth completes its orbit once every 365 ¼ days, of course, whereas Mars, being farther from the sun, traverses a greater distance and moves a bit slower, taking 687 of our days to complete one revolution. This means that every twenty-six months or so, the Earth and Mars line up in space shrinking the distance between them down to 35.8 million miles, making it the most efficient time to travel from one planet to the other. When reaching this alignment, the trip can be completed in seven to eight months.

In the year 2178, Spaceforce Incorporated and its CEO, Ryan Allen Kingsley, would embark on a twelve-year exploratory commitment with the US government agreeing to foot seventy-five percent of the bill. There were four separate expeditions necessary, traveling at an average speed of 25,000 miles per hour to achieve their goals. The first ship, which carried three astronauts and fifty robots, was sent to construct a small space station above the atmosphere of Mars. This station would serve as a docking port for future flights and additionally be utilized as a storage facility holding medical and building supplies and equipment as a backup to those that would eventually be stored on Mars itself.

The second mission would carry three astronauts brought to relieve the original three, who were sent to supervise the creation of the space station. This ship would also carry much of the materials necessary to build three separate structures on the surface: The terraforming of a main complex with living quarters, a secondary building for scientific research, including medical and surgical needs, and a third to fabricate a massive Terrarium, where food could be grown so the colonists would eventually achieve self-sufficiency. All the construction, although overseen by humans, would be carried out by the fifty robots, programmed to perfectly execute the plethora of requisite tasks.

Following the successful landing of the second mission to Mars in the year 2188, the selection of the colonists began back on Earth. It would take two years to complete the process, and the chosen forty would then train for eighteen months before their flight to Mars would leave Earth. The only limitation stipulated in the decision of whom they selected was that no young children and no single unattached person would be included. It was thought that the isolation of being away from Earth would be lonely enough, and a partner was considered essential. Even though there are no absolutes when it pertains to people remaining together, every selected couple and family underwent extensive analysis to determine the strength of their relationships in the hope of choosing those who were the most committed to one another.

People from different walks of life were chosen. Aside from a general practitioner physician, a surgeon, and two robotics technicians, the inclusion of other specific professions would be of lesser importance. The government did insist on sending a psychiatrist and a robot specially designed to be an assistant to the psychiatrist, given the emotional pressures of the expedition and the possibility of dealing with the unknown.

The first chosen were Dr. Olivia Manning and her husband, George, a college professor. Next, a historian, Professor Theodore Branch, his wife Elaine, also a college professor, and the psychiatrist Dr. Philip Liebenthal and his wife Connie were invited, joined by a Tai Chi practitioner, Brandon Holloway, and his wife Hope, a yoga instructor. There were also two families included. The Fields family, farmers from Montana, were selected with their two children and their spouses, as was the Patidar family from New York, parents Kapila and Parag, along with their daughter and her spouse. Kapila and Parag Patidar were the two robotics technicians chosen as colonists. The project also enlisted two computer specialists Lisa Davenport and her partner Amy. The list of forty was completed by the beginning of 2191, with diversity a primary focus and strength of character a strong consideration. Although strength of character is a trait that, until tested in the field, is extremely difficult to evaluate.

While the selection of the colonists had been progressing, the third spaceship to Mars lifted off at the end of the year 2189. The cargo on this flight was comprised of supplemental building materials, including those to construct the pressurized tunnels that would connect the three existing structures, allowing for movement among the main complex, science building, and Terrarium without the use of space suits. Included, as well, were the solar panels that would power the entire compound. Although the solar irradiance on Mars is little more than forty-three percent of Earth's because of its distance from the sun, advances in photovoltaic technology made these panels capable of keeping the complex and all its needs running smoothly. The panels were also self-cleaning, so ice, dust, and wind would not hamper their ability to function.

Additionally, this third mission to Mars brought the payload for the internal areas in each complex: the components to equip the mess hall, the furnishings, and photo digital wall panels to dress the common areas as well as the living quarters. Also, smaller necessary elements were on board, including 500 digital tablets and 500 phones, all of which were donated in exchange for the rights to use the "as used by the colonists on Mars" logo on their advertising. Mission 3 also carried with it three riding Rovers, two three-seaters and one five-seater, a medical analysis chamber, and all the necessary plants and seeds to begin growth inside the Terrarium, initiating a process that would hopefully start to mature by the time the 4th mission, 28 months later, brought the brave settlers to their new home.

The fourth ship would also bring enough food supplies to allow the robots in the mess hall to feed everyone for the first three years. Finally, in the year 2192, forty colonists and three astronauts made the eight-month journey to Mars. They docked at the space station and then made their way to the surface, settling in the deep impact basin, Hellas Planitia, to begin life in the first city on the 4th planet from the sun.

The flight onboard the spaceship traveling to Mars proved a joyous time for the colonists. The forty citizens of diverse backgrounds became one closely knit group, as a feeling of excitement highlighted the trip, and a shared reality in the exploration ahead resulted in an awareness of their dependence on each other, molding them into compatriots.

Once the colonists settled into their living quarters, as it is on Earth, smaller groups found their friendships deepened, while the overall community held onto a general sense of fellowship. The desolation of the vast, inhospitable territory existing outside the terraformed complex was a source of wonder, with the kinship amongst the forty, an emotional fortification against the isolation beyond the walls of their constructed environment. The daily routines inside the community emulated life on Earth in many ways. Dr. Olivia Manning, as a general practitioner, received patients for regular checkups or to treat any injuries, not requiring the services of the colony's surgeon, Dr. Emery Taylor. She was also responsible for administering medications.

Some prescriptions were for colonists with pre-diagnosed needs, while drugs such as Xanax, although its therapeutic value was understood given where they were, had to be prescribed carefully and closely monitored. Professor Theodore Branch, the historian, spent much of his time notating their experiences, his focus on writing a book about the colonists first five years on Mars. Professor Branch's wife, Elaine, and Olivia's husband, George, as teachers, offered continuing education courses on a wide range of subjects. Hope Holloway held yoga classes, and her husband Brandon taught Tai Chi in the science building, which was also home to a gym available for workouts supervised by a team of robots. Most of the heavy lifting throughout the compound was handled by robots but shifts working in the Terrarium were mandatory for the colonists, while working in the mess hall was optional and open to those with an interest in the culinary arts.

Resident psychiatrist Dr. Liebenthal, with the assistance of his droid Charlie, began a regimen to continually monitor the mental and physical health of the colonists, as directed by Spaceforce Incorporated and the U.S. Government. Each week, ten colonists were equipped with monitoring patches that recorded all vital signs for examination, making sure the strangeness of their surroundings was causing no deleterious effects. At ten colonists per week, each of the forty would be examined for a one-week period each month, a practice that would serve as a standard for as long as they inhabited their new home. Individual sessions in analysis with Dr. Liebenthal were also a requirement. Having a robot sit in on the sessions was disturbing at first, but Charlie had been programmed to mimic empathy. In time, the colonists found Charlie to be more empathetic than Dr. Liebenthal.

Eventually, the new inhabitants of the planet slowly developed a growing level of comfort. A little courage and a sense of security would, over time, allow for trips outside the complex. Donning space suits, some of the colonists began riding the three and five seat Rovers for recreation, the vehicles driven by robots who were able to safely maneuver through the rugged and mostly uncharted terrain of Mars. The colonists also enjoyed the ability to send and receive weekly communications to and from friends and family on Earth through video recordings as life in the new city proceeded smoothly for the next two years.

Then, the excitement inside the complex began increasing in anticipation of the first supplemental voyage set to arrive from Earth, only two months away. Aside from additional supplies and food to supplement the now thriving Terrarium, the colonists had been informed that the ship would be bringing hundreds of gifts from those they knew, as well as gifts, and a hard drive filled with digital cards of goodwill from people on Earth they didn't know, who saw them as celebrities and wanted them to feel their admiration and support. Also, in preparation for the arrival of the spaceship, ten robots had been assigned the task of gathering samples from beneath the surface of Mars, the first to be collected, cataloged, and crated: organic components of the planet readied for the journey back to Earth.

When the spaceship arrived, it docked at the space station and then the landing craft headed to the surface, carrying supplies as well as three astronauts to replace the three that had arrived over two years earlier. Before saying their goodbyes to the colonists, the departing astronauts gave their replacements a tour of the three complexes, familiarizing them with the science facilities, including the communications room. This room was off limits to the colonists. It was where transmissions between Mars and the U.S. government and the astrophysicists of Spaceforce were exchanged. It was also equipped with the computers used by the astronauts to monitor the airspace as far away as Jupiter, enabling them to track any movement beyond the atmosphere of their new home planet.

Meanwhile, boarding the recently arrived spacecraft, Dr. Olivia Manning supervised the unloading of the spacecraft's payload. In the first two years on Mars, Olivia had proven herself trustworthy and was well liked by the others. She had become the sort of de-facto leader of the group. Olivia directed the colonists as they unloaded hundreds of packages sent by family and friends. There were also the hundreds of packages sent by people on Earth they didn't know, parcels of goodwill, which evoked a sense of pride in the colonists. As they assisted each other in distributing the consignment there was a palpable feeling that they were a part of something greater than themselves, a sense that their small community, in reality, was much larger than just forty; the gifts and messages from the homes they left behind, and the offerings from strangers made them feel a little less isolated.

Amongst the packages was a medium-sized box addressed to Dr. Philip Liebenthal. The return address was one his wife Connie didn't recognize. When she asked the doctor about it, he informed her that it was from an old student of his. He opened the package in front of her, removing a bowl engraved with the words, "We're proud of you." Then the doctor took the apparently empty box and, under the guise of taking it for disposal, instead veered off and took it into his office. With the door locked, he removed the bottom cardboard piece that held the bowl in place and removed an envelope. Inside the envelope, Dr. Liebenthal found a brown folder, which he opened, finding papers inside marked "Top Secret" in red. The doctor did not appear surprised and proceeded to study its contents behind closed doors.

During the distribution of the presents from Earth, Hope Holloway approached Olivia Manning with an idea of what might be done with the over 3000 digital cards expressing felicitation received from all over the world, including many from the children on Earth. She proposed rearranging the cards, one hundred to a page, and then putting them on a loop to be continually displayed on one of the digital wall panels in the mess hall. Olivia, believing it to be a great idea, one that might continuously uplift the spirits of the colonists, gathered volunteers to assist in the project. Among them were Hope's husband, Brandon, Lisa Davenport, and her partner Amy, as well as Samuel and Betty Fields with their son and daughter and their spouses. Even with the process being mostly automated, it took three weeks to complete the task. At the project's unveiling, all forty of the colonists stood in the mess hall in front of the pictorial wall panel exhibiting the cards sent, watching page after page reveal the love of the people of planet Earth and their appreciation for the colonists' courage and commitment. The support represented by those small examples of solidarity on display was overwhelming. Parag and Kapila Patidar along with their daughter and her husband, were overcome with emotion when viewing hundreds of cards addressed directly to them from their native country of India.

As the colonists were enjoying and reading the messages of encouragement, an unusual sighting was discovered in the communications room on the equipment probing for any possible anomalies in the nearby cosmos. At first, Colonel Paul Davies, the astronaut on duty, didn't know what to make of the small blip appearing in front of him, seemingly out of nowhere. A communique from Earth directly from the Pentagon transmuted Colonel Davies' confusion into terror. The CEO of Spaceforce, Ryan Allen Kingsley, and the astrophysicists from his company had identified the object on the screen as an asteroid. The asteroid had broken free of the asteroid belt 40 million miles from Mars, escaping the gravity of Jupiter. Its trajectory was, at the moment, undeterminable.

Colonel Davies was ordered not to inform the colonists. Then, three hours later, with the other two astronauts present, Davies and his colleagues were informed that analysis was now indicating that the asteroid was currently ten million miles away from them. Its size was approximated at close to 800 feet across, its speed at 27,000 mph, and its trajectory placed the massive sky-rock on a collision course with Mars, its impact estimated at 100 miles from the location of the complex. Damage from this amount of force anywhere on the planet would threaten the integrity of the structures they had constructed and the pressurized containment of the oxygen-rich environment that ensured their survival. The astronauts were cleared to share the information with the colonists and wait for further instructions.

The colonists were still standing proudly together in front of the wall monitor displaying the messages of goodwill when Colonel Davies and his colleagues entered the mess hall. Calling for the attention of everyone there, the colonel explained the approaching threat. Using a remote, he switched the image on the wall panel that was exhibiting the source of Earth's support and encouragement to match the monitor in the communications room and the tracking of the asteroid. The explanation given by Colonel Davies, as they viewed the satellite image of the large mass hurtling towards them was difficult to accept. The reactions in the hall ranged from disbelief to confusion to extreme fear. Dr. Liebenthal quickly made his way to and from his office, returning with enough monitoring patches for everyone in the room. He urged the immediate attachment of the patches so he could begin keeping track of the effect of this development on all of them. Moments later, he began summoning the colonists and the astronauts into his office, one by one, for a quick session to offer comfort while he recorded their emotional responses to the event.

Aside from this brief diversion to the analyst's office, every colonist, astronaut, and every robot not otherwise occupied stood staring at the image of the asteroid, thinking about the catastrophe now advancing from only eight million miles away. By this time, most were consumed with fear, as Olivia and a few others advocated for a more composed approach, proposing that it was still just a possibility the asteroid would impact the planet. For the next ten days, the colonists attempted to recover some semblance of normalcy. However, as the sky-rock traveled closer to Mars, the calmer point of view lost steam. Now only three million miles from impact, at an increased speed of 48,000 mph, the projected course of this immense ball of destruction had not altered and was estimated to hit in eighty-three hours.

While returning often to stare at the wall monitor illuminating their fate, the colonists would individually visit Dr. Liebenthal, who continued to track their heart rate and other vitals, holding private sessions, on average, twelve hours a day. All these discussions were being recorded, as were the previous private sessions, without the knowledge of those seeking the doctor's assistance. He was aided by Charlie the robot, who was equipped with a clasped belt holding a box of tissues and small cups, which he filled with water when asked, using an internal tank built into his torso. Charlie's contribution might have been considered somewhat inconsequential when compared to the high stakes involved, but small gestures can help when dealing with such intense emotions. And the colonists had grown fond of Charlie and his empathetic programming.

Three additional days passed with no change in the trajectory of the asteroid, leaving nine hours remaining. The outlook was bleak. The asteroid's impact appeared imminent, and the colonists now followed its approach with a feeling of hopelessness. Then, with 75,000 miles between the asteroid and Mars, and the colonists an hour and a half from certain death, many closely following the path of the massive rock suddenly began screaming in joy. Some were slow to recognize what they were actually seeing. Colonel Paul Davies, sweat pouring down his face, confirmed the development. The asteroid's trajectory had changed course ever so slightly, possibly due to a collision with another object in space. Although they couldn't, at the moment, ascertain why, it was certain that the asteroid was now projected to bypass Mars, missing it completely.

The relief felt was incalculable. A celebration commenced in the mess hall. As the cacophonous cheers died down, Dr. Olivia Manning said a few words, praising everyone for their ability to contend with such an event and praying that this ultimate test of character would be the last. Everyone echoed her sentiments, enjoying their good fortune, even though they knew in their hearts that their harrowing escape served as a reminder of where they were and that living on another planet would always be a dangerous proposition.

After the threat to their survival had ended, Dr. Liebenthal conducted a final interview with each of the colonists and astronauts individually. Then, unbeknownst to any of them, he gathered all his notes from the sessions of the last few weeks, along with the data he collected from the health monitoring patches, and sent all of it back to Earth, directly to the Pentagon.

Day-to-day life on Mars reverted to customary routines in the aftermath of the asteroid scare, except for remnants of the psychological impact lingering to varying degrees. As it would on Earth, the remaining levels of fear registered differently, depending on the individual. Dr. Liebenthal's monitoring of the colonists' health resumed at its one-week-a-month schedule. However, his private sessions would persist more frequently than they had before. Charlie, empathetic as always, found it necessary to replenish his tissue box every few days. There was also an increased trepidatious feeling amongst the colonists as if they were waiting for the next celestial shoe to drop. As time went on, the freer attitude that had existed prior to the threat on their lives reemerged, and a little more than one year later, the overall morale of the colonists was lifted when a development in the life of their favorite daughter in arms, brought a sense of wonder back into the colony. Late in November of the year 2196, Dr. Olivia Manning, the thirty-year-old physician, space explorer, and fellow Mars resident, became pregnant.

Bringing a smile to the faces of everyone who encountered her in the compound, the possibility of new life, the first to be born on another planet, was reaffirming. The private sessions held by Dr. Liebenthal, suddenly diminished, with the underlying cause of this change, Olivia's pregnancy and its positive impact on the community.

In February of 2197, with the second supplemental supply ship from Earth only one month away, the mood of the colonists lightened even further. Any remaining fear from their brush with the asteroid seemed to have evaporated. The supplies they were anxiously awaiting included many items for the baby, such as diapers, formula to supplement Dr. Manning's intention to breast feed, a crib and a bassinet. With her baby, due to arrive in August, six months away, there was one necessary alteration to the colony's procedures. Olivia, as the settlement's general practitioner, could not be expected to treat herself. Therefore, the supervising surgeon, Dr. Emery Taylor, an original colonist whose services, up until now, had not been required, became the doctor in charge of Olivia's care. As the child's birth date grew nearer, he assumed her role as general practitioner to the colonists, as well.

Unfortunately, just one week later, an unforeseen tragedy jolted the spirits of the colonists. Samuel and Betty Fields, the farmers from Montana, were on an excursion outside the protection of the complex, riding one of the Rover transports when the computerized mapping system failed, causing their robot driver to crash into a rock. The Rover flipped on its side and slid along the Mars terrain, damaging the integrity of Samuel and Betty's spacesuits. It took just two to three minutes for them to die after being exposed to the Mars atmosphere, too little time for the robot to carry them to safety or for others to reach them with replacement protective gear.

The bodies of Samuel and Betty Fields were brought back inside the compound, where their devastated son, William, daughter Debra, and their spouses, Laura and Andrew, were waiting. The entire colony stood in solidarity behind them, stunned, each knowing that the accident could have happened to anyone of them. The two bodies were prepared for interment as their family was given the option of a burial on Mars or having them taken back to Earth on the return flight of the supply ship which was scheduled to arrive in three weeks time. It was decided that the bodies of Samuel and Betty Fields would be taken back to Earth. Their children, William, Debra, and their spouses were given the option of returning to Earth as well, but they unanimously opted to stay, believing that Samuel and Betty would have preferred they endure as colonists and continue to support the effort of which they had been so proud to be a part.

In a solemn but beautiful ceremony on Mars, Samuel and Betty Fields were honored as beloved colleagues and heroes before being laid into coffins, which were items of cargo contained in the original supply manifest. Items that everyone had hoped would never be needed. The second supply ship arrived on time in March of 2197, unloaded its supplies, and departed soon after. The caskets of Samuel and Betty were handled respectfully. Once on the spacecraft, the bodies were removed and stored in a frozen state, preserving them for their final resting place and a proper funeral, where they could be hailed as heroes by the people they served so courageously, and adorned with the formalities of pomp and circumstance they deserved.

The first deaths on the planet Mars had a negative effect on the morale of the colonists that lasted for months. It was quite some time before anyone felt secure enough to explore beyond the security of the compound's walls. Eventually, the investigation of the computer's GPS mapping system, which had failed, yielded the reason for the deaths of Samuel and Betty Fields. Discovered and analyzed by the colony's computer specialists, Lisa Davenport and her partner Amy, and with the assistance of robotics technicians Parag and Kapila Patidar, the problem was corrected. The Rovers were then deemed safe to ride again, and the moratorium prohibiting their use lifted, allowing excursions across the Mars' surface to resume. Even though the landscape was desolate, the feeling of freedom that the outings provided was liberating. Riding the Rovers and venturing outside, brought back some of the absent courage that had previously embodied the spirit of those chosen to make their unprecedented journey of exploration.

Then, on August 18th, 2197, a truly brave act brought absolute joy into the colony when Dr. Olivia Ellen Manning gave birth to the first baby born on another planet, a baby boy, Kyle Patrick Manning. The first picture taken was of the mother holding her newborn baby, with her husband George beside her, and the second photograph featured thirty-six honorary aunts and uncles surrounding them. Both photos were sent back to Earth and became as well-known as any pictures ever taken. The group image of Olivia, her husband, and baby Kyle, along with their extended family of fellow colonists, became the most viewed photo of the year. Less than two years later, in June of the year 2199, another supply ship arrived. This time, along with its regular haul, its cargo contained hundreds of gifts for

Kyle and his mother from the people on Earth, including enough toys and video games appropriate for varying ages to keep Kyle entertained for many years to come.

When the supply ship left its docking position on the space station and began the journey back to Earth, one of the astronauts expected to make the trip home was not on board. He had requested his assignment on Mars be extended. Colonel Paul Davies had become so attached to Kyle, and he to him, that the colonel didn't want to leave. Anytime Olivia was unable to locate her son in the main complex, she knew he could be found, where no other colonist was allowed, in the communications room in the science building. Kyle would often keep company with the colonel, watching the monitors tracking the skies, from the comfort of Colonel Davies' lap. Even though Kyle was too young to understand the purpose of the equipment, Colonel Davies described what they observed as if the boy did.

During one of these moments together, a blip of unknown origin appeared on the screen. As the colonel described what they were seeing as possibly a star or one of Jupiter's moons, the tracking system indicated that the object was in motion and moving towards them. The colonel pointed to the change of position, telling Kyle that it now appeared to be a faraway asteroid or meteorite, but definitely nothing to be concerned with, given its distance from them. But then the unknown object showed signs of a course correction as if it was self-maneuvering as opposed to an asteroid just tumbling through space. The colonel monitored the object's movements, while it continually appeared to self-adjust its path through the cosmos. Colonel Davies had no explanation for the phenomenon on his screen. It took him a moment to work through disbelief before accepting the only justification for the object's movement. It must be self-generated. There was only one explanation for an object in space with the ability to alter its own flight path. It had to be some sort of spacecraft, and because it was approaching from a direction farther from the sun than they were, it had to be coming from somewhere other than Earth. It was, without a doubt, a UFO, and as incredible as it seemed, it was most probably an alien spaceship.

Colonel Davies' first responsibility was to inform his superiors on Earth of the event. The colonel had to wait three hours for a response but finally received confirmation. His report was accurate, and the astrophysicists agreed it appeared to be a UFO. The colonel was given permission to share the sighting with the colony; however, as a precaution, for the time being, they were going to declare a blackout on all communications sent from the colonists to Earth. Until they had more information, there was no point in creating a panic. The colonel acknowledged his orders, took Kyle by the hand, and proceeded to the main complex where he gathered the colonists together and informed them of his findings. He also apprised them of the communications blackout, which the colonists accepted as prudent, understanding that the government may not want to alert the general public until more is known about the phenomenon.

Interestingly, the colonist's reaction to the possibility of an extraterrestrial encounter was different than it had been for the asteroid incident. Of course, there was quite a bit of fear; however, amongst some of the colonists, there was also an exhilarating anticipation of the unknown present. Dr. Liebenthal, as usual, appeared in control of his emotions. Immediately, he retrieved monitoring patches for everyone, the same action he had taken at the beginning of the asteroid threat, reassuming a routine of keeping track of the health of all of the colonists during a possible crisis. The doctor's wife, Connie's reaction was very different from her husband's. Standing alone, she appeared terrified. Olivia and a few others, noticing her condition, went to see if they could help her, while Kyle, two years old and fearless, stayed with his father, George. After accompanying Connie back to her quarters, Olivia prescribed a Xanax to help her rest. The other colonists gathered in small groups around the mess hall, either consoling each other or planning what they might do if they were indeed headed for a close encounter. Dr. Liebenthal began recording the different reactions to their new dilemma, as he set up mandatory private sessions to notate each individual's reaction, just as he had done during the asteroid event. Charlie was, as always, empathetic.

The following morning, the UFO was estimated to be less than four million miles from Mars, traveling at 52,000 mph, approximately three days away. Some of the colonists had been able to sleep; some had not. Some were able to eat; others were not. The wall monitor in the mess hall displayed the current tracking of the spaceship, as it had for the asteroid, and most of the colonists congregated there. Olivia, Kyle and George sat together and were joined by Lisa and Amy as well as Professor Branch and his wife Elaine. They began discussing an incident that seemed to be making the rounds. During the night, Dr. Liebenthal and his wife had been overheard arguing loudly, with Connie doing most of the yelling. As the table continued their discussion about the Liebenthals, Connie walked out of her private living quarters and joined them in the mess hall. To their amazement, she was calm, with no lingering affect from her fight with her husband or the intense fear that had consumed her the day before.

When Connie excused herself from the table after eating a hearty breakfast, the group she had been sitting with was stunned.

Everyone agreed: There was something very odd about her behavior. The inconsistency of her fearful demeanor stemming from the impending alien encounter, the fight with the doctor, and now total calm. The group tried to recall the extent of Connie's level of fear during the asteroid scare, but no one could. Connie's husband, Dr. Liebenthal, on the other hand, they knew for certain had been extremely calm through both major events; his only concern was the monitoring and notating of the colonists' reactions. Now, Connie has had a fight with her husband, only to end up free of the fear she had displayed just one day earlier. Something wasn't adding up. Without the prompting of any proof, an idea popped into Olivia's thoughts. She shared it with the group even though she realized the idea would appear insane. She posed, what if it was a hoax? What if there was no UFO? The intensity of the discussion that ensued brought others to the table, including Parag and Kapila Patidar, their daughter, and her husband. The more they spoke to each other, the less insane the idea seemed. Professor Branch added that if the extraterrestrial ship was a hoax, maybe the asteroid scare, an object that veered off with no explanation at the last moment, was a hoax as well. And if that is true, maybe all we are is a government experiment. The table sat stunned.

Professor Branch continued to support his premise, stating that throughout history, governments have used their citizens for experimentation for many reasons: to test strength, resolve, as well as courage, and an individual's dedication to their government's causes. Unbelievably, the idea that the entire Mars venture could be one large government experiment suddenly didn't appear crazy to any of them. Everyone present concurred that it was a premise that, at least, had to be investigated. However, they couldn't just torture Dr. Liebenthal in order to find the truth. Even if the government was testing them, the doctor may be innocent and just doing his job. They agreed to keep their theory to themselves, ponder a solution, and meet an hour later. When they did, Olivia and Professor Branch presented a plan. A plan, they believed might reveal the truth. And Charlie, the empathetic robot, was the key.

The plan Olivia and Professor Branch proposed was simple. The colony's robotics technicians, Parag and Kapila Patidar would take Dr. Liebenthal's robot assistant, Charlie, to the science lab for routine maintenance. It had been more than two years since Charlie's last checkup, so there would be nothing unusual about the request. In its absence, Dr. Liebenthal would be free to continue his sessions without Charlie or postpone them for the three-hour procedure necessary to test all of Charlie's primary and auxiliary programs. Parag and Kapila had previously ascertained, through the robot's technical specifications, that Charlie's empathy program held a full range of adjustable levels. The plan was to use Charlie's empathy programming to find out if Dr. Liebenthal was hiding something.

When the two robotics technicians examined the function, they discovered Charlie's empathy level's default was set at level three out of a possible ten. Parag and Kapila increased the setting to its highest mark. As Amy and Lisa, there for their computer expertise, and the Patidars watched for the changes that might result from their adjustment to its empathy program, they were amazed to see water begin disseminating from Charlie's eyes, artificial tears, dispersed from the water tank built into his torso. Charlie appeared to have no governor to limit its responses when adjusted to this level. It was completely open, vulnerable to their probing, prepared to reveal everything in its memory banks.

Over the next few moments, Charlie confirmed their fears. The asteroid scare had been faked, the alien event a hoax, and additionally, the entire venture to Mars was just a pretense, a veil covering the real purpose of their mission: To test and measure the resiliency of human beings when facing impossible odds in uncontrollable situations and against other-worldly threats. All of it, to gather information for the future in case relocating to another planet became necessary. Charlie revealed that the colonists weren't paving the way for more settlements to join them. They were an expendable group placed on Mars to be studied, with one of the key questions asked, being, whether a human's DNA could even cope with living somewhere other than their home planet of Earth. The colonists may have been living millions of miles away from those who sent them there, surrounded by thousands of miles of open territory, but they were the inhabitants of a fishbowl, just the same.

Charlie was then asked about Dr. Liebenthal's reports on the colonists, where they were stored, and with whom they might have been shared. Charlie divulged the truth. All of their private sessions with the doctor, along with the information collected from the patches monitoring their health, were packaged and delivered digitally to the U.S. government, and sent directly to the Pentagon.

With its empathy program reset to zero, courtesy of Parag and Kapila, an indignant Charlie led Lisa, and Amy, the Patidar family, Olivia, George, Kyle, and every other colonist, along with Colonel Paul Davies and the other three astronauts, as they crowded inside the door of Dr. Philip Liebenthal's office. The presence of the entire colony was an intimidating, frightening sight. Even the doctor's wife, Connie, was there to lend her support to the group. The fight she had had with her husband the night before was the result of Connie finding out about her husband's deception. Her sudden change in demeanor, from her initial fearful response to the approach of the alien ship to the calm she projected the following morning, was the outcome of her forcing the truth out of him and learning that there was no alien threat. The first person in the office to confront Dr. Liebenthal was William Fields, the son of Samuel and Betty Fields. William had to be restrained physically as he demanded to know whether the death of his parents was part of the experiment. The doctor, in fear for his life, confessed to everything Charlie had disclosed to them but pleaded they believe him when he told them that the Fields' deaths were a tragic accident and were never an intended consequence. No one was supposed to die as a result of the experiment. The apologies that followed fell on deaf ears. Dr. Philip Liebenthal was now a pariah, his wife proclaiming that if there was a judge on Mars, she would demand a divorce.

Alone in his office, Dr. Liebenthal retrieved the envelope that held the papers he had previously received marked "Top Secret." These government documents had educated the doctor to the events that were to occur, including advanced knowledge about the asteroid and alien events being faked. It also included instructions that outlined the doctor's assigned role in the facades. Dr. Liebenthal leafed through the pages until he found the one marked "emergency contact protocol." With the blackout in place, it was the only way of contacting Earth. He used the emergency procedure to contact his superiors and inform them of the recent development; that the colonists found out that the asteroid and alien threats were a hoax and realized that they had been enlisted to play a part in an experiment perpetrated by their own government. The doctor also made it clear that the colonists knew that he had been complicit in the deception and that he may, personally, be in danger.

Twelve hours later, all the monitors in the complex tracking the cosmos went dark. When Dr. Liebenthal attempted to use the emergency protocol to report the problem, he discovered the protocol was no longer operational. The colony of Mars had been completely cut off; abandoned by the people who should have been protecting them.

When the colonists realized that they had been deserted, depression set in all over the compound. This included Dr. Liebenthal, who realized that his message to Earth was the reason they were now totally isolated. However, no one was as depressed as Dr. Olivia Manning and her husband, George, whose only thoughts were for their son, Kyle. They lamented that even if the future went as well as it could, and the colony remained self-sufficient with everyone surviving, Kyle would grow up with no one by his side, eventually ending up completely alone, the last man standing on Mars. Over the following ten days, with no contact from Earth, the colony's depression turned to anger and disbelief over what their fellow human beings had done to them.

With no operating instrumentation, the colonists were blind to any movement in the skies above Mars. As a result, they were unaware that a spaceship had entered the atmosphere and was situated directly above them. It wasn't until the wall monitors in the mess hall suddenly began to function again that they were alerted to something happening outside the compound. Their screens, reactivated by an external power source from somewhere nearby, revealed the image of a spaceship of unknown origin. Bewildered, the colonists watched as a landing craft of significant size separated from the larger spacecraft and floated down towards the surface. Once it landed, lettering appeared across the monitors inside the complex. They read, "We are here to take you home."

On Earth, governments from all over the globe had been following this anomaly from the moment it had been detected passing Saturn, as every device monitoring the cosmos, government and privately owned, had lit up, signaling a warning never before seen. From SETI, the Search for Extraterrestrial Intelligence, and NASA's Office of Planetary Protection to the AATIP, the Advanced Aerospace Threat Identification Program, and the UAP, Unidentified Aerial Phenomenon, every agency tracking the solar system was reporting the same story. Something was coming. Something inexplicable, traveling at speeds that were impossible for anything man-made. The White House, the Kremlin and Beijing were all on high alert. There was a palpable fear present amongst the high-ranking officials all over the world, as they followed the object, this UFO, as it moved past Jupiter. By the time the unknown phenomenon suddenly stopped above the planet Mars, news of the event had spread to the four corners of the globe. As the Earth's superpowers predictably readied a military response, the citizens of the planet had varied reactions to finally having the answer to the question, are we alone in the universe. There was panic, but for others, there was the same wondrous anticipation felt by some of the colonists on Mars when they thought they had seen evidence of extraterrestrial life.

On Mars, the alien landing craft had positioned itself near the hatch the colonists used to exit the complex when exploring the Mars surface. A short, pressurized tunnel was extended, then attached to the outside of the hatch and sealed so the colonists could board the alien spacecraft without the use of spacesuits.

There was an understandable hesitation, a fearful distrust of the alien's offer of assistance before Olivia called for courage. Despite the risk, she and her husband had to leave for the sake of their son. She also admitted that given recent events, she had more faith in the benevolence that might exist in the unknown than she had confidence in her own kind. Amy and Lisa stepped forward to join her, as did Professor Branch and his wife Elaine, followed by the Patidar family, Colonel Davies and Connie Liebenthal. The group continued to grow until all the colonists and astronauts agreed it was time to go. Even Charlie and his fellow robots fell in behind the colonists. No one would be left behind. Finally, Dr. Philip Liebenthal, hoping for acceptance, waited for approval. The thirty-eight colonists, four astronauts, and fifty robots glanced back at Dr. Liebenthal before Olivia grabbed his hand and said, "Let's go." Once aboard the alien craft, although never seeing the physical form of their rescuers, they were secured on board and assured by an electronic voice, translated into the English language, that they were safe.

The spaceship continued its journey and slowed down once it had easily penetrated the outer atmosphere of Earth. The main ship hovered in place before releasing and lowering its landing craft and its inhabitants to the Earth's surface. The craft landed in Washington, DC, touching down gently on the front lawn of the White House, effortlessly crushing the iron gates protecting the perimeter of this great center of American democracy. Every digital screen, every billboard, and every television in the world was then hi-jacked by the extraterrestrial marvel and forced to feature the same image, showing the spaceship opening a side portal and extending a large ramp smoothly to the ground. Fortunately for the Earth, the scene did not provoke any military response. The world looked on as fifty robots were the first to exit the landing craft, followed by the colonists and the astronauts. They all stood on the White House lawn, still bitter and angry but, at the same time, relieved. Before the alien craft retracted its ramp, shuttered its portal, and returned to the mothership, the same electronic voice the colonists had heard spoke again. And even though the voice was electronically produced, there was a distinct inflection to its tone, projecting an emotion that could only be characterized as disappointment. The voice imparted a warning. The aliens assured the people of Earth that the message that followed represented the position of all intelligent life in the galaxies beyond the Milky Way.

"If you can abandon your own - those who served you so valiantly, then you must be considered a threat to life everywhere. We will be watching."

The alien spaceship disappeared as quickly as it had arrived, while aid for the returned colonists spilled out onto the White House lawn, and the entire planet felt the relief of being given the opportunity to change. The opportunity, but most likely, if past is prologue, without the ability.

THE PAST CAPTURES US FOREVER

Final words from our Benefactor.

For those of us who commissioned this project in our present,
These stories exist only in our future.

But just as with Our Future, just as with All Futures,
Eventually, they will Exist Only In Someone Else's Past.
Taking Their Permanent Place Somewhere
On The Timeline of Existence.

Ultimately,
All Of The "Futures to Come,"
When They Become the Past,
Continue to Exist
In Close Proximity to Where We Will Always Be,
Captured Forever "Somewhere" In SpaceTime.

The Future Leaves Us All Behind
The Past Captures Us Forever.